Praise for *Cold Snap*

"Winner and still champion Jones takes this one on points. His second collection of rock-hard stories goes the distance, surviving on adrenaline, killer instinct, and artistry."

— starred *Booklist*

◆

"At least as powerful and as gritty with existential courage as *The Pugilist at Rest*. . . . Jones leaves a chunk of primal matter, painful to hold, thrown up from volcanic depths."

— *Time* magazine

◆

"A wild talent. . . . His stories have the same frightening allure as the sarcophagus at Chernobyl: You want to go in there to the smallest, darkest chamber, where the action is."

— *Boston Globe*

◆

"The stories in *Cold Snap* confirm the critical consensus — there is indeed a new kid on the block. . . ."

— *Chicago Tribune*

◆

"If you missed him the first time, try him now. Jones is better than good. . . ."

— *Men's Journal*

◆

"In its linguistic exuberance . . . *Cold Snap* is reminiscent of the works of Thomas Pynchon and Stanley Elkin. Like those fine stylists, Mr. Jones writes it all out. He takes risks and lets the words fly."

— *Washington Times*

"Extraordinary . . . a compelling reading experience."
— *San Francisco Chronicle*

◆

"Towers above the dull, doleful strain of much current fiction. . . . The author's vivid, often hilarious voice will keep you laughing in the dark."
— *Details*

◆

"*Cold Snap* does to readers what *Pulp Fiction* did to movie-goers — takes you on a wild careening ride. . . ."
— *Philadelphia Inquirer*

◆

"Horrifically fascinating. . . . Jones continues to examine the horrible and wonderful qualities that bracket quotidian existence."
— *Voice Literary Supplement*

◆

". . . Thom Jones's stories are anything but grim; they quiver with their own manic life. The thrilling urgency of his voice transcends his subject."
— Joyce Carol Oates, *New York Times Book Review*

◆

"Jones's voice never falters. . . . It is Jones's rich genius that he can create empathy where it is least expected."
— *San Francisco Review of Books*

◆

"*Cold Snap* oozes adrenaline. . . . Filled with an edgy rush of unknown possibility, his stories give survival a whole new meaning."
— *People*

Cold Snap

Books by Thom Jones

The Pugilist at Rest
Cold Snap

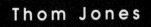

Thom Jones

stories

Cold
Snap

BACK
BAY
BOOKS

little, brown and company : boston new york toronto london

First Paperback Edition

The characters and events in this book are fictitious. Any similarity to real persons, living or dead, is coincidental and not intended by the author.

Grateful acknowledgement is made to the following publications in which some of these stories were first published: *The New Yorker:* "Cold Snap," "Superman, My Son," "Way Down Deep in the Jungle"; *Playboy:* "Pickpocket," "Quicksand," "Dynamite Hands"; *Harper's:* "I Need a Man to Love Me" (published under the title "Nights in White Satin"); *Esquire:* "Ooh Baby Baby"; *Buzz:* "Pot Shack."

Excerpt from "Coconut" by Harry Nilsson, © by EMI Music.

Library of Congress Cataloging-in-Publication Data
Jones, Thom.
   Cold snap : stories / Thom Jones. — 1st ed.
     p. cm.
   Contents: Cold snap — Superman, my son — Way down deep in the jungle — Quicksand — Pickpocket — Ooh baby baby — Rocketfire red — I need a man to love me — Pot shack — Dynamite hands.
   ISBN 0-316-47307-3 (hc)
   ISBN 0-316-42757-3 (pb)
   1. Africa — Social life and customs — Fiction. 2. Manners and customs — Fiction. I. Title.
PS3560.0546C65 1995   94-49539
813'.54 — dc20

10 9 8 7 6 5 4 3 2 1

Designed by Barbara Werden

MV-NY

Published simultaneously in Canada by Little, Brown & Company (Canada) Limited

Printed in the United States of America

For my daughter Jennifer

Now the spirit of the Lord departed from Saul, and an evil spirit from the Lord tormented him. And Saul's servants said to him, "Behold now, an evil spirit from God is tormenting you. Let our Lord now command your servants, who are before you, to seek out a man who is skillful in playing the lyre: and when the evil spirit from God is upon you, he will play it, and you will be well."

—1 Samuel 16:14–16

Contents

Cold Snap

Cold Snap

SON OF A BITCH, there's a cold snap and I do this number where I leave all the faucets running because my house, and most houses out here on the West Coast, aren't "real" — they don't have windows that go up and down, or basements (which protect the pipes in a way that a crawl space can't), or sidewalks out in the front with a nice pair of towering oak trees or a couple of elms, which a real house will have, one of those good old Midwest houses. Out here the windows go side to side. You get no basement. No sidewalk and no real trees, just evergreens, and when it gets cold and snows, nobody knows what to do. An inch of snow and they cancel school and the community is paralyzed. "Help me, I'm helpless!" Well, it's cold for a change and I guess that's not so bad, because all the fleas and mosquitoes will freeze, and also because any change is *something,* and maybe it will help snap me out of this bleak post-Africa depression — oh, baby, I'm so depressed — but I wake up at three in the morning and think, Oh, no, a pipe is gonna bust, so I run the water and let the faucets drip and I go outside and turn on the out-door faucets, which are the most vulnerable. Sure enough, they were caking up, and I got to them just in the nick of time, which was good, since in my condition there was no way I could possibly cope with a broken water pipe. I just got back from Africa, where I was playing doctor to the natives, got hammered with a nasty case of malaria, and lost thirty pounds, but it was a manic episode I had that caused Global Aid to send me home. It was my worst attack to date, and on lithium I get such a bad case of psoriasis that I look like alligator man. You can take Tegretol for mania but it once wiped out my white count and almost killed me, so what I like to do when I get all revved up is skin-pop some morphine, which I had with me by the gallon over there and which will keep you calm — and, unlike booze, it's something I can keep under control. Although I must confess I lost my medical license in the States for substance abuse and ended up with Global Aid when the dust settled over that one. God's will, really. Fate. Karma. Whatever. Anyhow, hypomania is a good thing in Africa, a real moti-vator, and you can do anything you want over there as long as you keep your feet on the ground and don't parade naked on the president's lawn in Nairobi and get expelled (which I did and which will get you expelled; okay, I lied, you can't do *anything* — so sue me). On lithium, while you don't crash so bad, you never get high, either, and all you can do is sit around sucking on Primus beer bottles, bitching about how hot it is when there's so much work to do.

While I'm outside checking my faucets, I look my Olds-mobile over and wonder was it last year I changed the antifreeze? Back in bed, it strikes me that it's been three years, so I go out and run the engine and sit in the car with my teeth chattering — it's thirteen below, geez! And pretty soon the warm air is defrosting the car and I drive over to

the hardware section at Safeway and get one of those antifreeze testers with the little balls in it. At four in the morning I'm sitting in my kitchen trying to get it out of the
plastic jacket, and it comes out in two parts, with the bulb
upside down. No doubt some know-nothing Central American put it in upside down for twenty cents an hour in some
slave factory. I know he's got problems — fact is, I've been
there and could elucidate his problems — but how about
me and my damn antifreeze? I mean, too bad about you,
buddy, how about me? And I'm trying to jury-rig it when I
realize there is a high potential for breaking the glass and
cutting my thumb, and just as that voice that is me, that is
always talking to me, my ego, I guess, tells me, "Be careful,
Richard, so you don't cut your thumb" — at that instant, I
slice my thumb down to the bone. So the next thing you
know I'm driving to the hospital with a towel on my thumb
thinking, A minute ago everything was just fine, and now
I'm driving myself to the emergency room!

Some other guy comes in with this awful burn because
a pressure cooker exploded in his face, and he's got this
receding hairline, and you can see the way the skin is peeled
back — poached-looking. The guy's going to need a hair-
piece for sure. A doctor comes out eating a sandwich, and
I hear him tell the nurse to set up an I.V. line and start
running some Dilaudid for the guy, which he deserves, considering. I would like some for my thumb, but all I get is
Novocain, and my doctor says, "You aren't going to get
woozy on me, are you?" I tell him no, I'm not like that, but
I have another problem, and he says, "What's that?" and I
tell him I can't jack off left-handed. Everybody laughs, because it's the graveyard shift, when that kind of joke is
appropriate — even in mixed company. Plus, it's true.

After he stitches me up, I'm in no pain, although I say,
"I'll bet this is going to hurt tomorrow," and he says no,

he'll give me some pain medication, and I'm thinking, What a great doctor. He's giving me *pain medication*. And while he's in a giving mood I hit him up for some prostate antibiotics because my left testicle feels very heavy.

"Your left testicle feels *heavy*?" he says skeptically.

Yeah, every guy gets it, shit; I tell him my left nut feels like an anvil. I mean, I want to cradle it in my hand when I'm out and about, or rest it on a little silk pillow when I'm stationary. It doesn't really hurt, but I'm very much conscious of having a left testicle, whereas I have teeth and a belly button and a right testicle and I don't even know. I tell him I don't want a finger wave, because I've been through this a thousand times. My prostate is backing up into the seminal vesicles, and if you don't jerk off it builds up and gets worse, and the doctor agrees — that does happen, and he doesn't really want to give me a finger wave, especially when I tell him that a urologist checked it out a couple of months back. He puts on a plastic glove and feels my testicle, pronounces it swollen, and writes a script for antibiotics, after which he tells me to quit drinking coffee. I was going to tell him that I don't jerk off because I'm a sex fiend; I have low sex drive, and it's actually not that much fun. I just do it to keep the prostate empty. Or should I tell him I'm a doctor myself, albeit defrocked, that I just got back from Africa and my nut could be infected with elephantiasis? Highly unlikely, but you never know. But he won't know diddle about tropical medicine — that's my department, and I decide I will just shut my mouth, which is a first for me.

The duty nurse is pretty good-looking, and she contradicts the doctor's orders — gives me a cup of coffee anyhow, plus a roll, and we're sitting there quietly, listening to the other doctor and a nurse fixing the guy with the burned forehead. A little human interaction is taking place and my depression is gone as I begin to feel sorry for the guy with the burn, who is explaining that he was up late with insomnia cooking sweet potatoes when the pressure cooker blew. He was going to candy them with brown sugar and eat them at six in the morning and he's laughing, too, because of the Dilaudid drip. After Linda Ronstadt sings "Just One Look" on the radio, the announcer comes on and says that we've set a record for cold — it's thirteen and a half below at the airport — and I notice that the announcer is happy, too; there's a kind of solidarity that occurs when suffering is inflicted on the community by nature.

My own thing is the Vincent van Gogh effect. I read where he "felt like a million" after he cut off his ear. It only lasted for a couple of days. They always show you the series of six self-portraits that he painted at different times in his life as his mental condition went progressively downhill. Van Gogh One is a realistic-looking pic, but as life goes on and his madness gets worse he paints Van Gogh Six and it looks as though he's been doing some kind of bad LSD, which is how the world had been looking to me until I cut my thumb. It gave me a three-day respite from the blues, and clarity came into my life, and I have to remind myself by writing this down that all the bad stuff does pass if you can wait it out. You forget when you're in the middle of it, so during that three-day break I slapped this note on the refrigerator door: "Richard, you are a good and loving person, and all the bad stuff does pass, so remember that the next time you get down and think that you've always been down and always will be down, since that's paranoia and it gets you nowhere. You're just in one of your Fyodor Dostoyevski moods — do yourself a favor and forget it!"

I FELT so good I actually had the nerve to go out and buy a new set of clothes and see a movie, and then, on the last day before the depression came back, I drove out to Western State and checked my baby sister, Susan, out for a day trip. Susan was always a lot worse than me; she heard voices and pulled I don't know how many suicide attempts until she took my squirrel pistol and put a .22 long-rifle slug through the temple — not really the temple, because at the last minute you always flinch, but forward of the temple, and it was the most perfect lobotomy. I remember hearing the gun pop and how she came into my room (I was home from college for the summer) and said, "Richard, I just shot myself, how come I'm not dead?" Her voice was calm instead of the usual fingernails-on-the-chalkboard voice, the when-she-was-crazy (which was almost always) voice, and I realized later that she was instantly cured, the very moment the bullet zipped through her brain. Everyone said it was such a shame because she was so beautiful, but what good are looks if you are in hell? And she let her looks go at the hospital because she really didn't have a care in the world, but she was still probably the most beautiful patient at Western State. I had a fresh occasion to worry about her on this trip when I saw an attendant rough-handling an old man to stop him from whining, which it did. She'd go along with anything, and she had no advocate except me. And then I almost regretted going out there, in spite of my do-good mood, because Susan wanted to go to the Point Defiance Zoo to see Cindy, the elephant that was on the news after they transferred the attendant who took care of her, for defying orders and actually going into the elephant pen on the sly to be her friend.

There are seven hundred elephants in North American zoos, and although Cindy is an Asian elephant and a female and small, she is still considered the most dangerous elephant in America. Last year alone, three people were killed by elephants in the United States, and this is what Susan had seen and heard on the color television in the ward

6   Thom Jones

dayroom, and she's like a child — she wants to go out and see an elephant when it's ten below zero. They originally had Cindy clamped up in a pen tighter than the one they've got John Gotti in down in Marion, Illinois, and I don't remember that the catalogue of Cindy's crimes included human murder. She was just a general troublemaker, and they were beating her with a two-by-four when some animal activist reported it and there was a big scandal that ended with Cindy getting shipped down to the San Diego Zoo; I think there was some kind of escape (don't quote me on that) where Cindy was running around on a golf course in between moves, and then a capture involving tranquilizer darts, and when they couldn't control Cindy in San Diego they shipped her back up here to Tacoma and put her in maximum-security confinement. It was pretty awful. I told Susan that over in India Cindy would have a job hauling logs or something, and there would be an elephant boy to scrub her down at night with a big brush while she lay in the river, and the elephant boy would be with her at all times, her constant companion. Actually, the elephant would be more important than the boy, I told her, and that's how you should handle an elephant in America — import an experienced elephant boy for each one, give the kids a green card, pay them a lot of overtime, and have them stay with the elephants around the clock. You know, quality time. How could you blame Cindy for all the shit she pulled? And in the middle of this, Susan has a tear floating off her cheek and I don't know if it's a tear caused by the cold or if she was touched by Cindy's plight. The reason they sent my sister to the nuthouse was that you could light a fire on the floor in front of her and she would just sit there and watch it burn. When our parents died, I took her to my place in Washington state and hired helpers to look after her, but they would always quit — quit while I was over in the Third

World, where it's impossible to do anything. It was like, *Meanwhile, back in the jungle/Meanwhile, back in the States* . . . Apart from her lack of affect, Susan was always logical and made perfect sense. She was kind of like a Mr. Spock who just didn't give a shit anymore except when it came to childish fun and games. All bundled up, with a scarf over her ears, in her innocence she looked like Eva Marie Saint in *On the Waterfront.*

We drove over to Nordstrom's in the University District and I bought Suz some new threads and then took her to a hair salon where she got this chic haircut, and she was looking so good that I almost regretted it, 'cause if those wacked-out freaks at the hospital weren't hitting on her before they would be now. It was starting to get dark and time to head back when Susan spots the Space Needle from I-5 — she's never been there, so I took her to the top and she wandered outside to the observation deck, where the wind was a walking razor blade at five hundred and eighteen feet, but Susan is grooving on the lights of Seattle and with her homemade lobotomy doesn't experience pain in quite the way a normal person does, and I want her to have a little fun, but I'm freezing out there, especially my thumb, which ached. I didn't want to pop back inside in the sheltered part and leave her out there, though, because she might want to pitch herself over the side. I mean, they've got safety nets, but what if she's still got some vestige of a death wish? We had dinner in the revolving dining room, and people were looking at us funny because of Susan's eating habits, which deteriorate when you live in a nuthouse, but we got through that and went back to my place to watch TV, and after that I was glad to go to sleep — but I couldn't sleep because of my thumb. I was thinking I still hadn't cashed in the script for the pain pills when Susan comes into my bedroom naked and sits down on the edge of the bed.

"Ever since I've been shot, I feel like those animals in the zoo. I want to set them free," she says, in a remarkable display of insight, since that scar in her frontal lobes has got more steel bars than all the prisons of the world, and, as a rule, folks with frontal-lobe damage don't have much insight. I get her to put on her pajamas, and I remember what it used to be like when she stayed at home — you always had to have someone watching her — and I wished I had gotten her back to the hospital that very night, because she was up prowling, and suddenly all my good feelings of the past few days were gone. I felt crappy, but I had to stay vigilant while my baby sister was tripping around the house with this bullet-induced, jocular euphoria.

At one point she went outside barefoot. Later I found her eating a cube of butter. Then she took out all the canned foods in my larder and stacked them up — Progresso black beans (*beaucoup*), beef-barley soup, and canned carrot juice — playing supermarket. I tell her, "Mrs. Ma'am, I'll take one of those, and one of those, and have you got any peachy pie?"

She says, "I'm sorry, Richard, we haven't got any peachy pie."

"But, baby, I would sure like a nice big piece of peachy pie, heated up, and some vanilla ice cream with some rum sauce and maybe something along the lines of a maraschino cherry to put on the top for a little garnish. Nutmeg would do. Or are you telling me this is just a soup, beans, and carrot-juice joint? Is that all you got here?"

"Yes, Richard. Just soup and beans. They're very filling, though."

"Ahhm gonna have to call Betty Crocker, 'cause I'm in the mood for some pie, darlin'."

Suzie looks at me sort of worried and says that she thinks Betty Crocker is dead. Fuck. I realized I just had to sit on the couch and watch her, and this goes on and on, and of course I think I hear someone crashing around in the yard, so I get my .357 out from under my pillow and walk around the perimeter of the house, my feet crunching on the frozen snow. There was nobody out there. Back inside I checked on Susan, who was asleep in my bed. When I finally saw the rising of the sun and heard birds chirping to greet the new day, I went to the refrigerator, where I saw my recent affirmation: "Richard, you are a good and loving person," etc. I ripped it off the refrigerator and tore it into a thousand tiny pieces. Only an idiot would write something like that. It was like, I can't hack it in Africa, can't hack it at home — all I can hack is dead. So I took all the bullets out of the .357 except one, spun the chamber, placed the barrel against my right temple, and squeezed the trigger. When I heard the click of the hammer — voilà! I instantly felt better. My thumb quit throbbing. My stomach did not burn. The dread of morning and of sunlight had vanished, and I saw the dawn as something good, the birdsong wonderful. Even the obscure, take-it-for-granted objects in my house — the little knickknacks covered in an inch of dust, a simple wooden chair, my morning coffee cup drying upside down on the drainboard — seemed so relevant, so alive and necessary. I was glad for life and glad to be alive, especially when I looked down at the gun and saw that my bullet had rotated to the firing chamber. The Van Gogh effect again. I was back from Van Gogh Six to Van Gogh One.

THEY'RE calling from the hospital, because I kept Susan overnight: "Where is Susan?" "She's watching *Days of Our Lives*," I say as I shove the .357 into a top drawer next to the phone book. "Is she taking her Stelazine?" "Yes," I say. "Absolutely. Thanks for your concern. Now, goodbye!"

Just then the doorbell rings, and what I've got is a pair of Jehovah's Witnesses. I've seen enough of them on the Dark Continent to overcome an instinctive dread, since they seem to be genuinely content, proportionately — like, if you measured a bunch of them against the general population they are very happy people, and so pretty soon we're drinking Sanka and Susan comes out and they are talking about Christ's Kingdom on Earth where the lion lies down with the lamb, and Susan buys every word of it, 'cause it's like that line "Unless they come to me as little children . . . " Susan is totally guileless and the two Witnesses are without much guile, and I, the king of agnostics, listen and think, How's a lion going to eat straw? It's got a G.I. system designed to consume flesh, bones, and viscera — it's got sharp teeth, claws, and predatory instincts, not twenty-seven stomachs, like some bovine Bossie the Cow or whatever. And while I'm paging through a copy of *Awake!*, I see a little article from the correspondent in Nigeria entitled "The Guinea Worm — Its Final Days." As a doctor of tropical medicine, I probably know more about *Dracunculus medinensis*, the "fiery serpent," or Guinea worm, than anyone in the country. Infection follows ingestion of water containing crustacea (*Cyclops*). The worms penetrate the gut wall and mature in the retroperitoneal space, where they can grow three feet in length, and then generally migrate to the lower legs, where they form a painful blister. What the Africans do is burst the ulcer and extract the adult worm by hooking a stick under it and ever so gently tugging it out, since if you break it off the dead body can become septic and the leg might have to be removed. The pain of the Guinea worm is on a par with the pain of gout, and it can take ten days to nudge one out. The bad part is they usually come not in singles but in multiples. I've seen seven come out of an old man's leg.

If and when Global Aid sends me back to Africa, I will help continue the worm-eradication program, and as the Witnesses delight Susan with tales of a Heaven on Earth I'm thinking of the heat and the bugs in the equatorial zone, and the muddy water that the villagers take from rivers — they pour it in jugs and let the sediment settle for an hour and then dip from the top, where it looks sort of clean; it's hard to get through to them that *Cyclops* crustacea may be floating about invisibly and one swallow could get you seven worms, a swallow you took three years ago. You can talk to the villagers until you're blue in the face and they'll drink it anyhow. So you have to poison the *Cyclops* without over-poisoning the water. I mean, it can be done, but, given the way things work over there, you have to do everything yourself if you want it done right, which is why I hate the idea of going back: you have to come on like a one-man band.

On the other hand, Brother Bogue and the other brothers in the home office of Global Aid don't trust me; they don't like it when I come into the office irrepressibly happy, like Maurice Chevalier in his tuxedo and straw hat — *"Jambo jambo, bwana, jambo bonjour!"* — and give everyone one of those African soft handshakes, and then maybe do a little turn at seventy-eight revolutions per minute: "Oh, *oui oui*, it's delightful for me, walking my baby back home!" or "Hey, ain't it great, after staying out late? Zangk heffen for leetle gorls." Etc. They hate it when I'm high and they hate it when I'm low, and they hate it most if I'm feeling crazy/paranoid and come in and say, "You won't believe what happened to me now!" To face those humorless brothers every day and stay forever in a job as a medical administrator, to wear a suit and tie and drive I–5 morning and night, to climb under the house and tape those pipes with insulation — you get in the crawl space and the dryer-hose vent is busted and there's lint up the ass, a time bomb for spontaneous combustion, funny the house hasn't blown already (and furthermore, no wonder the house is dusty), and, hey, what, carpenter ants, too? When I think of all that: Fair America, I bid you adieu!

But things are basically looking up when I get Suz back to the hospital. As luck has it, I meet an Indian psychiatrist who spent fifteen years in Kampala, Uganda — he was one of the three shrinks in the whole country — and I ask him how Big Daddy Idi Amin is doing. Apparently, he's doing fine, living in Saudi Arabia with paresis or something, and the next thing you know the doc is telling me he's going to review Susan's case file, which means he's going to put her in a better ward and look out for her, and that's a load off my mind. Before I go, Suz and I take a little stroll around the spacious hospital grounds — it's a tranquil place. I can't help thinking that if Brother Bogue fires me — though I'm determined to behave myself after my latest mishap — I could come here and take Haldol and lithium, watch color TV, and drool. Whatever happened to that deal where you just went off to the hospital for a "little rest," with no stigma attached? Maybe all I need is some rest.

Susan still has those Jehovah's Witnesses on her mind. As we sit on a bench, she pulls one of their booklets out of her coat and shows me scenes of cornucopias filled with fruit and bounty, rainbows, and vividly colored vistas of a heaven on earth. Vistas that I've seen in a way, however paradoxically, in these awful Third World places, and I'm thinking, Let them that have eyes see; and let them that have ears hear — that's how it is, and I start telling Suz about Africa, maybe someday I can take her there, and she gets excited and asks me what it's like. Can you see lions?

And I tell her, "Yeah, baby, you'll see lions, giraffes, zebras, monkeys, and parrots, and the Pygmies." And she really wants to see Pygmies. So I tell her about a Pygmy chief who likes to trade monkey meat for tobacco, T-shirts, candy, and trinkets, and about how one time when I went manic and took to the bush I stayed with this tribe, and went on a hunt with them, and we found a honeycomb in the forest; one of the hunters climbed up the tree to knock it down, oblivious of all the bees that were biting him. There were about five of us in the party and maybe ten pounds of honey and we ate all of it on the spot, didn't save an ounce, because we had the munchies from smoking dope. I don't tell Suz how it feels to take an airplane to New York, wait four hours for a flight to London, spend six hours in a transient lounge, and then hop on a nine-hour flight to Nairobi, clear customs, and ride on the back of a feed truck driven by a kamikaze African over potholes, through thick red dust, mosquitoes, black flies, tsetse flies, or about river blindness, bone-break fever, bilharziasis, dumdum fever, tropical ulcers, AIDS, leprosy, etc. To go through all that to save somebody's life and maybe have them spit in your eye for the favor — I don't tell her about it, the way you don't tell a little kid that Santa Claus is a fabrication. And anyhow if I had eyes and could see, and ears and could hear — it very well might *be* the Garden of Eden. I mean, I can fuck up a wet dream with my attitude. I don't tell her that lions don't eat straw, never have, and so she's happy. And it's a nice moment for me, too, in a funny-ass way. I'm beginning to feel that with her I might find another little island of stability.

ANOTHER hospital visit: winter has given way to spring and the cherry blossoms are out. In two weeks it's gone from ten below to sixty-five, my Elavil and lithium are kicking in, and I'm feeling fine, calm, feeling pretty good. (I'm ready to go back and rumble in the jungle, yeah! *Sha-lah la-la-la-lah.*) Susan tells me she had a prophetic dream. She's unusually focused and articulate. She tells me she dreamed the two of us were driving around Heaven in a blue '67 Dodge.

"A '67 Dodge. Baby, what were we, the losers of Heaven?"

"Maybe, but it didn't really matter because we were there and we were happy."

"What were the other people like? Who was there? Was Arthur Schopenhauer there?"

"You silly! We didn't see other people. Just the houses. We drove up this hill and everything was like in a Walt Disney cartoon and we looked at one another and smiled because we were in Heaven, because we made it, because there wasn't any more shit."

"Now, let me get this straight. We were driving around in a beat-up car — "

"Yes, Richard, but it didn't matter."

"Let me finish. You say people lived in houses. That means people have to build houses. Paint them, clean them, and maintain them. Are you telling me that people in Heaven have jobs?"

"Yes, but they like their jobs."

"Oh, God, does it never end? A *job!* What am I going to do? I'm a doctor. If people don't get sick there, they'll probably make me a coal miner or something."

"Yes, but you'll love it." She grabs my arm with both hands, pitches her forehead against my chest, and laughs. It's the first time I've heard Susan laugh, ever — since we were kids, I mean.

"Richard, it's just like Earth but with none of the bad stuff. You were happy, too. So please don't worry. Is Africa like the Garden of Eden, Richard?"

"It's lush all right, but there's lots and lots of dead time," I say. "It's a good place to read *Anna Karenina*. Do you get to read novels in Heaven, hon? Have they got a library? After I pull my shift in the coal mine, do I get to take a nice little shower, hop in the Dodge, and drive over to the library?"

Susan laughs for the second time. "We will travel from glory to glory, Richard, and you won't be asking existential questions all the time. You won't have to anymore. And Mom and Dad will be there. You and me, all of us in perfect health. No coal mining. No wars, no fighting, no discontent. Satan will be in the Big Pit. He's on the earth now tormenting us, but these are his last days. Why do you think we are here?"

"I often ask myself that question."

"Just hold on for a little while longer, Richard. Can you do that? Will you do it for me, Richard? What good would Heaven be if you're not there? Please, Richard, tell me you'll come."

I said, "Okay, baby, anything for you. I repent."

"No more Fyodor Dostoyevski?"

"I'll be non-Dostoyevski. It's just that, in the meantime, we're just sitting around here — waiting for Godot?"

"No, Richard, don't be a smart-ass. In the meantime we eat lunch. What did you bring?"

I opened up a deli bag and laid out chicken-salad-sandwich halves on homemade bread wrapped in white butcher paper. The sandwiches were stuffed with alfalfa sprouts and grated cheese, impaled with toothpicks with red, blue, and green cellophane ribbons on them, and there were two large, perfect, crunchy garlic pickles on the side. And a couple of cartons of strawberry Yoplait, two tubs of fruit salad with fresh whipped cream and little wooden spoons, and two large cardboard cups of aromatic, steaming, fresh black coffee.

It begins to rain, and we have to haul ass into the front

seat of my Olds, where Suz and I finish the best little lunch of a lifetime and suddenly the Shirelles are singing, "This Is Dedicated to the One I Love," and I'm thinking that I'm gonna be all right, and in the meantime what can be better than a cool, breezy, fragrant day, rain-splatter diamonds on the wraparound windshield of a Ninety-eight Olds with a view of cherry trees blooming in the light spring rain?

Superman, My Son

WILHELM BLAINE pulled his red Volvo wagon under the lone, stubby fig tree in front of his son Walter's California-beige stucco home. Somebody needed to get off their rear, get out here, and do a little landscaping. But Blaine knew it wasn't so bad behind the large cedar fence. It was a little enclave, really, with the pool, the Jacuzzi, the barbecue setup, and the rattan chairs. You could do a Winston Churchill — sit under lofty palms, sip a little brandy, smoke an expensive cigar, and discuss the weighty matters of the world.

Blaine ran down his electric windows and the hefty scent of gardenia from the backyard hit him in the face. Behind the fence, Walter's wife Zona pruned, watered, and fertilized — but out front, nothing. The fig tree was in need of serious medical attention, and in general the whole neighborhood was taking a precipitous slide. Blaine saw lots of "For Rent" signs. Almost every driveway seemed overloaded. If it wasn't a pickup truck with jacked-up monster wheels, it was a pin-striped van or a Harley low rider amid broken bicycles and rusty automobile transmissions. When the subdivision was new, Walter had paid $240 K for his place, but Blaine had just seen a chicken prancing across a sun-torched lawn before he hung the left on Millpine Drive.

Blaine inched a few feet farther as he anticipated the amount of time he would spend inside. The Volvo would be an oven when he came out. Would Walter be laid out in a sluggish, torpid depression — insensible to reason or to the comforting reassurance of a father's voice? Or would he be mad as Saul, spewing poison and virulent accusations? Then there was Freddy, just back from Africa. Freddy could bullshit for hours. Blaine pondered these various intangibles. It would either be a lion's den or a morgue in there. He wanted to park the car so that it would be in at least partial shade. He looked back over his shoulder to the east, calculating, and caught a faceful of the 9:30 A.M. sun.

Poor Walter. He was a manic-depressive, and on this most recent flipout, according to Zona, he had somehow got buck-naked outside one of their supermarkets and dropped into the position of a Greek Olympian about to launch the discus. Zona said he locked up like a coiled spring. There was no discus to hurl but rather the Revised Standard Bible that he carried with him everywhere. And he would not let go. No amount of persuasion did any good. Walter *became* a statue, and they had to pick him up and take him to the emergency room just like that. The paramedics were furniture movers on that run. The incident did not have the feel of Walter's routine flipouts, either. Maybe this was a big one. Too bad Walter hadn't let the book sail. There was such a thing as religious toxicity. It was the worst poison of all. But Blaine wasn't going to go inside and say so. He wasn't going to get heavy-handed or come on too strong. He had done enough of that in the old days. He was just going to listen.

Zona had implied that Walter's ineffectual psychiatrist was some sort of "Christian" therapist. He had talked Walter out of his contortions, given him some Xanax, joined his hands in prayer, and then let Zona and Freddy drive Walter home. Blaine was glad he had missed the whole scene. He was worried about Walter but had troubles of his own. There were many things to do. Deals to be made. You just couldn't retire anymore. God almighty no! You had to work right up until the day you died.

Blaine revved the motor for a second and then switched off the ignition. The Volvo was his only means of transportation now, and he had come to love the car, the way it automatically "found" all his destinations in town. He had sold his Ferrari for interest on taxes due — no principal paid off or anything, just penalties. The next thing to go would be the house. But before he did that he had to pour a small fortune into finishing his courtyard.

One of the workers employed on that project, a cheerful green-card, had stolen his Patek Philippe. The guy had been dumb enough to "admire" the watch prior to the theft. Blaine had him figured but realized there was little he could do. The police certainly wouldn't care. Not about a mere property crime. Okay, the poor bastard needed the money, and Blaine left valuables around. The temptation must have been incredible. In the old days, Blaine would have hardly cared, but the Shoprite Food Value Emporium empire was falling to pieces. It was getting impossible to compete with the bigger stores, and Blaine was literally getting taxed out of business — getting reamed to keep people like the green-card afloat in various social programs of dubious worth. The thanks he got was grand theft — grand theft one day and armed robbery the next. Almost immediately after the green-card incident, Blaine had made hot tracks to his bedroom safe for his coin collection — close to fifty thousand in value — and had driven the wagon to a coin shop in downtown Sacramento and then, oh, man — a chain of events ensued that still had him reeling.

There were four black men inside the store when the proprietor buzzed him in through the security gate. Blaine's pockets were laden with gold, and he could literally smell the trouble — on top of the alcohol there was a toxic smell of adrenaline coming from these thugs, and they were getting right into the proprietor's face. "How much this one? How many Rolexes you got, man? You got some in the back? I don't like these here."

It was a tremendous relief to see them go, but suddenly they were back — one of them claiming to have left a pair of sunglasses behind. The Vietnamese coin dealer, Phat H'at, or the Fat Hat, as he was known, buzzed them back in. You would have thought the old man had developed an instinct for trouble, but he acted like a complete fool. Blaine had his coins out on the counter by then, and the bandits quickly brandished little snub-nosed .38s. Hat went for his nickel-plated .45, but one of the men was over the counter faster than a cat. "Motherfucker! One more move out of you and you dead."

Blaine had been glad that the bandit had some agility. He didn't want any shooting, although once the .45 was out of the way the robbers fired three shots into the security camera, *Ka-Pow! Ka-Pow!* Orange-and-blue flames burst out of the gun barrels. *Ka-Pow!* The harsh sound of the gunfire caused exquisite pain in his ears. One of the robbers scooped Blaine's coins into a bag, then executed a deft pirouette and expertly snatched the Cartier off Blaine's wrist and popped it into a pocket. Another man, wearing a ski mask, grabbed Blaine's wallet and began to rifle through it.

"You are welcome to all of it, gentlemen," Blaine had said, hands up, suddenly giddy. The savoir-faire with which he delivered these words seemed to calm the gunmen a little. It took the tension down a couple of notches. The biggest one pulled most of the green out of Blaine's wallet, but twelve bucks floated to the floor, and Blaine took a small satisfaction in stepping on the money. It was sort of a stupid thing to do, but Blaine felt possessed of a kind of Mel Gibson movie-house invulnerability. His left foot was on the ten, his right on the two singles, and he felt splendidly frozen in time, as if he were in a white tie and tails doing a kind of lithe Fred Astaire — as if he suddenly knew what life wanted of him.

While the bandits fled the shop, Fat Hat ducked into the back room and emerged with a twelve-gauge. Blaine's happy spell was broken. "Hey, there! Wait a minute! Those hoods will come back in here and shoot us both," he said.

"Why you smiling? Why you smiling?" Hat said. "Taking sixteen Rolexes. Got alla my cold, hard cash. Got all your gold, man!"

The Asian darted out into the parking lot, squatted, and leveled the gun from left to right. His movements resembled some ridiculous, partly forgotten foreign army-training maneuver — an action long ago imprinted in an Alzheimer's-demented brain. The bandits were peeling rubber, fishtailing away in an old diesel-powered Oldsmobile Toronado. One of them leaned out the window and blasted a couple of shots back, causing Fat Hat to drop prone and hug the asphalt. Blaine saw the blue-and-orange muzzle flame a second before he heard the shots. He watched the car swing out onto the freeway until the only sign of it was the lingering, thick white smoke of the tail exhaust. And very soon that was gone. The entire incident had lasted no more than a minute or two.

Fat Hat ran back inside and dialed 911. Then he turned on Blaine. "Them get away. Too fast for me. Getaway driver an' shit. Piss on this whole damn country, anyhow. I'm packing up and could go back to Mauritius! No gun in your face alla time! Why you smiling? Stop that smiling, vexing me! Damn you, man. Why you smiling?"

"I'm smiling because . . . I'm alive." Blaine picked up his last twelve dollars. "And because I've got enough money to buy lunch."

IN some perverse way, the robbery had been fun. It was an adventure. His gold was gone, but if thieves didn't get it, Walter's ineffectual psychiatrist would. Blaine returned to the thought of Wally frozen in a discus-thrower's position. His track specialty in high school had been the discus throw. Zona had told Blaine that Walter had been convinced the Bible was a tiny spaceship containing a crew of three hundred and fourteen perversely evil, micro-sized men who were extorting pocket change from some street bum Walter had recently met during his manic space walk. Walter was going to uncoil and hurl the little bastards to the farthest reaches of the Milky Way. Or something. He never really let the thing fly. Should have, probably. A normal person might find comfort in the fundamental religions, with their laws, promises, and the so-called covenant with God. But why listen to a bunch of cockamamie? Wasn't it better to pursue your own truths? Very few had the courage or the elasticity to go it alone, though. And to view Christianity through the lens of manic psychosis was dangerous. Blaine had shucked his own Bible in Germany just after the war. Blaine was a full-blooded German himself. He even took heat for it at the time ("You're one of *them*, Blaine, a fuckin' kraut"), but he saw what the Germans had done and he had hated them for it. He knew the tendencies. His personality was marred by them, but at least he knew them. You didn't have to let a bug crawl up your ass and get all hellbent and mean or trample over people to make money. You could treat people right without fearing or trying to please God. You could do it simply because it was human to do it, because love was a more ennobling tendency than hate, and if you were lucky, maybe you could live with yourself and sleep nights.

But Walter didn't have Blaine's German genes. Blaine and his wife, Joanna, had adopted Wally. The boy was just three when they got him. This whole manic-psychosis business had to be genetic. He had been a happy kid back in Appleton, Wisconsin. Blaine had racked his brain trying to think of some way in which he had failed his son. There was nothing major. Blaine recalled the streams of dogs, birds, and rabbits, and Walter's pals and girlfriends. Walter hadn't been a very good student, but he had one stupendous season as an all-state catcher on the baseball team. Blaine could still remember the fastball Wally drove deep into the right-centerfield seats, breaking up a no-hitter in the state championship game. The opposing pitcher was brimming with confidence, and he challenged Walter with a fat one right down the middle. *Boom!* As soon as Wally made contact, everyone knew that ball was gone. It was one of those tape-measure jobs — four hundred and four feet. What a day that had been; probably the kid's best day. The very next week, Walter came within a half inch of setting a state record in the discus throw. The first athlete at Appleton to double-letter in spring sports. Blaine bought Walter a brand new Corvair a few days later, and in less than a month, Walter was in the hospital; he had experienced his first manic flipout and rolled the car. There were subsequent hospitalizations for psychiatric treatment. Successions of therapists. Years of nothing but pain and trouble, really. Hell, trouble was the one constant in life. Pain and trouble. They pervaded everything.

Blaine stepped under the fig tree and examined its leaves. It had once been lush and productive of fruit, and now it was barren. Did it suffer — actually *suffer* on some level? He studied the tree with wonder, stroking its rough trunk. Love could save this plant. Zona could get her ass out here and save this plant if she *felt* like it. But you couldn't stay on top of everything. Blaine walked away from the fig tree. See you later. He was in up to his neck on several levels, and he realized now why he was stalling. He did not want to go inside.

It was a relief to duck into the vestibule and get out of the blazing sun. Blaine was sweating in his seersucker suit. He pushed the doorbell, swept his fingers through his mane of chestnut brown hair, and then rammed both hands in his pockets as he rocked back and forth on his heels. The right words would be there for him.

ZONA Blaine clomped down the stairs wearing a short robe and a pair of her husband's slip-ons. She still had nice legs, and, in spite of her pool-lounging in the hot valley sun, she had nice skin. She was cradling a basket full of laundry and talking to her bird, Boo Boo, who was perched high on her shoulder. She looked into the front room and said good morning to Walter's cousin, Freddy, who was leaning forward on the couch with a cup of coffee so hot he was fanning it with a copy of a bird magazine. Freddy didn't look so good. It had been a real shocker to Zona when she first got a load of him at the airport. He was beyond what one might term "a whiter shade of pale," and he had dropped fifty pounds. He claimed it was malaria.

Zona swung open the garage door and loaded the washer. She was back in a second and said, "This bird is crazy."

"Can it talk?" Freddy said.

"You should hear him. I go out into the garage and he says, 'Whacha doin'?' I say, 'I'm doing the laundry, Boo Boo.' He says, 'Need any help?' "

"No!" Freddy declared.

"I'm not kidding. 'Need any help?' "

"That's wild. What else does he say?" Freddy cranked the footrest of the lounger down and made an assault on the hot cup of coffee. Zona wondered how he could drink it so hot.

"He does a one-way telephone conversation: 'Yeah . . . uh-huh . . . yeah?' Then he'll pause, you know. 'Oh, yeah? Uh-huh. That's right.' Pause again. 'Oh, yeah? Ah-ha-ha-ha!' "

Freddy said, "Is it like parakeet chatter? Or is it like human?"

"It's just like human. Parakeets — " Zona screwed up her face and cocked her head to the side. " 'Pretta bird, chich chich chich. Pretta bird.' That's all you get from parakeets."

"Parakeets have got that tinny quality," Freddy said. He picked up a bright blue butane lighter and shook a Kool from his pack. "What about Blaine's parrot? That bird can talk."

"Roberto? 'I ham joost hey line man for zee county.' "

Freddy lit his cigarette and inhaled deeply. "Roberto bit me on the cuticle last time I was out here. Took out a chunk of meat. I still got the scar."

"African grays," Zona said. "They are mean, but they're the best talkers. 'Hey, hey, pretty wooman. Wot harrh you wearing such hey sexy blouse for? You h'rr making me so hot, bébé.' "

"He's a smooth one, all right. He gets you to trust him and then he bites you. Does he bite Blaine?"

"He bites them one and all. Roberto is a real card. He's a character," Zona said.

"Who taught him all that Spanish? He must be a pre-owned bird. It's always a sex trip or that stupid song."

"*Bésame Mucho,*" Zona said.

"Yes. I hate that song. It makes me depressed. If I bought a pre-owned bird, I'd get it from a soul brother, not some bean head. It always starts in with that song at six in the morning. And, it's like, loud."

Blaine remained in the porchway with his hands in his pockets, rocking on his heels, wondering if the doorbell had shorted out. But then he heard voices inside. He gave the door a little rap. He was thinking of the stickup, wondering if his insurance would cover it. Well, it would or it wouldn't.

He gave the door a second sharp rap and stepped inside. Blaine liked his entrances to seem like explosions. His voice was a rich baritone, and he liked to ham. "Is somebody in here badmouthing my parrot?"

"Hey, hey, hey!" Freddy said. He got up to shake hands with his uncle, but they ended up in a tight, back-slapping embrace. It had been three years. The family had been dying out fast. Freddy was the last of the Blaine line, and, by the looks of him, Blaine wondered how long Freddy would last. He looked terrible.

Blaine held his nephew at arm's length and studied his face. "My God, Freddy, it's good to see you again. Jesus! How are you feeling?"

"Not too bad. How are you? Lucky to be alive, ain't you? Stick 'em up, dude!"

"Oh, Christ," Blaine said dismissively. "I was just thinking about those cocksuckers. They got away clean. I'm lucky to be alive. Or not so lucky, when you consider the state of the world. A bullet between the eyes might have been a blessing. I'm seventy-two, for Christ's sake. I am probably

Superman, My Son   27

nourishing monstrous occlusions and tumors of which I'm not yet aware but will be presently. Ha! But what about you? What about this number you pulled on the airplane?"

"I hate to go into that," Freddy said. "I'll just get riled up again."

"No, tell me." Blaine said. He was an expert at drawing people out, and he loved lurid tales. Blaine winked at Zona, who ran upstairs to put on some clothes.

"I haven't done anything like that in years," Freddy said. "I thought I was in control, that those days were over. But sometimes there is a black-and-white situation where anger seems completely justified."

"I want to hear the whole story. Don't shortchange me," Blaine said, as he selected a pipe from Walter's pipe rack and began loading it from a canister of coarse tobacco.

Freddy took a quick hit off his cigarette. "Well, imagine," he said. "From Douala, in Cameroon, to Kinshasa, to Dar, to the Africa House in Zanzibar — party, party for a couple of days — and then on to Paris, customs at L.A., blah blah, and then here. Until the water bed in the guest bedroom last night, the last time I was in between sheets and really slept was at the Hotel Akwa on the Boulevard de la Liberté in fucking Douala — the armpit of Africa. That was just before the latest round with this fucking malaria. None of it was too bad, until I hit that airline strike in Los Angeles. I was supposed to be in business class, but they somehow had me in the last seat in the tail section — one of those seats that don't tilt back. You can take that shit when you're young, but I was having my — you know, my epileptic twitches, and I'm back there going off like a machine gun, rat-a-tat-tat, and in the meantime the steward is dishing shit out to everybody, like we're in prison and he's the yard boss. I got into it with him. I just let him have it, that's all. Zona, is there any more coffee?"

"How many cups have you had already?" Zona said. She had fixed her hair in a ponytail and had thrown on a cotton sundress.

"Just two."

Zona looked to her father-in-law. "All he does is sit there, drink coffee, and smoke strong cigarettes. He won't eat. I didn't think doctors smoked anymore."

"Who said doctors had good sense?" Freddy said. "Doctors can be the craziest sumbitches in the world. Behind the bulwark of authority, self-assurance, and the seemingly judicious intelligence of the white coat, too often unrighteousness, lunacy, and sheer incompetence sit at the helm. Thus it is in medicine as in all walks of life; in medicine, more so. Drug addicts, suicides, desperate people. I mean, I publish in the journals. I have a certain renown. So you see what the world's coming to." Freddy presented Zona with the empty mug. "Please, baby, more. I've got jet lag and a real bad case of the poontang blues."

Zona went into the kitchen, and Blaine leaned forward and whispered, "You get much pussy over there — you know, in Africa?"

"Yeah, sure," Freddy said nervously. "A little. Some one-night stands with the ever-circulating network of aid workers. Some of the hard cases will go to the ground and marry natives. A lot of the Catholics sublimate. I can do that, too. I can sublimate."

"You mean you just don't do it?" Blaine said.

"Well, it's pretty risky. AIDS is everywhere. It used to be bad in the big cities, but now it's all over. It puts the fear of God into you."

Zona returned with a coffee tray. "Tell Willy how you lost your shoe."

Freddy began to fan his mug as soon as Zona filled it. "I'm sure Uncle Willy would rather hear about Walter."

Blaine wiggled a little bag of NutraSweet, ripped off the top, and dumped the contents into his cup. "Zona filled me in about Walter late last night. You tell me about the flight from hell."

Freddy sipped his coffee. "Am I talking too fast?" He didn't wait for an answer. "I am now and was then all whacked-out on Mefloquine. I was not really lucid, but still it dawned on me that whenever anybody had a request that was within this steward's power to fulfill, he just said, 'Yeah, just a minute,' and didn't *do* anything. We were just sitting dead on the ground like for about an hour and a half, and the steward took that rude L.A. tone, 'Everybody on the plane is a revenue-paying customer. If you want another seat you'll have to trade with somebody once we get into the air.' I just lost it. 'Who in the *hell* do you think you are, jacking everybody around? Motherfucker, I have been out in the damn jungle in Cameroon. I have been on an airplane or in a transient lounge for two and a half days, and you think you got it bad 'cause you're working a double shift. Well, how do you think *I* feel?'

"He came right back. 'Fuck you!' he says, and then, bingo, we started wrestling in the aisle, and two cops grabbed me. 'You're under arrest!' I've been three years in Central Africa and nothing happens to me until I get back to the imperialistic, fascist state!"

Blaine had thought he would come into the house and have words for whatever hit him, but the spectacle of Freddy left him speechless.

Freddy gulped down more coffee, lit another Kool, and, thus freshly armed, leaned forward and continued. "People were still trying to get on the plane, it was a big cluster fuck, and the police were dragging me away; I lost a shoe, and some little Greek lady got up and said, 'Hold it right there! That man did nothing wrong! *That man did nothing wrong.* It was *him*, Mr. Sunny Jim there!' and she's pointing to the steward. 'It was all his fault.' So there is some justice in the universe. The cops stopped, like, 'Oh, yeah?' and the steward said, 'Screw this job, who needs it?' I mean, this is the kind of shit that happens on a cross-country Trailways bus ride when some maniac is stoked on fortified wine. And I never did find my shoe. Off to baggage claim wearing socks." Freddy had a pencil-thin mustache and a short goatee, which he fingered nervously while he patted perspiration from his forehead with a folded linen tea napkin. Blaine stared at him.

"Stop looking at me like that," Freddy said. "I get crazy when I tell that story. I'm better now, really, if I could just — if God would just have mercy on me and let me get a little sleep." He laughed nervously. "So tell us about the robbery. Four of them, with gunfire. Was dey blood? Was dey niggazzh?"

"They were thugs," Blaine said. "They just pumped a few shots into the ceiling, that's all. Why do you denigrate them? You are over in Africa for three years, ostensibly saving African lives, dispensing care — "

Freddy flicked his hand at a fly. Blaine took note of the limp wrist action and the way Freddy crossed his legs. In spite of a lifelong fondness for Freddy, Blaine felt himself disapproving of his nephew's whole demeanor.

"It's just a term of speech, Uncle Willy. You yourself referred to them as 'cocksuckers.' Was this coin dealer insured?"

"I still don't know," Blaine said. "My lawyer's handling it. It's depressing. I am down to selling paintings and coins so I can fix up that courtyard. In the morning, I'm importing a fountain from Italy, before lunch I am robbed, and in the afternoon I'm shopping for a double-wide."

"You're such a kidder," Freddy said. "Zona, did you hear that, babe? He's getting a double-wide."

"I'm serious," Blaine said. "I've got some scrub acreage. I'll plop it down there. *Pow!*" Blaine slapped his hand on the coffee table. "Home, sweet home. I'll sit there and call it good." He relit his pipe. "Where is Walter, for God's sake? How is he?"

Zona gave Blaine a cup of coffee. "He's up in the bedroom."

"Won't come out?" Blaine said.

"No," Zona said. "I've been trying to baby him but . . . well, you know Walter. He's the biggest and best manic depressive in the Golden State. When he's up, *fa-gam!* The planet Krypton. He can fly there in an hour. But when he's down, he's really down. A major crash."

Blaine's face became a mask of concern. "He's back on the lithium, isn't he?"

"Yes," Zona said, "and I could sue that damn psychiatrist! 'Try the Tegretol a little longer.' 'He doesn't need any damn Tegretol,' I said. 'You sit there real calm and say, "Try the Tegretol a little longer; check back in two weeks," and Walter is running around in a three-piece wool suit and no underwear!' He's got the Samsonite out and he's packing. I say, 'Walter, where are you going?' He says, 'I'm blasting back to Krypton. To be among my own kind.' And — *fa-gam!* — out the door he goes, wearing a damn three-piece wool suit, no underwear, a horrible tie, nine pounds of wing tips and no socks; he's got huge blisters on his heels and doesn't even seem to know. It has to be at least a hundred and twelve out and he's wearing that ugly damn brown suit of his, copping a load of b.o. — when he finally ditched it, I burned the damn thing. When you get b.o. into wool, it never comes out. Pick it up with a pole. He says, 'Where's my brown suit?' 'Walter, that suit is out of style.' 'It's so old it went out of style and came back in,' he says. I said, 'They never quite do, they never quite do, and every fool knows that.' "

"But he's on the lithium now?" Blaine asked. His focus was on Zona now. He was completely concentrating on her.

"Finally," Zona said. "I'm about ready to lose my mind. He packed up that Samsonite and was off. I'm not lying. The Eye of Horus and Rosicrucians. I'm serious."

"Can I go up and see him?" Blaine said.

"I don't think that would be a very good idea," Zona said. "His remarks concerning his father have been kind of volatile lately." She picked up one of Freddy's Kools and lit it. "Damn, three months without a cigarette," she said.

"Well, I guess every son wants to kill his dad at some level," Blaine said. "But I thought the Tegretol was doing him good."

"It was at first. His psoriasis cleared up entirely. He was going to his recovery meetings, to Bible study, to bird meetings. When Walter is straight, he's totally on the ball. But this shrink had him on Prozac, too. Got him horny. Let me tell you. Five times a day! I said, 'Walter, I'm not made out of steel. You may be Superman but I'm a forty-six-year-old woman with a hysterectomy last year. Give me a break.' "

Freddy began to finger his goatee again. "Psoriasis. In terms of diseases, it's a metaphor for rage."

"What's that supposed to mean?" Blaine said.

"You are Walter's father," Freddy said. "You would have the insight. The skin is a very emotive organ. Don't get so touchy."

Blaine leaned forward with his forearms balanced on his knees. He gave a little sigh and turned up his palms. "We adopted Wally when he was three," he said. "Most of the pyschic damage had to have been done long before. We were good parents. Who knows? Maybe manic psychosis is genetic. The psoriasis comes from the pills. Of course, what he says may be true. He may indeed come from Smallville.

Perhaps he truly is Superman. He went through the windshield of a Corvair without a scratch."

"It's a possibility we should consider," Freddy said. "Superman."

Blaine turned to Zona. "What about Turkey? Can't you go back there for the psoriasis?"

"Turkey?" Freddy said, pinching his chin.

"Yes," Blaine said. "There's this village in Turkey that has a kind of hot springs with these weird little fish in it, and what you do is sit in the springs and the fish come up and nibble your skin. There's something in their saliva, or whatever, that causes the skin to heal over. Two weeks and you're in remission."

"I'm not going back to damn Turkey," Zona said. "They don't have any magic carpets. What they got is buses with bald tires, nonexistent shock absorbers, and all the windows stuck shut! Damn! I'm a California girl. I like air conditioners, clean water, and a certain amount of oxygen in my atmosphere." Zona shot a stream of smoke out of the side of her mouth. "And they've got laws from day one over there. They used to hang you for drinking coffee and smoking."

"Pretty soon they'll be doing it here," Freddy said. "Have you noticed that now you can't offend with the sexist or racial remark, but smokers are open game? I mean every news broadcast, the front page of every paper. A cigarette was just a cigarette twenty years ago, but now the smoker is a pariah."

"That's true," Blaine said. "All that hate has to come out. The world needs scapegoats. No one will embrace the other — the inner dark man."

"And in another ten years coffee drinkers will be on the list," Zona said, taking a measured drag on the cigarette. "Coffee makes people violent or something."

"They should tax it, if you want to know," Blaine said.

"I mean, if you get right down to it, how much would you pay for a Kool and a cup of rocket fuel before you had to get dressed and hit the road?"

Freddy fiddled with his lighter. "Getting up in the morning, for coffee and a cigarette? I don't know, considering my present financial circumstances, which are meager, every last dime . . . seven hundred."

"You see. You aren't the only one, either; there are thousands like you," Blaine said. "We could wipe out the national debt."

Freddy shook a Kool from his pack and lit it. He put an arch in his voice, "Excuse me, do y'all mind if I smoke?"

"I like them too much," Zona said as she mashed hers out. "I better go check on Walter."

Blaine waved his daughter-in-law over to him and spoke quietly. "Was there some kind of precipitating event? What the hell *really* happened?"

"A neighbor — this guy, this asshole hurt his back at work and is collecting disability. If you ask me, it's a bullshit claim. He sits in his garage and drinks beer all day, or you'll see him doing real heavy labor, like he's got the strongest back in the world. Anyhow, he comes over here and says Walter's birds are too loud. Calls the city. They come out and say Walter isn't zoned for an aviary. You know how Walter lives for those birds. Well, not only do we have to get rid of the birds, move them out to the stables, but they want us to tear up the construction. If I were a man I would take that guy out with one punch. One punch! End of conversation. End of problem."

"I can't believe Walter is cowed by some guy with a bad back," Freddy said. "He's a damn Sumo."

Zona said, "Yes, but he's not mean, and he really gets into the Christian lifestyle. So now it takes a half hour to drive out to the stables. It takes an hour to cut up fruit. You have to bleach the tables, the cutting boards, and all the paraphernalia because of salmonella, which can wipe out a flock overnight. Lories eat fruit and nectar; they aren't seed eaters. That's the big downside on lories. You do that twice a day and try to run a business and it will snap you. Of course, the city is right. We aren't zoned for an aviary. So there you are."

"And I've got to sell the stables," Blaine said. "I wish we'd dumped the business ten years ago and bugged out for Mexico. We got an offer for seven million at the time, but we were taking in a hundred and ninety-five thousand a month clear. Now I'm stuck. Our traffic is down by half, the lease payments and payroll are killing us. The next thing, I really will be living in a double-wide. In fact, I don't see any way to avoid it."

"We'll all be living in the double-wide when I pay for this last caper," Zona said. She picked up the laundry basket and headed upstairs.

Blaine looked over at Freddy. "So you really love it over there, in Central Africa?"

"I do," Freddy said. "I feel that my life has meaning there. I can't do any good over here. I'm just not built for here. In Africa, I thrive, although it's very hard. Africa generates and consumes at an accelerated rate. You can feel it buzz. An hour of rain can turn a desert green in a day, the grass will grow three inches in a week, and two more days of sun can turn the green brown. Production, consumption. It's so instant. It's just . . . super. You can understand the whole 'cradle of civilization' business the minute you take a breath over there. They gave me a medical leave. I just came home to recover. This is a horseshit life back here."

"Joanna and I did Kenya and Tanzania just before she died — what, two summers ago? I guess that's just Disneyland compared to Cameroon, but I think I know what you mean."

At these words, Freddy did an ultra-femme double take, and Blaine's suspicions were confirmed. He thought of AIDS, and found himself cringing inwardly, as if in the presence of a vampire.

"Shit," Freddy said, "I didn't know you guys went to Africa. What about your pathological fear of lions? You told me when I was little that a lion was going to eat you."

"You are right. I thought a lion would get me. As a kid, I saw the picture. My mother said it was a dream. They took me to the doctor, but it wasn't a dream. It was some sort of ESP. I was terrified that Barnum and Bailey would drive by in a convoy, have an accident, and let a lion loose — that it would make its way to my house and eat me. This was my greatest fear."

"But you went to Kenya. Why would you go *there*? To tempt fate?"

Blaine said, "Well, when we rented the cherry farm out, up in Oregon — didn't I tell you this? When we rented the cherry farm to those hippies, the lions almost did get me."

"What lions on the cherry farm?" Freddy said.

"Jesus!" Blaine said. "I drove up to the cherry farm in Salem to check on the property when your dad was in the nuthouse. I knew something was going on, and I was right."

"What?"

"Well, hell, the tenants were five months behind in the rent," Blaine said. "Dope-smoking hippies. I rented them the place because they were Walter's friends. 'Oh, Mr. Blaine, we'll take care of the place just like it was our own.' Shit! Everything was either missing or ruined. They even cut a hole in the front door so their Rottweiler could go in and out. They had opium poppies in the front yard — the little pods were oozing juice from razor slits. I figured that if they're growing opium in the yard, they had to have grow lights in the basement. I told the hippie housewife I was going to go down in the basement to check on the furnace, and she panicked — *no, no, you can't do that*. When a little kid started crying upstairs, I had my chance. Down into the basement, I turn around and there's a fully grown African lion — "

"Jesus Christ!"

Blaine came up from the couch with his palms out as if he were summoning up a vision in a crystal ball. His eyes darted from left to right as he reenacted the scene. "A fully grown lioness crouching down in the seven o'clock position, and from the front comes a male. I knew then that my picture was coming true. The male let out a growl that shook the rafters, almost knocked me down — Christ! Ten seconds later the hippie earth-mother bitch is down the stairs with an umbrella, popping it in the female's face. Those were a long ten seconds." Blaine sat back on the couch and sipped his coffee. "The coin shop was a romp."

"God! Mary Poppins," Freddy said, squealing with delight.

"She says, 'Back, Sheena!' " Blaine extended his left leg, pulled his pant leg loose and laughed.

Freddy rattled off a laugh of his own and dabbed at his face with another of Zona's linen tea napkins. "Jesus! You never told me this."

Blaine scowled as he took a swig of coffee. "Freddy, you've got that too-much-Elavil, no-energy fairy voice again."

"My voice isn't *that* bad," Freddy said. "I'm starving, sleep-deprived, malarial, and if I don't take a leak pretty soon, I'm going to piss my pants! Give me a break, dude."

At this Blaine slapped his thigh and laughed. "It is that bad," he mimicked. Then he was on his feet again, acting out the scene in the basement. He would imitate a lion, then himself, then the hippie housewife, and then a lion again. *"Back, Sheena!"*

Freddy mopped his face. "Zona, he's making me laugh. I'm gonna pee on the rug!" He jumped up, and cupping his genitals, began to dance like a pair of scissors. "Quick: what happened to the lions? A zoo?"

"Euthanized," Blaine said. "But the point is my picture was right in the ballpark. I went to Africa because lions in Africa weren't my problem. It was lions in Oregon."

"My voice isn't *that* bad. It's . . . normal."

"It's airy-fairy," Blaine said. He held his hand out and let it quaver. "I'm just telling you because you're my nephew, and somebody has to point these things out. It was really bad when you said, 'Excuse me, do you mind if I smoke?' "

Freddy threw his head back and laughed. "That was *intentional!* I was doing the nineteen-thirties movie thing. You're just getting crabby because you need to eat. Did you have anything for breakfast?"

"A doughnut," Blaine said.

"Well, you were sugared up and now you're down. You came in booming with good cheer and now you're Mr. Crab Patch. Maybe we should make some eggs or something?" Freddy said.

Zona came downstairs with a thick red copy of the *Physicians' Desk Reference* and shoved it at Freddy's chest, knocking him back on the couch. "Page 2,257," she said. "Interpret the lingo, buster."

"What's going on up there?" Blaine said.

Zona said, "I put Boo Boo in with Walter. They're talking."

"They're talking? You mean like 'How're ya doin'?' " Freddy said.

Zona stroked her cheek, " 'Whacha doin'?' 'Just layin' here, Boo.' 'Are you feeling bad, Captain?' 'I feel pretty rough. I sure do.' 'Give me a kiss.' Talking like that."

"Well, at least he's talking. Last night — last night was *bad*," Freddy said.

"It's tearing me up," Blaine said, reaching through the buttons of his shirt to rub his chest. "This on top of everything else."

Zona rapped the *P.D.R.* with her knuckles. "How long before the pills kick in?"

Freddy's finger ran expertly down a column as he scanned the entry for Eskalith. " *Typical symptoms of mania include pressure of speech, motor hyperactivity, reduced need for sleep, flight of ideas, grandiosity, elation, poor judgment, aggressiveness and possibly hostility. When given to a patient experiencing a manic episode,* Eskalith *may produce a normalization of symptomatology within one to three weeks.'* Why, it sounds great. We could all do with some."

There was a large crash and the sound of heavy footfalls upstairs. "Goddammit! Who's laughing down there?" The voice came down like thunder, with an overlay of fear and paranoia.

"I'll be right back," Zona said. She rushed up the stairs, swung open the bedroom door, stepped inside, and pushed it shut.

"Shit," said Blaine. "I'm going up there."

"Zona can handle it. He finds men threatening. We better wait. He's got the strength of twenty."

"Maybe you're right," Blaine said. "She's really been good for him. An angel. Really."

"Most women couldn't handle the psoriasis, let alone the — "

"She doesn't even see it; it's not a consideration," said Blaine. He sat with both arms extended on the top of the couch and managed to sneak a look at his new Timex Indiglo.

*   *   *

AT last, Walter appeared at the top of the stairs. He was a huge man, balding, with a six-week beard. He cinched the tie on his white terry-cloth bathrobe. He held a worn Bible in his hand and looked crazed. Zona followed him as he grabbed the railing and worked his way down the steps.

"Hi, Dad. Hi, Freddy," Walter said meekly. He paused on the third step from the bottom and looked down at the two men.

"Walter wants some breakfast," Zona said. "Or should we have lunch? It's getting late. Would you guys like to eat?"

"We were just talking about that," Freddy said. "Eggs. Protein. Whole-wheat toast. Tomato juice. I'm a nervous fucking wreck. I look like hell. At least Walter *looks* like a human being. I'm just a skeleton in a bag of of skin. And I don't have AIDS and I'm not gay, if that's what you're all thinking — so you can quit boiling the silverware."

Walter stared awkwardly at the two men and then raised his left hand like an Indian. "I would like to read something. A prayer."

"Read?" Blaine said.

"Great," Freddy said. "I'm going to piss my pants, but first a prayer."

Walter fumbled through his Bible. At first it seemed that he was okay, and then it appeared that the effort was almost too much for him to bear. He had to grab the bannister to steady himself. His lips were dry, and he kept running his tongue over them. Large beads of perspiration began to form on his forehead. The onionskin pages of his Bible were sticking together. He flipped through them, stopping occasionally to study the text. From the look on his face, it seemed that he was trying to decipher an incomprehensible language. The Bible began to wobble in his huge hands like a divining rod. "I'm sorry," he said. "Geez! Are you guys hot? Is it hot down here?"

"It's just hotter than a *mother*fucker," Freddy said. "Africa hot! The Libyan desert at high noon!"

"It's warm," Zona said. "Air conditioner or no. But you're sweating because of the lithium, and Freddy has a fever. Don't indulge yourselves with symptomatic lingo. It just makes everything worse."

"You're right baby," Walter said. He opened the Bible again, and, leaning against the wall, studied the page, while Blaine, Zona, and Freddy waited expectantly. At last Walter was ready. A gleam came to his eye. He was running with sweat. He pulled the Bible up close to his face, as if he were severely nearsighted. He read at an infuriatingly slow pace, but his audience watched with rapt attention:

> He who dwells in the shelter of the Most High,
> who abides in the shadow of the Almighty,
> will say to the Lord, "My refuge and my fortress;
> my God, in whom I trust."
> For he will deliver you from the snare of the fowler
> and from the deadly pestilence;
> he will cover you with his pinions,
> and under his wings you will find refuge;
> his faithfulness is a shield and buckler.
> You will not fear the terror of the night,
> nor the arrow that flies by day,
> nor the pestilence that stalks in darkness,
> nor the destruction that wastes at noon-day.
>
> A thousand may fall at your side,
> ten thousand at your right hand;
> but it will not come near you.
> You will only look with your eyes
> and see the recompense of the wicked.

Because you have made the Lord your refuge,
the Most High your habitation,
no evil shall befall you,
no scourge come near your tent.

For he will give his angels charge of you
to guard you in all your ways.
On their hands they will bear you up,
lest you dash your foot against a stone.
You will tread on the lion and the adder,
the young lion and the serpent you
will trample under foot.

"Because he cleaves to me in love, I will deliver him;
I will protect him, because he knows my name.
When he calls to me, I will answer him;
I will be with him in trouble,
I will rescue him and honor him.
With long life I will satisfy him,
and show him my salvation."

By the time Walter finished, his robe was soaked, and the sweat was popping off his face, plopping down on the pages of the Bible. His hands were shaking. He continued to work his tongue over his cracked lips. He closed the book and pressed it to his breast.

"I'm still a little bit messed up," Walter said. "But I think I'm going to be okay. The lithium is starting to work. That's why I'm sweating so bad. I'm dehydrated, too. Honey, can I have some Diet Shasta — black cherry, two cans?"

Zona put her arm around his shoulder. "You're just going to be fine, babe. Just fine. I'll get you the pop and then fix all you boys up with some grub."

Freddy got up and hugged his cousin. "It's cool, Wally. I love you, man. But I gotta hit the water closet. Was it a good trip?"

"It was righteous, cuz. I saw the alpha and the omega, but I'm back now. Go forth and pee," Walter said. "And then *everybody* get back out here so we can do a big circle hug and sing joyous praise for a multitude of blessings."

"Fuck you," Freddy said.

"That's right, Walter, just fuck it, huh?" Zona called from the kitchen. Her tone was light.

When it was his turn, Blaine embraced Walter and at once recalled the joy he felt forty-seven years and some before, when he first held this stranger, the adopted little boy.

The Blaine line would end with Walter and Freddy. Zona was sterile, like Joanna. Unless by some remote stretch Freddy got married, it was over, and Blaine was sure now that Freddy was gay and suffering from the first symptoms of AIDS. Blaine took in all these thoughts in a rush, and through eyes slightly blurring with tears, he glanced outside and saw how the shadow of the withering fig tree had disappeared at noon, leaving his Volvo a victim of the blistering sun. Heat waves shimmered off the faded paint job. Most people at least had the satisfaction of knowing that they would live on in their grandchildren. Even atheists took consolation in that.

Blaine gave Walter a tight hug. His son was soaking wet. "You had me worried there, kiddo. It's good to have you back."

"Thanks, dad," Walter said. "I'm okay now. It's all right."

Blaine broke loose from Walter and with a croaking voice called to Zona, "Just a minute, beautiful. Let me give you a hand out there." As he stepped away from the living room, Blaine dabbed the tears from his eyes, quickly blew his nose, and fought to regain his composure before he "exploded" around the corner singing, *"Bé-sa-me, Bé-same mucho, como si fuera esta noche la última vez...."*

Way Down Deep in
the Jungle

DR. KOESTLER'S baboon, George Babbitt, liked to sit near the foot of the table when the physician took his evening meal and eat a paste the doctor had made consisting of ripe bananas and Canadian Mist whiskey. Koestler was careful to give him only a little, but one scorching afternoon when the generators were down and the air conditioners out, Koestler and Babbitt sat under the gazebo out near the baobab tree that was the ersatz town square of the Global Aid mission and got blasted. It was the coolest spot you could find, short of going into the bush. The baboon and the man were waiting for a late supper, since the ovens were out, too. Cornelius Johnson, the mission cook, was barbecuing chickens out in the side yard — not the typical, scrawny African chickens, but plump, succulent ones that Johnson made fat with sacks of maize that the generous donors to Global Aid had intended for the undernourished peoples of the region.

It had been a grueling day, and Koestler was drinking warm whiskey on an empty stomach. At first, he was impatient for a meal, then resigned to waiting, then half smashed and glad to wait, and he began offering Babbitt straight shots of booze. When he saw the look of sheer ecstasy that came over Babbitt's Lincolnesque face, he let the simian drink on, convinced that the animal was undergoing something holy. And perhaps he was, but after the initial rush of intoxication, Babbitt made the inevitable novice drinker's mistake of trying to amplify heaven. He snatched the whole bottle of Canadian Mist and scampered off into the bush like a drunken Hunchback of Notre Dame. Koestler had to laugh; it seemed so comical — the large Anubis baboon was unwilling to share the last of the amber nectar with his master. Well, there was always more where it came from, but suddenly Koestler wondered about the rapidity with which Babbitt had been slamming it down. He was afraid Babbitt would poison himself. Koestler took off into the bush after the animal, and he was instantly worried when he did not find Babbitt in any of his favorite trees. But Babbitt, who was perched higher than usual, announced his presence by launching the empty bottle down at Koestler like a bomb, just missing him. It was a calculated attempt at mayhem, Koestler realized, as Babbitt began to rant and rave at him with an astonishing repertoire of hostile invective that not only puzzled Koestler but wounded him to the core. Koestler had been Babbitt's champion and staunchest defender. Virtually no one on the compound had any use for the large and powerful baboon. As Sister Doris, the chief nurse, liked to say, Babbitt was aggressive, noisy, a biter, a thief, and a horrendous mess-maker with no redeeming quality except the fact that he was one of God's creatures. Father Stuart quickly pointed out that crocodiles were God's creatures, too, but that didn't mean you had to let them move in with you. Almost every day someone would come up to Koestler and besiege him with complaints about the animal. Only Father Stuart had the nerve to confront Babbitt directly, once using a bird gun to shoot Babbitt's red ass with a load of rock salt, an incident that caused the priest and the doctor to cease speaking to each other, except through third parties. Koestler and the priest had become so estranged that Koestler refused to dine with the rest of the staff, and this suited him fine, since he no longer had to sit through the sham of hymns, prayers, and all the folderol that surrounded meals in the lodge.

Koestler was a loner, and preferred his own company to that of anyone else after long, hard days ·of bonhomie with the junior physicians and the in-your-face contact with patients — patients not only deprived of basic necessities but lacking such amenities as soap, mouthwash, and deodorant. Koestler found that it was useful, and even necessary, to remain remote — to cultivate the image of the chief — since an aspect of tribalism invaded the compound in spite of the artificial structure of the church, which was imposed on it and which never seemed to take very well in the bush. The new-fangled wet blanket of civilization was thrown over ancient customs to almost no avail. But there were ways to get things done out here, and Koestler embodied those most notable characteristics of the New Zealander: resourcefulness, individualism, and self-reliance. In fact, Koestler carried self-containment to a high art. He had a lust for the rough-and-tumble, and preferred the hardships of Africa to the pleasant climate and easygoing customs of his homeland. As Koestler was fond of thinking, if Sir Edmund Hillary had a mountain to conquer when he climbed Everest in 1953 and breathed the rarefied air there, Koestler had baboons to tame and tropical diseases to vanquish in the here and now of Zaire. Koestler modestly considered himself New Zealand's gift to equatorial Africa.

* * *

NOW Babbitt was high up another tree, raising so much hell that the majority of the Africans — workers and convalescents — had assembled to watch. Babbitt scrambled back and forth along a limb with a pencil-size twig in his fingers, mimicking the manner in which Koestler smoked his Dunhill menthols à la Franklin Delano Roosevelt. Babbitt's imitation was so precise that it seemed uncannily human. Then, having established his character, he did something far worse: he imitated the way Koestler sat on the toilet during his bowel movements, which were excruciatingly painful because of Koestler's piles.

This was all much to the delight of the Africans, who roared and fell to the ground and pounded it or simply held their sides and hooted hysterically. Babbitt, who was so often reviled, feared, and despised, now gave the Africans enormous pleasure. They roared anew each time Babbitt bared his teeth and shook his fist like evil incarnate, once nearly toppling from his limb before abruptly grabbing hold of it again. Babbitt's flair for the dramatic had roused the Africans to a fever pitch. Some of the natives began to dance as if invaded by unseen spirits, and this frightened Koestler marginally, as it had during his first days in Africa. Koestler thought that when the Africans were dancing — especially when they got out the drums and palm wine — they were as mesmerized by unreason as the mobs who once clamored to hear the irrational, primitive, but dangerously soul-satisfying ravings of Hitler and other megalomaniacs and Antichrists of his ilk.

The doctor retained his composure throughout the episode and, speaking to his pet in reasonable tones, attempted to persuade him to come down. Koestler knew that baboons did not climb trees as a rule, and while Babbitt was not an ordinary baboon, he was very unsteady up in a tree, even when sober. But the more sweetly Koestler coaxed, the more Babbitt raged at him. Koestler instructed Johnson — the only African who was not holding his sides with laughter — to run back to the compound and obtain a stretcher to use as a safety net in case Babbitt passed out and fell from the tree, but as the doctor was intently giving Johnson these instructions, a wedge of smile cracked the African's face and he fell to howling as well.

"So, Cornelius, this is how it is with you," Koestler said with a certain amount of amusement. "You have betrayed me as well." As the others continued to hoot and wail, Koestler remembered that his friend Jules Hartman, the bush pilot, would be flying a pair of new American docs in later that day, and considered what a marvelous story this would make. He wanted to join in the fun, but as Babbitt began to masturbate, Koestler's impulse to laugh and give in to the moment was quickly vanquished by feelings of shame, anger, and real concern at the possibility of Babbitt's falling. Furthermore, it was his job to see that things didn't get out of control. An inch freely given around here quickly became the proverbial mile. The doctor raised his voice just slightly, insisting that the audience make a pile of leaves underneath the tree to break Babbitt's fall, which seemed all but inevitable. *"Mister* Johnson, see that this is done immediately," Koestler said. "I had better see heel-clicking service, do you hear me?"

Johnson wiped the smile from his face and began abusing the Africans. Soon a formidable pile of leaves had been gathered, but then Koestler, who was plotting the trajectory of the possible fall, was distracted when a small boy charged onto the scene and summoned the doctor to the clinic. A child had been bitten by a snake and was dying, the boy said. Koestler hastened back, the heavily laden pockets of his bush shorts jingling against his legs as he trotted along-side the young messenger, trying to get the boy to identify the type of snake responsible for the bite so he would be able to respond immediately with the appropriate dosage of antivenin, based on the victim's body weight, the bite pattern and location, the amount of edema present, and a number of other factors, including the possibility of shock. His alcohol-benumbed mind was soon clicking like a computer.

The child's father, tall, lean, but regal in a pair of ragged khaki shorts — his ebony skin shiny with oily beads of perspiration and covered with a number of pinkish-white keloid scars — stood impassively outside the clinic with a hoe in one hand and a dead cobra in the other. The man muttered something about how the snake had killed his cow, how quickly the animal had fallen stone dead. In fact, he seemed more concerned about the dead animal than about his child, which, after all, was only a girl.

Inside the surgery, Sister Doris was already at work on the girl, who had been bitten twice on the left leg. Koestler assumed that the snake had deposited most of its neurotoxic venom in the cow; if the girl had not been bitten second she would have been as dead as the cow, since the snake was large and the girl was small and frail.

Koestler cautiously administered a moderate dose of antivenin, antibiotics, and Demerol for pain. Then he auscultated the child's chest. Her lungs sounded fine, but since the natives were enamored by hypodermic needles, he gave her a B_{12} shot — the magic bullet he used on himself to relieve hangovers. Before long the child's color improved, and only then did Koestler's thoughts return to Babbitt's latest caper. It seemed like an event that had happened in the distant past.

Mopping perspiration from his face, Koestler stepped

outside and told the girl's father that his daughter was very strong, that the bite had been one of the worst Koestler had ever seen, and that the daughter was very special to have survived it. Actually, the little girl would probably have survived with no intervention whatever. But to survive a serious snakebite gave the victim unique status among the natives. Koestler hoped the father would now see his child in a new light, and that she would in fact have a better life from here on in. Sister Doris picked up on this and embellished the story until the crowd that had gone to witness Babbitt's debauchery had gathered outside the surgery to examine the dead snake and catch a glimpse of the young girl who would have unspecified powers and privileges for the rest of her life.

KOESTLER returned to the office in his small brick duplex — a mere hundred square feet cluttered with a large desk, five filing cabinets, books, whiskey bottles, medical paraphernalia, ashtrays, and a triocolored, fully assembled human skeleton. Koestler shook the last Dunhill from his pack and lit it. How long had it been since he had eaten last? He had a full-blown hangover now, and the cigarette, which tasted like Vicks VapoRub and cardboard, practically wasted him. He heard Johnson's feet flip-flopping along in an oversized pair of Clarks which Koestler had handed down to him, and looked out to see Johnson rushing toward the office, anxiously followed by a couple of boys who were carrying Babbitt toward the gazebo on a stretcher.

Koestler was not pleased. In the first place, Johnson had let the chickens burn in all the excitement, and now Koestler's fears about Babbitt were realized as he listened to the story of how the baboon had passed out and dropped from the tree with his arms tucked to his sides. He pictured the monkey falling like a black leaden weight, an oversized version of the Maltese Falcon. He would not tell Hartman of the incident after all, since if he did he would never hear the end of the pilot's ridicule about Koestler's misplaced love for the absurd animal. Absurdity was a very big part of his life, even as he strove to attain a kind of nobility in spite of it. Koestler became completely fed up with Babbitt as Johnson explained that the animal was basically unhurt. Koestler wondered if he should get himself a dog for a pet, since every other creature on the planet seemed inclined to shun him. It must be some vibe he gave off, he thought. Beyond superficial relationships, he was alone. Even Hartman, once you got past the fun and games, did not really care one whit about him. Not really. My God, he felt vile! Koestler suddenly realized how his devotion to the monkey must have seemed to the staff: as inexplicable as he had found Philip Carey's pathetic, masochistic attachment to Mildred, the green-skinned waitress in *Of Human Bondage,* a book he had read many years ago as a kid in Auckland, the very book that had pushed him into medicine and off to faraway tropical climes.

To be this much alone offered a vantage point from which he might look into the pit of his soul, but what good was that? How much truth could you bear to look at? Particularly if it left you a drunken sot. Koestler forked down a can of pink salmon; then, to clear his palate of fish, he chewed on stale twists of fried bread dusted with cinnamon and sugar while from his window he watched Johnson and the boys lift Babbitt onto the veranda of the gazebo, out of the sun. In a moment, Johnson was back in Koestler's office in his floppy pair of Clarks, so large on him they were like clown shoes.

"Him falling hard. Missing the falling nest altogether," Johnson exclaimed.

"Well," Koestler said with satisfaction, "you know how it is — God looks out after drunks and such. Maybe it will teach the bugger a lesson." Koestler fixed a Cuba libre and asked Johnson to salvage some of the overroasted chicken or run over to the kitchen and rustle up something else, depending on what the staff had been eating. According to Johnson, it had been hartebeest, which Koestler, as a rule, found too stringy. He told Johnson to smother some of it in horseradish and bring it anyway. That was about all you could do. There was a tinned rum cake he had been saving since Christmas. He could have that for dessert.

Koestler looked out his window as the sun flared on the horizon and sank behind a curtain of black clouds, plunging the landscape into darkness just as his generator kicked in and the bright lights in his office came on and his powerful air conditioner began to churn lugubriously. He took a long pull on his drink, found another pack of cigarettes and lit one with a wooden match, and waited for the liquor to do its job. Johnson was slow on the draw. An African glacier. It was just as well. Koestler would have time to eradicate his hangover and establish a pleasant alcoholic glow by the time Johnson returned with the food. In the meantime, he got busy with paperwork — stuff that was so dull it could only be done under the influence. Hartman and the green docs were already overdue, and he knew he would be tied up with them once they got in. In the beginning, new physicians were always more trouble than they were worth, and then, when they finally knew what they were doing, they lost heart and returned to lucrative practices back home. The altruism of most volunteers, Koestler thought, was pretty thin. Those who stayed seemed to do so for reasons that were buried deep in the soul.

*   *   *

KOESTLER woke up at dawn feeling very fit, while Babbitt spent the morning in abject misery. He would retreat to the corner of the doctor's office and hold his head in his hands; then he would approach Koestler (who was busy at his desk), pull on the doctor's pant leg, and implore him for help. Koestler cheerfully abused the animal by uttering such clichés as "If you want to dance, Georgie, you have to pay the fiddler. Now stop pestering me," and "You've sold your soul to the Devil, and there's not a thing I can do for you! Are you happy with yourself now?"

When Koestler finished his paperwork, he showed the baboon some Polaroids he had taken of it vomiting in the night. "Look at you," he said. "This is utterly disgraceful. What would your mother think of this? I've got a good mind to send them to her."

Babbitt abruptly left the room to guzzle water from a rain puddle but quickly returned when some Africans outside, who had witnessed the folly of the previous afternoon, began laughing derisively. He fled to his corner and held his head and, to Koestler's amazement, he was still there when the doctor came back to the room for a wash before dinner. The animal presented himself to Koestler like the prodigal son.

"I could fix it all with a shot, Georgie, but then you'll never learn, will you? Zip-A-Dee-Doo-Dah and out drunk again."

Babbitt buried his head in his hand and groaned mournfully.

Koestler finally took pity on him and gave him a B_{12} injection with five milligrams of amphetamine sulfate. In a half hour, Babbitt seemed as good as new, apart from a sore neck. The doctor took care of this by fixing Babbitt up with a small cervical collar cinched with Velcro. Koestler expected Babbitt to rip it off, but the animal was glad for the relief it provided. Koestler watched as Babbitt retreated to a hammock that hung in the gazebo under the baobab tree. In almost no time, he was sleeping peacefully. At the sight of Babbitt snoring in the absurd cervical collar, Koestler began to laugh, and he forgave his pet for most of the nonsense he had pulled during his drunken spree.

After Johnson served breakfast, Koestler took a stroll around the compound, barking orders at everyone in sight. The Africans ducked their heads submissively in his presence. Good, he had them cowed. He would ride them hard for a few weeks to reestablish his absolute power. If he had given them their inch, he would get a yard back from them. When he stuck his head into the mission school for a minute, Brother Cole, who was demonstrating to the children how to write the letter "e" in cursive, took one look at the doctor and dropped his chalk. Koestler imagined that he saw the man's knees buckle. No doubt Father Stuart, with all his carping, had blown Koestler up into a bogeyman. He rarely showed himself at the school. The children whipped their heads around, and when they caught sight of the "big boss," their heads just as quickly whirled back. Koestler tersely barked, "Good morning, please continue. I'm just checking on things. Don't mind me." Ha! Feared by all.

By the time Koestler completed his Gestapo stroll, the compound was as quiet as a ghost town. He went into the clinic at nine, and with the help of the nurses completed over forty-five procedures by four-thirty. No record by any means, but a good day's work.

LATE that afternoon, Koestler took his dinner in the gazebo as usual and got drunk with Hartman and the two new young docs, who had spent the greater part of the day with the mission's administrator. Both Americans were shocked by the heat, the long flight, and, no doubt, by the interminable introductions to the staff and the singsong ramblings of that repetitive bore Father Stuart, who delighted in giving visitors a guided tour of the compound. The doctors seemed happy to be knocking back high-proof alcohol, and when Koestler fixed the usual bowl of banana mash and Canadian Mist before bridge, a number of rhesus monkeys rushed in from the jungle to accept the magical paste and soon were drunk and rushing around the compound fighting and copulating. Babbitt, who had ditched his cervical collar, was having none of the paste. The baboon seemed chastened and wiser. Koestler noted this with satisfaction and felt completely reconciled with his pet.

One of the newbies, a wide-eyed young doctor from Hammond, Indiana, said, "I see that the whole fabric of the social structure breaks down when they drink. It's like some grotesque parody of humans, but with none of the subtleties — just the elementals."

"It doesn't take Jane Goodall to see that," said Hartman. He had flown the Americans in that morning, and had got a head start on the Canadian Mist that afternoon. To Koestler's eye, the pilot appeared to be on the road to a mean, brooding drunk, rather than the more typical Hartman drunk — that of merriment, cricket talk, vaudeville routines, and bawdy songs. Koestler had recently run some blood work on his friend and knew that Hartman's liver was getting a little funny, but he could only bring himself to give Hartman a perfunctory warning and a bottle of B vitamins, since Koestler liked to match Hartman drink for drink when he made his twice-weekly drops at the mission and, as Koestler told Hartman, chastising him would seem like a ridiculous instance of the pot calling the kettle black. Like himself, Hartman was an old hand in Africa, and while he was not a Kiwi, he was close, having been raised in Launceston, Tasmania. Those pretentious types from mainland Australia looked down their noses on Taz, as they did on New Zealand — the poor sisters.

While Hartman had the typical apple cheeks and large ears that made Tasmanians look almost inbred, he liked to claim that he was Welsh. "May the Welsh rule the world!" he often said, but at other times he admitted that a year in Wales, with forays into much detested England, had been the most boring of his life. Whenever the subject came up, whether he was drunk or sober, the English were "Those bloody Pommy bastards!"

From the moment Babbitt had refused the alcohol mash, the doctor had been in a good mood, and now he began to pontificate. "As a rule, a baboon will only get drunk once, a monkey every day. Incredible animals, really, are baboons. Very smart. Did you know they can see in color? Actually, their visual powers are astounding.

"What happened to its neck?" the young doctor from Hammond, Indiana, asked. "It keeps rubbing its neck."

"It's a long story," Koestler replied. His cheerful countenance turned sour for a moment. "George Babbitt is a long-term experiment. He's come from the heart of darkness to the sunshine of Main Street. My goal is to turn him into a full Cleveland."

"What's a full Cleveland?" Indiana asked.

"A full Cleveland is a polyester leisure suit, white-on-white tie, white belt, white patent-leather shoes, razor burn on all three chins, and membership in the Rotary Club and the Episcopal church."

"You forgot the quadruple bypass," the other newbie, who was from Chicago, said.

"Well, he's got a running start there," said Koestler. The baboon had stationed himself between Hartman and Koestler. Hartman held the stump of a wet cigar in his hand and seemed poised to relight it. Babbitt was intent on his every move.

"Georgie smokes a half a pack of cigarettes a day," Hartman said.

"Used to smoke — " ·

"Still does," Hartman said. "Whatever he can mooch from the Africans."

"Well, I'll soon put an end to that," said Koestler. "He's getting fat and short-winded. His cholesterol is up there. How long has he been smoking this time, the bloody bugger? He'll end up with emphysema, too. And how come I didn't know about this? I used to know everything that went on around here! I've got to cut back on the juice."

"Dain bramage," said Hartman.

"It's not funny," Koestler said.

"What's the normal cholesterol for a baboon?" Indiana asked. His cherubic face made him seem impossibly young.

"Forty to sixty or thereabouts," Koestler replied. "I couldn't even get a reading on his triglycerides — his blood congeals like cocoa butter."

Indiana began to giggle. "Jeez, I still can't believe that I'm in . . . Africa."

"Tomorrow you will believe," said Koestler. "You will voice regrets."

"I mean, I *know* I'm in Africa. I knew that when Mr. Hartman landed that DC-3. Talk about a postage-stamp runway — and those soldiers! Are those guns *loaded?*"

"That runway is a piece of cake," Hartman said. "More than adequate. And the guns *are* loaded. The political situation is very uptight these days. Not that we can't handle that; it's just that it's getting impossible to make a decent wage. I've got a mind to sell the plane and head back to Oz. I'm getting too old for this caca."

"You won't last a week in Australia and you know it," Koestler said. "All the oppression of civilization. Sydney's getting almost as bad as Los Angeles. Every other bloody car is a Rolls or Jaguar. Not for you, my friend. You'll have to put on a fucking necktie to take in the morning paper."

"Darwin's not so bad," Hartman said, punching at a large black fly. "In Darwin an eccentric can thrive. Colorful characters. Crocodile Dundee and that sort of thing. I can make milk runs to New Guinea, do something — "

Suddenly Hartman seemed drunk, and he glowered at Indiana. "If you think this runway was crude, sonny boy, you've got a fuckin' long way to go." He sailed the half-empty bowl of banana mash into the wisteria bushes, and a few of the monkeys went after it, scrapping over the paste.

"Well, it wasn't exactly O'Hare International," Indiana said. "And how come the Africans sandbagged the tires?"

"To stop the hyenas from eating them," Koestler said. "It's hell to procure tires in these parts."

"Eating tires?" Indiana said. "You're shitting me!"

"The object of our little get-together is to ease you into your new reality," Koestler said. "If you get hit with everything too fast, it can overwhelm. Tomorrow will be soon enough. The leper colony — a rude awakening."

"What kind of scene is that?" the young doctor from Chicago asked. He was a dark man, with a hawk nose and a thick head of hair as black and shiny as anthracite; he was short, muscular, and had copious body hair. Koestler took him to be about thirty.

"It's a bit smelly. Poor buggers. Pretty much Old Testament, if you know what I mean. Your leper is still the ultimate pariah. In the beginning, there's 'gloves and stockings' anesthesia, and in the end, if we can't interrupt the course of the disease, a great deal of pain. They only believe in needles — they love needles. So use disposables and destroy them. That's the first rule. The second rule is this — if you have a patient who requires one unit of blood, do not give it to him. If he requires two units of blood, do not give it to him. If he requires three units of blood, you will have to give it to him, but remember that that blood will most likely be contaminated with HIV, hepatitis B, and God knows what all, despite the assurances from above."

"AIDS — *Slim*," Hartman said evenly. "The only safe sex is no sex. Do not even accept a hand job."

"I've heard that they take great offense if you don't eat with them," Indiana said. "I've heard they'll put the evil eye on you if you don't eat with them."

"It's true," Koestler said.

"So you eat with them?"

"Hell no! I don't get involved with them on a personal level. You cannot let your feelings get in your way. If you do, you will be useless. Move. Triage. Speed is the rule. You'll see the nurses doing things that your trauma docs can't handle back in the States. Hell, you'll see aides doing some very complicated work. It comes down to medical managing. The numbers defeat you."

Johnson came out to the gazebo bearing a tray of chilled coconut puddings. He set a dish next to each of the men and then began to light the Coleman lanterns and mosquito coils as the sun did its orange flare and fast fade into the horizon. As it disappeared, Koestler said, "Thank God. Gadzooks! Sometimes too hot the eye of heaven shines, huh, boys? Especially when you're smack-dab on the equator."

The new men said nothing but watched as, one by one, Johnson picked up the last of the drunken rhesus monkeys by their tails and flung them as far as he could before padding back to the kitchen.

Indiana looked out at the monkeys staggering in circles.

"They don't know what to do — come back for more or go into the jungle."

"Those that make for the bush the leopard gets. It's one way to eradicate the bastards," said Koestler darkly.

"I see — method behind the madness," Chicago said.

"Johnson's been using his skin bleach again." Hartman observed. "He's gone from redbone to high yellow in a week. Wearing shoes, yet. The Eagle Flies on Friday Skin Pomade for some Sat'day-night fun."

"It's not only Saturdays," Koestler said. "He goes through two dozen condoms a week. His hut is littered with the wrappers. He's insatiable."

"Well, at least you got that part through to him. Use a rubber."

"Johnson is no dummy, Jules. He knows the score, believe me. He's very germ conscious. That's one thing. A compulsive handwasher. I trust him with my food absolutely."

As Indiana spooned down the pudding, he looked nervously at Hartman, who was bulky man and was glowering at him. "What's this 'redbone, high yellow' stuff?" Indiana said.

Hartman said nothing and continued to stare at the young doctor. Indiana looked at the other men and then laughed, "Hey! What's with this guy?"

Chicago picked up his pudding and began to eat. "And now for something completely different," he said. "The evil eye."

Hartman's face brightened. He relaxed his shoulders and laughed softly. "I remember a doctor — an American, tropical medic — didn't believe in the superstitions, and in the course of things he humiliated a traditional doctor. The old boy put a curse on this hotshot, and it wasn't more than a week before the American stepped on a snake. I had to fly him to Jo'burg, since he was really messed up, was this chap. A year, fourteen months later he's back, forty pounds lighter, and a rabid animal bites him on the second day in. It took us three weeks to get a rabies vaccine, and it came from a dubious source. He took the full treatment, but came down with the disease anyhow. Bitten on the face. Travels to the brain faster. Funny thing about rabies — makes a bloke restless. Nothing to do for it, either. Dr. Koestler, Johnson and I had to lock him up in one of those chain-link-fenced compartments in the warehouse."

"Excessive scanning," Koestler said. "Hypervigilance. You could see the whites of his eyes — "

"From top to bottom," Hartman said. "Very paranoid, drinking in every sight and sound."

"What made it worse," Koestler said, "was the fact that he knew his prognosis."

"Yeahrr," said Hartman. "The paranoiac isn't necessarily wrong about things — he just sees too much. Take your hare, for instance. Your hare is a very paranoid animal. Your hare has basically been placed on the planet as food. He doesn't have a life. When you are an instant meal, you are always on the lookout. So, paranoid. Well, our friend was a lion, which all doctors are, present company included — they're tin gods from Day One — and, while it may work in America, it doesn't cut any ice down here; he humiliated this old witch doctor, so there wasn't any way out. No need to go around asking for trouble in this life, is there? The hare sees too much, the lion not enough — and there's the difference between happiness and hell, provided you are a real and true lion, not some bloody fool who is misinformed."

Hartman had the fleshy, broken nose of a pug, and as he spoke he kept brushing at it with his thumb. He sneezed three times in rapid succession.

"The curious thing," Koestler said, "is that the stupid bleeder died professing belief in science. He had a little slate and a piece of chalk, and when we finally went in to remove the body, I read his last words: *Amor fati!* 'Love your fate.' A stubborn bloody fool."

"Wow," Indiana said. "What did you do for the guy? Did he just die?"

"Of course he died. 'Slathered like a mad dog' is no mere cliché, let me tell you. I was inexperienced back then and had to play it by ear. All you had to do was say the word 'water' and he had esophageal spasms. You try to anticipate the symptoms and treat them, but we just aren't equipped here. The brain swells, you see, and there's no place for it to go."

Koestler accidentally bumped his pudding onto the floor with his elbow, and Babbitt quickly stepped forward and scooped it up in neat little handfuls.

Indiana picked up his dessert and tasted another spoonful. "This is good."

"Good for a case of the shits. Did you boys bring in any paregoric?"

"Lomotil," Chicago said. "Easier to — "

"Transport," Hartman said, picking up a greasy deck of cards and dealing them out for bridge.

"Mix it with Dilaudid and it will definitely cure diarrhea," Koestler said.

"You got some cholera in these parts?" Chicago said. He was beginning to sound like an old hand already.

"No," Koestler said vacantly. "Just the routine shits." He picked up his cards and fanned through them.

As Indiana finished his pudding, Johnson padded back out to the gazebo with a bowl of ice, another quart of Canadian Mist, and four cans of Coke Classic.

"I had this patient call me up at three in the morning," Indiana said.

"Called the doctor, woke him up," Chicago recited.

Indiana said, "Hypochondriac. Right. She's got lower GI pain. Diarrhea. Gas. The thing is — she's switched from Jello-O pudding to Royal pudding."

"Doctor what can I take?" Chicago sang.

"I said, 'Delilah, remember how you — Delilah, I don't think you have a ruptured appendix. Delilah! Remember when you switched from RC Cola to Pepsi?' "

"Doctor — to relieve this bellyache," Chicago sang.

"I said, 'Put the lime in the coconut. Yeah, it does sound kind of *nutty*. That's good. Now, haven't you got a lime? You've got lime juice. One of those little green plastic lime things? Okay, that's good, now listen closely — *You put de lime in de coconut an' shake it all up; put de lime in de coconut and you drink it all down.* Trust me, Delilah, an' call me in de morning.' "

"And she never called back," Hartman said soberly. "Very clever."

"Let me get this straight," Koestler said. "You put de lime in de coconut?"

"Yeahrrr," said Hartman. "Jolly good."

"It's not bad, but that's his only routine," Chicago said. "I've spent seventy-two hours with the man, and that's it. That's his one trick. Plus, he's a fuckin' Cubs fan."

"Hey," Indiana said. "Long live Ernie Banks! Speaking of weird, we brought in three cases of sardines," Indiana said. "What's with all the sardines?"

"They are an essential out in the bush," Koestler said, removing a can of King Oscar sardines from his pocket and shucking the red cellophane wrapping. "Look at that, a peel-back can. No more bloody key. It's about time."

Hartman said, "They've only been canning sardines for ninety years."

Koestler jerked the lid back and helped himself to a

half-dozen fish, his fingers dripping with oil. "Why, Jules, don't take personal offense. I'm sure His Majesty has enough on his mind without worrying about zip-open cans." Koestler offered the tin around, and when everyone refused, he gave the rest of the fish to Babbitt. "King Oscar sardines are worth more than Marlboro cigarettes in Africa," he declared.

"King Oscar, the nonpareil sardine," Chicago said.

Indiana filled his bourbon glass with Coke, Canadian Mist, and a handful of ice cubes, which melted almost instantly.

Hartman fixed his hard stare on young Indiana. "What exactly brought you to Africa, sonny boy?"

"I came to serve humanity, and already I'm filled with a sense of the inexplicable. I can't believe I'm in Africa. And fuck you very much."

"Speak up. You sound like a bloody poof — 'I came to serve humanity,' " Hartman said.

"And you sound like a major asshole. Why don't you try a little anger-management training?"

"Bloody poof, I knew it. Nancy girl!"

"Fuck!" Indiana said. "You're drunk. I'm not even talking to you."

"Won't last a week. Mark my words," Hartman said.

"Tomorrow you will believe," Koestler said. "The leper colony."

"Separates the men from the boys," said Hartman.

"Way down deep in the jungle," said Chicago, "we have the leper colony. We have Hansen's disease. That which we call leprosy by any other name would smell just as sweet: indeterminate leprosy, tuberculoid leprosy, lepromatous leprosy, dimorphous leprosy. 'What's in a name?' "

To Koestler's astonishment, Chicago pulled out a fat

joint and torched it up. He took a long drag and passed it to the other American.

"I did a rotation at the leprosarium in Carville, Louisiana, when I was in the Navy," Chicago said. "I learned how to understand the prevailing mentality of the patient suffering from Hansen's disease."

"Put yourself in their 'prosthetic' shoes, did you?" Hartman said.

"The kid's right," Chicago said. "You're a hostile person. Shut up and listen. I mean, these patients are in denial until a white coat gives it to them straight. Zombie denial, man. You should see the look on their face. It's not a look like you've got cancer, which is a good one, instant shock. The you've-got-Hansen's look is more like, 'I have of late — but wherefore I know not — lost all my mirth — ' "

"I know that look," Koestler said. "I see it every morning whilst I shave. Jules, the man knows Shakespeare."

"I suppose a leper colony in Africa is a hut made out of buffalo shit — "

"In your leper colony over there in the States," Hartman said, "are all the lepers bloody nigs?"

"You really are a racist, aren't you?" Indiana said.

Koestler attempted to deflect this inquiry. "I believe the current phraseology is 'African-American,' Jules, or, if you must, 'black.' "

"Some are black. Some are white. Some are Hispanic," Chicago said. "That word of yours is not in my vocabulary, and if you say it again — "

"You'll what?"

"Jules, please," said Koestler. "Don't be bloody uncouth."

Hartman pitched his head forward and pretended to sob over his cards. "I'm an uncouth ruffian, I won't deny it." He gulped down some whiskey and said, "When that faggot over there wants to fly home for ballet lessons, it won't be in my plane."

"Aryan Brotherhood," Indiana said.

Koestler raised his hand to silence the doctor while he turned on Chicago. "Where on earth did you score that joint?" he asked. "Did you give it to them, Jules?"

"Actually, it was your man, Johnson," Indiana said. "God, am I ever high. Everything is so . . . surreal."

"Johnson? That bugger!" Koestler said. "He's got his hand in everything."

Koestler put the wet end of the joint to his lips and took a tentative puff. As he did, Chicago pulled out another and lit it.

"Fuck," Koestler said. He took another hit. A much bigger one.

Chicago handed the new joint to Koestler's baboon, who greedily inhaled the smoke, and for the next few moments the whole curious party sat around the table attempting to suppress coughs.

"I'm so fucking high," Indiana said. "Jesus."

"A minute ago *I* was drunk; now *you* can't tie your shoelaces," Hartman said. "Poofter!"

"Let's have a little music," said Koestler. He flipped on the shortwave and fiddled with the dial. "I have got nothing but bloody Radio Ireland recently, half Gaelic, and then an hour of bird calls! Needs a new battery." He slapped at the radio and then, with Dixieland accompaniment, an Irish tenor was singing, *"I've flown around the world in a plane — "*

Koestler joined in. *"I've settled revolutions in Spain — "*

He flipped the dial and slapped the set until he hooked into American Armed Forces Radio. After an announcer listed the major-league ball scores, Jimi Hendrix came on blaring "Red House."

The men sat back and listened to the music. Koestler popped up to turn up the volume, his weather-beaten face collapsing inward as he took in another draught of marijuana smoke, closed his eyes, tossed his head back, and got into the song. He was soon snaking about the duckboard floor of the gazebo, playing air guitar to the music.

"Hey, if Father Stuart could only see us now," Hartman said. "Father Stuart *can* see you now!" The priest flipped on an electric torch and stepped out of the darkness up into the gazebo. "This is a hospital, not a fraternity house! Kindly remember that. People are trying to sleep. Can't you think of others for a change?" He turned to the new doctors. "I'm glad to see that you two lads are off to an auspicious beginning."

The priest, dressed in a bathrobe and flip-flops, snatched the shortwave, switched it off, slung it under his arm, and clopped back toward the lodge. The beam of his flashlight, which was tucked between his shoulder and chin, panned the wisteria bushes, the ground, the sky, and the buildings of the compound as he attempted to push down the telescopic antenna on the radio. For a moment, the men sat in stunned silence. This was followed by an explosion of laughter.

Koestler started up as if to go after the priest, but then thought better of it and sat down at the table. He reached into his bush shirt and removed another can of sardines, handing them to Babbitt, who quickly tore off the lid, ate the fish, and then licked the olive oil from the inside of the can. "You might not believe it, but Georgie can open a can of sardines even with a key," Koestler said proudly.

"Fuck, he's got the munchies," Indiana said, as he fell into a paroxysm of laughter.

Chicago studied the red sardine jacket, giggling as he read: "Add variety and zest to hot or cold meatless main

dishes. . . . By special royal permission. Finest Norway brisling sardines."

"Brisling?"

"It's that advertising thing," Chicago said. "Brisling is
Norwegian for 'sprat,' which means small marine fish. Not
each and every small fish you pull in is certifiably a herring;
some other small fish get picked up by the school. No false
advertising this way."

"Wow," Indiana said sardonically. "Are you Norwegian or something?"

"Lebanese," Chicago said. "I already told you that."

Indiana said, "Who runs that country, anyhow? I was
there, and I don't know that much. All I remember is that
they won't even give you the time of day."

"No way," Chicago said. "The people are friendly as
hell. The government of Norway is a hereditary constitu-
tional monarchy, a parliamentary democracy, and the king is
endowed with a certain amount of executive power. In reality, however, the king is limited in the exercise of power."

"He's a Norway freak!" Indiana said.

"More likely he's got a photographic memory," Hartman said.

"Touché, Mr. Hartman," Chicago said.

"I still can't believe I'm in Africa," Indiana said.
"Heavy. Fourteen-year-old kids with machine guns — and,
my God, look at the stars. There are so many of them."

"Stop acting so fucking incredulous," Hartman said.
"You're really getting on my nerves."

"Watch Sister Doris," Koestler said. "She's forgotten
more about jungle medicine than I'll ever know."

"Doris? Man, she's unattractive. She's ugly, man," Indiana said.

"She'll be looking pretty good in about five months;
that is, if you last that long," Hartman said. "You'll be

having some pretty intensive fantasies about that woman. Are you going to last, sonny boy?"

"Fuck off. I got through a residency at Bellevue. I guess I can hack Africa."

"The thing about Doris," Koestler said, slicing the air with the edge of his hand, "is that she's what we call an A-teamer. The A-team takes all of this business seriously. Tight-asses. Father Stuart is A-team beaucoup. There are B-teamers, who take a more casual approach. You will line up with one of these factions. Personally, if the political thing doesn't ease up a bit, I'm going to boogie out of this hellhole. I've no desire to have my throat slit. Stuart and Doris will stay until the last dog is hung."

"Go back to Kiwiland and listen to them harp about All Blacks rugby and that bloody yacht trophy," Hartman said. "Family's gone. Africa's your home, man."

"I've got a few cousins left in Auckland, and I do miss New Zealand beer, rather," Koestler said. "I'm not going to hang around and get my throat cut. I'd rather try a little lawn bowling."

"The natives are restless?" Indiana said.

"Yes, Percy le Poof," Hartman said. "The natives are restless."

"Politics as usual. So far, it hasn't filtered down to the villages," Koestler said. "It's a lot safer here than in Newark, New Jersey, I would imagine."

Suddenly the men fell silent and examined their cards. Swarms of insects buzzed the gazebo in successive waves.

Despite the mosquito coils, the insects attacked ferociously. Hartman was the first to hop up, and he moved with a quickness that startled the others. With no warning, he roughly grabbed Indiana's head in the crook of his muscular forearm and savagely rubbed his knuckles over the top of the young doctor's head. His feet shuffled adroitly, like those of a fat but graceful tap dancer, as he yanked the doctor in various directions, never letting him set himself for balance. Hartman ran his knuckles back and forth over the young man's crew cut, crying, *"Haji Baba!* Hey, hey! *Haji Baba!* Hey, hey!"

"Ouch, goddamn!" Indiana shouted. He was tall, with a basketball-player's build, and he finally wrested himself out of Hartman's powerful grip. He stood his ground, assuming a boxer's pose. Both he and Hartman were suddenly drenched with sweat. "You fucker! Shit!"

Hartman threw his hands in the air, his palms open in a gesture of peace. As soon as Indiana dropped his guard, Hartman waded in throwing roundhouse punches. One of these connected, and a chip of tooth pankled off a can of Coke Classic on the table. Indiana pulled Hartman forward, going with the older man's momentum. At the same time, he kicked Hartman's feet out from under him, and the two men rolled off the gazebo, and Indiana rose astride Hartman's broad back like a cowboy. Indiana had Hartman's arm pulled up in a chicken wing with one hand while he felt for his missing front tooth with the other.

"You son of a bitch!" Indiana said. "Fat bastard." He pounded Hartman's large ears with the meaty side of his fist. "I'll show you who's a faggot. How do you like it?"

He continued to cuff the pilot and cranked the arm up higher until Hartman cried, "Oh God, stop!"

"Had enough? Had enough?"

"God, yes. God, yes. I give!"

Indiana released his grip and got up. He was covered with black dirt. He was studying an abrasion on his knee when Hartman leaped atop him pickaback and began clawing at his face.

Hartman cried, "Son-of-a-bitch, I'll kill you!" Once again the two men began rolling about in the dirt. This time

Hartman emerged on top, and his punches rained down on the younger man until Chicago and Koestler each snatched him by one of his arms and dragged him off and flung him back into his chair. He started to get up, but Koestler shoved him back down with both hands and then pointed a finger in his face.

"You're drunk. Knock this shit off immediately!"

Hartman clutched his chest and panted frantically, wheezing. Rivulets of sweat coated with black dust rolled down off his face and dropped on his lap like oily pearls. Koestler poured out a large glass of whiskey and handed it to Hartman and said, "Here, old man. Drink yourself sober."

"Just having a bit of fun is all," Hartman said agreeably. "Didn't mean anything by it." Indiana drew away from Hartman, who managed the entire glass of whiskey in three gulps. "I believe all that marijuana got me going. No offense intended. Apologies all around."

Hartman took a mashed cigar out of his pocket, twisted off the broken end, and lighted it. He puffed rapidly without inhaling and wafted the smoke in front of his face to clear away the mosquitoes. Then he pulled himself up, set his glass on the table, and said, "It's been a long day, and here I am, shitfaced again. Good night, all."

Hartman hastily made his way up the path toward the sleeping quarters beyond the surgery. As he went, he laughed again and repeated the famous Monty Python litany, "And now for something completely different — sawing logs. Ah, zzzzz! Ah, zzzzz! Ah, zzzzz!"

Indiana turned to Koestler. "What is with that guy?"

"Don't mind Jules. He's a jolly good fellow. You'll grow to love him. And he won't remember a thing about tonight. Blackout drunk, this — presumably. I might not remember any of it, either."

From the distance, an elephant blared, a big cat roared,

the hyenas began their freakishly human wailing, and the whole cacophony of jungle sounds took over the night.

WAS it a minute or an hour later that Babbitt hopped on Hartman's empty chair and seemed to beseech the card-players to deal him in? The men had drifted off into their separate thoughts. Babbitt grabbed the bottle of Canadian Mist from the card table and, brandishing sharp canine teeth that shone like ivory in the glow of the Coleman lanterns, caused both the young doctors to duck to the floor before he quickly sprang off into the black jungle. Even Koestler hit the deck, wrenching his knee. When he got up, he brushed himself off and said, "That settles it, I'm getting myself a dog."

"Christ, that's one mean son-of-a-bitch!" said Chicago. "And I thought you said a baboon will only get drunk once. Here I thought he was poised to go for that goat-shit cigar. I mean, so much for your full Cleveland."

"Georgie is not your average baboon," Koestler said with a shrug. "Especially when he's stoned. When you've got a stoned baboon, all bets are off."

Indiana looked at Koestler. "What are we going to do? Are we going after him?"

"Not likely — anyhow, you need to clean up. Put something on those scratches. They can go septic overnight in this climate."

"But the leopard."

"Not to worry. I'll send Johnson and some of the men out with flashlights and shotguns. I'm absolutely fried from that joint. I'm not going out there — although we have to do something about that cat. He's getting altogether too bold, and we have children about. I'm going to have to roust Johnson. Anyhow, welcome to the B-team, gentlemen — Har har! Try to get some sleep. Tomorrow is going to be a rather difficult . . . a rather gruesome . . . well, shall I say, it won't be your typical day at the office? Up at dawn and that sort of thing." Koestler tossed back the last of his drink. "Rude awakening, the leper colony. Not for the faint of heart."

The young doctors grimly nodded an affirmation as Koestler made a pretense of cleaning up around the card table. He watched the two men stumble back to their rooms in the dorm, and when they were out of sight, he picked up one of the fat roaches that were left over from their party. He lit it with his Ronson and managed to get three good tokes off it. He heard the leopard out in the bush.

Who was it? Stanley? Was it Sir Henry Morton Stanley who had been attacked by a lion, shaken into shock, and who later reported that he had felt a numbness that was a kind of bliss — a natural blessing for those creatures who were eaten alive? Not a bad way to go. Of course, leopards were smaller. Slashers.

Koestler picked up Indiana's drink, which was filled to the brim; it was warm, and the Coke in it had gone flat. It didn't matter. There seemed to be a perfect rightness to everything. That was the marijuana. Well, what difference did it make? It was his current reality. When he finished the whiskey, Koestler got up and clicked on his small chrome-plated penlight and followed its narrow beam into the bush. The beam was just long enough to allow him to put one foot in front of the other. Finding Babbitt would be almost impossible. *Amor fati.* Choose the right time to die. Well, there was no need to overdramatize; he was just taking a little midnight stroll. The leopard, unless it was crazy, would run from his very smell.

*　　*　　*

AS soon as Koestler got under the jungle canopy, the air temperature fell ten degrees. The bush smelled damp and rotten. Yet, for the first time in thirty years, Koestler felt at one with the jungle. A little T-Bone Walker blues beamed in from some remote area of the brain: *They call it Stormy Monday, but Tuesday's just as bad.*

At the sound of Koestler's heavy boots, the nocturnal rustlings of the bush grew still. Koestler could then hear drums from the nearby village. There had been an elephant kill. Somehow his peripheral awareness had picked up on that news at some point during this most incredible day. Elephant kill. House of meat. Cause for celebration. The doctor proceeded into the darkness. The penlight seemed to dim; were the batteries low? Beneath the sound of the drumbeats, Koestler heard a branch snap. He stood stockstill in the middle of it all. He flipped his penlight right and left, and in a low, piping voice, said, "Georgie, Georgie? Where are you, my little pal? Why don't you come on back home? Come back home to Daddykins."

Quicksand

AD MAGIC, the celebrated direct-mail wizard for the Global Aid hunger effort, spent a full day and two dark nights of the soul in his bathroom at the Hotel Arusha. It was a nasty, humid little room about the size of a small French elevator. It smelled of old sewage and fresh bilious vomit even with the door open and the bathroom air commingling with the dead, heavy air of his suite. He had a case of the Congo trots that seemed to go on forever. The malaria Ad Magic picked up in Rwanda was making a comeback now that he was unable to keep his Mefloquine down. Malarial fever had a way of elongating time into delirious expanses of paranoia and despair. Yet the bone-rattling chills that would follow were somehow worse, like impending death, and he alternated between fever and chills with something like documentable regularity. In between these sieges Ad Magic fell into a heavy slumber punctuated with horrible hypnogogic dreams, or wide-awake bouts of visceral evacuation. The heart of darkness Conrad wrote about so vividly was available in modern-day Arusha just as much as in some ghastly trip upriver on the Zaire. It seemed that he had fallen into an eternal vortex of hell. And when Ad Magic's physical torments didn't awaken him, the sounds of drunken copulations in the adjoining rooms did. He began to imagine that the so-called three-star hotel was little more than a whorehouse.

The nights were especially bad. Commencing at dusk the sounds of drunken foolishness in the back alley picked up and gradually built into the roar of full-blown evil. Africans were back there drinking rum, palm wine, and banana beer, knocking out a demonic beat on upturned fifty-gallon drums. Ad Magic was too weak and frightened to step out in the hall and summon help. "Please, bwana, call an ambulance?"

Why, they would only laugh.

He had a headache that had him cross-eyed and during the peak of a fever would bring his anguish to a pitch that seemed beyond the limits of misery, that seemed unendurable but would finally push his brain into some ethereal hyperspace that was not altogether unpleasant. Soon thereafter the chills had him clutching his single blanket with chattering teeth, as wretched as a cold wet dog. Through all of this his broken thumb continued to throb unbearably, sometimes ascending to the throne of his most paramount agony. In addition to the intense pain, the thumb reminded him of the shocking scenes he had recently witnessed in Rwanda, coloring his recollections with a dread that had not occurred to him as he saw them unfold originally. Watching the massacre had been "watching TV" until the exhaustion of malaria, diarrhea, and thumb. Ad Magic recalled that when the cities and villages of Rwanda were almost deserted, what little jungle there was in the country had become as crowded as Times Square on New Year's Eve. And, moreover, it had been almost as cold. How surreal! Ad Magic had seen his share of Third World bullshit, but Rwanda was the topper. In the end the exhaustion became too much and he fell into the dreamless sleep of a dead man.

When he awoke his stomach had finally calmed and the malaria settled in the middle ground. He was not altogether refreshed but managed to rouse himself, shave, shower, and quickly run a comb through his hair. Then he made his way down to the dining room. Although he knew he was still deranged at some level, it seemed imperative for him to eat.

The dining hall was opaque with the blue smoke of harsh tobacco and cooking fumes. It was evening and as the road traffic breezed by in the hot night, thick puffs of dusty red, diesel-smelling air wafted in through the large louvered windows of the restaurant. The dining room was done up in a Masai motif with shields and spears hanging on the walls in between a pair of mangy lion heads covered with cobwebs and red road dust. The wall also featured the heads of a greater kudu, a leopard, a water buffalo, and finally that of a hippo whose partially open mouth contained a fake cigar. As ridiculous as the wall-mounted head seemed, Ad Magic knew that hippos were extremely dangerous. Year after year they killed more human beings in Africa than any given species of animal, crocodile, snake, or spider. Ad Magic waved at a pair of Methodist missionaries he had met before his attack and flashed them a smile. The missionaries were seated at a large table illuminated by a pair of forty-watt ceiling bulbs encased in crepe Japanese shades. They were taking a major detour to drive Ad Magic and a young physician from Copenhagen to the Global Aid mission at Mocherville. That was a nice little piece of luck since Ad Magic was already overdue in Zaire. The entire party had been kind enough to delay their trip until Ad Magic was able to recover. Pastor Dave summoned him over to the table with a wave but first Ad Magic stopped at the bar, ordered a double whiskey and a bottle of Simba beer, downed them instantly, and asked the waiter to send another round to the table. Before the waiter arrived Ad Magic felt acutely well. So well, in fact, that when the waiter arrived with his setup, Ad Magic ordered the house special, vegetable curry on rice. It was going for something like ninety cents American.

After the trio of old African hands made small talk awhile, the newcomer, Dr. Erika Lars, made her appearance at the table midway through the meal. She was a stunning beauty. Women like Lars seldom turned up in places like this. It was only then that Ad Magic recalled her coming into his bathroom at the peak of his diarrhea crisis. She caught him on the floor tucked in the fetal position clenching a blanket. His underwear were around his ankles and he cursed, demanding that she leave. Instead, she gave him a painful injection. Remembering the squalid scene now, he found himself too embarrassed to speak.

A furious assault of spiced curry came from the kitchen until the road breeze picked up and rustled the palm fronds just outside the hotel. An overhead fan with burnt bearings pounded steadily but with little effect. As Lars pulled off her sweater, she drew her blouse taut and Ad Magic got a load of her breasts. Jeez! He realized that he was staring but couldn't help it. Lars hunched forward, shyly, as if to diminish them. She was far more beautiful than he had remembered. To avoid staring and to better contain his embarrassment, he turned toward the bar, tossed off his second double whiskey with a debonair flick of the wrist, and began sipping his second bottle of Simba. His rationale was that the alcohol would finish off the last of the intestinal bacteria that had made him so sick in the first place and that further doses of follow-up whiskey would dispatch any germs that he would incur from the rice curry.

At the bar, a half-dozen wealthy Africans wearing chunky Rolex watches were snapping orders at the barman, a short Arab in a fez and a grimy white bar coat. An old Art Deco radio on a glass case behind the bar played "Moon River." The radio had an amazingly good sound.

While Dr. Lars pondered the hand-written menu, Ad Magic dived into the ninety-cent vegetable curry served with hot pipi peppers. There was enough food to feed an army. It was value for the dollar. As Pastor Dave and his wife, Cissy, drank Nescafé and fired questions at Lars, Ad Magic astonished everyone by finishing his enormous meal in less than three minutes. When the waiter brought him a brandy, Ad Magic whipped out a Marlboro. It was his first cigarette in days. After four long drags he knew he had made a colossal mistake. Not only was the cigarette a grave error but the brandy, the curry, and the whiskeys and beer before it. A jar of Gerber's Baby Custard would have been more appropriate. He braced himself on his narrow chair and held on to the edge of the table as his face went pale. The virus — he felt that he was about to leak from every orifice and turn into a pile of green goo. Dr. Lars set her menu down, leaned forward, and placed the cool back of her hand against his forehead and cheek. "Oh dear," she said with a Danish accent. "You don't look well at all."

Ad Magic popped up and converted a sentence into a word, "Nine-seconds-to-make-the-toilet!" He delivered this declaration so emphatically, the whole room fell silent as everyone turned to stare. It seemed that even the glass-eyed animals on the walls trained their enamel-painted pupils on him as he padded out of the room with his ass cheeks squeezed together.

Once safely out of view, he bounded up the back stairs, scrabbled open his double-locked door, and burst into the bathroom. When the worst of it was over he curled into the fetal position and prayed, "Oh, God, please, I'll do anything! Just . . . cut me a little slack."

When the cramps began to subside there was a sharp,

insistent knocking at his door. Ad Magic flushed the toilet and mopped his face off with a dingy hotel towel that smelled of mold and brought him within an ace of vomiting yet again. He swished some Scope in his mouth, stepped into his bush shorts and answered the door. Dr. Lars stood at the portal with an amber bottle of paregoric. "Hiya," she said, pushing her bangs back. "I thought you could use something to help with your tummy troubles." She handed him the medicine. "This should stop the cramping and calm things down in your lower GI tract."

Ad Magic knew that paregoric contained opium and wasted no time shaking up the bottle and taking several large slugs of the chalky mixture. From his bureau he shook a couple of malaria tablets in his hand and chased them with more paregoric.

"Uh . . . I just wanted to tell you that I thought your letter with the mealies sample was fabulous."

"It was?" Ad Magic said. Fine beads of perspiration broke out on his face. "Hell, I take no credit for that letter. The Holy Spirit wrote that one."

"Don't be modest, that was a wonderful concept. I mean attaching a little glassine bag of mealies made it all so real for the reader. It just brought the whole point home. It completed the picture. There's such incredible donor fatigue, but your letters. Well, they're marvelous. For less money than it takes to feed the average St. Bernard, feeding an African family of seven. What person with the least shred of human feeling can say no? After I ate my sample, I immediately wrote a check and drove it straight to the post."

"That's exactly what you were supposed to do. When you set them aside for later — to think it over — nothing ever comes of it. But the samples weren't really mealies," Ad Magic said. "I sort of cheated. And in truth, what with graft, transportation, thievery, and so on, it cost less for two to dine at a Tokyo nightclub than it does to give a single African a handful of Kansas corn." Ad Magic took another slug from the paregoric bottle.

"What?"

"How long have you been in-country, baby?"

"Three months, *baby!*"

"It's frustrating is all. Everything just seems to keep getting worse. Mealies letters, for God's sakes."

"What was in it, it was delicious?"

"You'll get pissed if I tell you," Ad Magic said.

"Oh come on now," she said with a laugh. "Since I've come to Africa I've eaten monkey, goat, fried grubs, crocodile even — "

"You'll be disappointed in me — I mean you guys take the Hippocratic oath and are ethical and everything. Ad writers are a different breed. What kind of car do you drive?"

"A Saab."

"A Saab! Well, then I *really* can't tell you. You'll hate me forever."

"No I won't. Cross my heart and swear to die," Lars said. She was a blond pushing thirty. Crow's-feet and wrinkles were beginning to establish themselves on her face but the bone structure would hold up for life. She had a pretty nose, and from Ad Magic's experience with fashion models in the days when he worked as a commercial ad writer, he knew a good nose was the foremost requisite for the sort of beauty that would survive into middle age. He felt like proposing marriage to her right on the spot. Lars had a great face. She had plump high cheekbones, full lips, and large green eyes. And then there were the breasts which simply defied the laws of physics. Maybe she had a job done on them. Maybe there was a colleague in Copenhagen that practiced cosmetic surgery. The width and thickness of the brassiere that was visible beneath Lars's T-shirt was formidable. Maybe it was Howard Hughes's last masterwork? Ad Magic took a step back to get an overall idea of proportions. Lars's arms and shoulders seemed slender. She had good muscle tone and he realized they only seemed slender relative to the size of her breasts. Her forearms and wrists were substantial. He hoped she wouldn't ruin everything by having thick ankles.

"Thanks for the medicine. That was very nice of you. Do you think you could you take a look at my thumb? It's just killing me. And this malaria is bad. I haven't been able to keep any pills down. I've been hallucinating, it seems, for a lifetime. Am I dreaming or are you real?"

"I'm real," Lars said with a laugh. Her teeth glistened white. Her tongue and gums flashed healthy and pink. Ad Magic escorted her into the room, closed the door, and followed her over to the dim light by his bed. Lars wore a madras skirt that hung to her ankles but the ankles were trim. She had a narrow waist, shapely hips, and unless she was related to Popeye, she had to have long thin legs.

"A pediatrician from Denmark. Hmmm. They know of me there? Did you read my letter about potable water in the Cameroon? I wonder how it held up through the translation."

"It was fabulous. I read it in Danish. I liked the business about 'living waters.'"

"You didn't think that was too . . . biblical? Too corny?"

"Not at all. In the context of the letter the whole image was perfect and very subtle actually. You're a very sophisticated writer. Ever since I got into this field I've heard scads about you, and now it's as though I'm meeting a celebrity. Anybody with half a brain can get through medical school but to actually move people, to involve them as you do — I had no idea you would be so handsome," she blurted.

"You mean to make them give up some of their green?" he said. Sick as he was, Ad Magic saw that she was attracted to him. The word "handsome" escaped from her mouth like a Freudian slip. Lars seemed to realize this since she flushed. "Are you going to tell me what was in my little packet of mealies?"

Ad Magic shook his finger at her in a teasing, admonishing fashion, worrying at the same time that his breath was vile. "Oh, Lars, ho, ho, ho. I can't tell. It's a trade secret like the recipe for Pepsi. You don't think the 'living waters' thing was kind of . . . overly theatrical."

"It was wonderful but it's going to take more than water to right the situation in Goma. It's going to take some of that American 'green' — lots!" Lars pushed her bangs back again. Preening behavior. She wore no makeup. Her hair was lank with the humidity. With a shampoo, some face powder, and red lipstick she would be a knockout. He wondered if she had been three months plus without sex as well. She seemed eager for him to make his move but Ad Magic had serious doubts about his breath. Then his stomach growled and he winced from the cramps. "Unngh!" he said. "I know I just got the shits, but I've been having this pain in my side, too, before this all started. It really gets bad if I take vitamins or eat dairy — I mean I know I'm fairly young, but you don't think I could have . . . cancer?"

"Oh, you silly hypochondriac," Lars said. "Of course you don't have cancer."

"How can you just say that? I mean without a CAT scan or something?"

Lars patted the bed. "Lie down," she said. As Ad Magic lay on the bed, his stomach growled again and they both laughed. Lars slipped her cool hands under Ad Magic's shirt. "What are you doing?"

"Feeling your liver," she said. She slid Ad Magic's shirt

up and placed her ear on his stomach. "Pretty wild in there," she said, "bowel sounds. Where do you have the pain?" Ad Magic took her wrist and placed her hand on the spot. "If you press on it, it sort of goes away."

Lars began to massage the spot. "There's a ninety-degree crinkle in your bowel at that spot and it can get spastic when you eat irritating foods. It's nothing — "

"Really?"

Lars began to laugh. "You *silly* hypochondriac, you. Now let's have a look at that thumb." Lars carefully removed the dressing.

"You've got a lot of pressure under the nail and the bone is crushed. No wonder it hurts. What happened to you?"

"Rwanda," he said. "When I got to the fucking refugee camp in Tanzania and showed the doctors my thumb, they just laughed like, 'We've got *real* things to worry about.' I said, 'I'm Derek Van Horne.' And it was like, 'So what? Get the fuck out of here.' So I wrapped it myself. And speaking of refugees, let me give you a little piece of advice — you want to bring somebody back from the brink of starvation, powdered milk, beef, or whatever doesn't cut it. It will kill them by the second day. It takes sardines, mackerel, or cod liver oil if you can't get fish. EPH. Omega 3's. That's what they need. Not crude protein. Those assholes in Tanzania are pushing powdered milk. It's a joke."

Dr. Lars got up from the bed and removed a paper clip from a manuscript that was lying on Ad Magic's bureau. "You still haven't told me what happened to your thumb."

"Government soldiers bashed it. Chased me over the edge of a damn ravine — head over heels like a Peter Sellers movie. I landed in a muck-fucking quicksand pit loaded with crocodiles. I lost my shoes. It was insane. I still can't believe it."

Lars straightened out the paper clip and then heated it

with a butane lighter that sat on the bureau next to Ad Magic's red and white packet of Marlboros. In seconds the end of the paper clip glowed red. Worried about his breath, Ad Magic took another swallow of paregoric. He hoisted his window and looked down at the street drummers. "Why, Lars, it's Martha and the Vandellas: Your love is like quicksand. I'm sinkin' deeper. Goopy lose-ya-good-shoes-forever quicksand. The sharp whine of mosquitoes. Spotlights, gunfire, red beady crocodile eyes, *'Oh God, I'm being eating. Oh, God, I'm dead! Goodbye forever! Send Anaud to Uganda! Aiiee!'*"

Ad Magic popped the fingers on his good hand and continued to rumba to the street drums. " 'I'm sinkin' deeper.' " Lars took his injured hand. She reheated the paper clip. "Hey," Ad Magic said, "what are you doing?"

"Don't worry," she said. "Trust me. Be a brave little soldier, now." Lars plunged the red end of the paper clip into the base of Ad Magic's thumbnail, filling the air with the pungent smell of burned hair. When she made a second hole a narrow stream of blood shot across the room. "Oh man," Ad Magic said, sagging visibly. "That feels better! You scared the shit out of me but, oh boy. Holy cow. What a relief!"

"Didn't I tell you so?" Lars said with a laugh. "You're so tense. Roll over on your belly," she said pulling him to the bed. Soon her cool fingers were massaging his back and neck. Ad Magic let off a long sigh as the rush of paregoric on an empty stomach hit home and the pleasant sensation of warmth filled his abdomen. In another moment he seemed to float an inch above the mattress. He closed his eyes and saw marvelous swirling lights. "That feels so good," he said. "Don't ever stop. All that shit in Rwanda . . . I've been as scared as a rabbit ever since I got here. This has been a fucked-up trip."

Her fingers left his skin suddenly and Lars seemed to be

rustling out of her shirt. Ad Magic listened as she unclasped her bra. It sounded like she was opening up a bank vault. *Could it be possible?* Suddenly he could feel the sweep of her long hair and the points of her firm breasts on his back as she licked, kissed, and nibbled his ears. He quickly grew hard and as he rolled over, Lars pulled off her panties and mounted him. Her breasts stood erect with the nipples tilted up utterly. Implants or real?

Lars bent forward and let Ad Magic bury his face in those marvelous breasts. In order not to come, he forced himself to think of the numbers that had accrued to date on his mealies letter. He thought of the metric tons of corn that had been purchased with the funds. He thought of the overhead, transportation costs, and the percentage of money Global Aid owed him over and above his salary on a sliding scale rate. Suddenly Lars found the right position and began to groove on his cock like a bronco rider. She let off a long shuddering groan and then reverted to the push-up position. Ad Magic quit his mental calculations and concentrated on her firm breasts for the very few seconds that passed before he exploded inside her.

LARS did not get off him but leaned back pinching her nipples as she continued to thrust in a wholly new fashion. Ad Magic worried that she would expect him to remain hard. He did not think himself capable of such a feat but to his amazement, by watching her breasts his erection remained intact, hardened like industrial-grade diamond. "I'm fucking. I'm fucking. I'm *actually* fucking. I am getting laid," he whispered.

The farther Lars leaned back, the more confident Ad Magic became in his staying power. Her cool body warmed up and began to run with sweat. As the back bend became more extreme, Ad Magic thought that she would snap his penis off. Yet there was pleasure in the pain. He slipped out, and she roughly grabbed his dick and reinserted it. Ad Magic suddenly found himself doing a kind of neck bridge to accommodate her. As with so many of the beautiful women he had known in the fashion industry, making love to Lars was becoming very hard work.

Lars got off him and let off a small series of dog yelps as he entered her from the missionary position. Lars began having several successive low-grade orgasms. She wet her middle finger in her mouth and stuck it up Ad Magic's raw ass. He just about hit the ceiling over that one and began banging her as hard as possible, as if to fuck her to death, and it was then that she gave off her greatest cry. "Finally," Ad Magic thought.

But Lars took Ad Magic's head in her hands and rammed her tongue into his mouth. The furnace heat she was putting out was incredible. She worked her mouth down his neck to his chest, arms, and the fingers of his good hand. He held the sore thumb above his head in abeyance until Lars went down on him in such an experienced and smooth fashion that Ad Magic realized he was about to receive the blow job of a lifetime. Forgetting about the pain in his thumb, he clasped both hands gently on her head, closed his eyes, and drifted off into ecstasy. It was as if Rwanda and the whole nightmarish trip to Africa had never happened. Lars seemed tireless and when Ad Magic opened his eyes and saw those shimmering breasts, he became harder than a teenager on testosterone and in moments he came.

AD Magic awoke to the feel of Lars's cool fingers on his cheek. When he looked up at her, she was fully dressed. "Did we do it, or have I been dreaming?"

Lars winked at him. "Oh, it was a dream. What kind of gal do you take me for? This has strictly been a professional visit."

He smiled at this. "I knew it had to be too good to be true." He swept his hair back with his fingers. "Tell me something, Lars. Do you ever feel like a marionette in a Punch and Judy show?"

"No," she said. "What kind of question is that?"

Ad Magic realized he was still grooving on the opium. He reached for a cigarette and smoked it cool style, pouting his lips and inserting it into the center of his mouth. "Scatman Crothers as Mr. Clotho: *Ahm just a porter on the Pushman line.*"

Lars smiled.

"Scatman Crothers in *The Shining*: 'How would y'all like a nice big dish of chocolate ice cream, Doc? Heh heh heh.' "

Lars smiled revealing her teeth.

"Scatman Crothers as Jimmy Durante — "

Lars unbuttoned her blouse, tossed it on a chair, and reached behind her back to unclasp her bra. When her breasts sprang loose, she said, "Yes? Jimmy Durante. Yes?"

"Make dat Ralph Kramden, darlin', 'Homina, homina, homina!' "

PASTOR Dave Mosely walked around his dirty gray Peugeot 505 station wagon shifting luggage on the roof rack, loosely securing ropes, lighting and relighting a big bowl calabash pipe as he experimented with various load arrangements. He was a large stout man, with a full gray beard.

Ad Magic's pupils were dilated and his eyes had a glassy opiate sheen as he took the last few slugs from his gigantic bottle of paregoric. It was warm out and kept getting hotter as Pastor Dave continued to fiddle around with the Peugeot. Ad Magic wondered when the man would ever be ready and zigzagged back to his room to pay one last visit to the toilet. As the sun rose higher, Ad Magic, who was dressed in the thinnest of cottons, watched the stout minister stand in the hot sun in a thick cabled wool sweater with increasing dismay. Mosely was now checking not only the air pressure of the tires, but also that of the spare. Ad Magic made another trip to his room. When he returned Pastor Dave had the narrow hood of the Peugeot up and his head was buried underneath. Christ! Now what? Ad Magic dreaded a protracted conversation with the minister but at last he could stand it no longer and approached Pastor Dave, tapping him on the shoulder. "Are you putting in new head gaskets or . . . w'aaaht?"

Pastor Dave stepped back, struck a wooden match, and lit his pipe. He took several pulls on it and then held it out before him like a beloved object. He took another few pulls and fast-sinking blue and white smoke poured out of the bowl like mist coming off a hunk of dry ice. "I'm afraid the water pump is shot. Are you feeling any better?"

"I feel fine," Ad Magic said. "I thought we were leaving at nine. The water pump is broken?"

"Oh. Not to worry. This is Africa, son." Pastor Dave puffed on the calabash as he surveyed the landscape. It was such a bright and clear day that the low flat crater of Mt. Ngorongoro seemed deceptively near. The minister nodded at the mountain, summoning Ad Magic to do the same. "Oh the hell with that," Ad Magic said, waving it off. "If you seen one fucking crater, you've seen them all."

"Oh ho," Pastor Dave said. "It's the fever still. You're not feeling well, are you? It's a wonderful day."

. "It's not that I'm not feeling well. It's just that I

thought we agreed to leave at nine. How are you going to run down a water pump? I suppose you want to boil out the radiator, too."

"Joshua is rounding one up now," Pastor Dave said. "Cissy has gone along to keep him away from the beer halls."

"God! They have an auto parts store in Arusha?" Ad Magic said.

"Not really. There's a junkyard."

"The whole city is a junkyard!"

"Well, a case could be made. Anyhow, they've gone there to scavenge a water pump. I thought I'd take the time to adjust the timing and top off the oil. I really need to throw a new set of rings into this beast. It burns a quart with every fill-up. I'm almost three-quarters of a quart low and I hate to top up since we'll have an open can of oil to carry — "

"Just dump it all in," Ad Magic said abruptly.

"Well, you can do that but then there's too much pressure and it can blow the seals . . . especially on a hot day — "

"Then add three-fourths of a quart and throw the oil away. You can't carry an open can in the car. Somebody's going to knock it over."

"I was thinking of that," Pastor Dave said. "But I hate to waste oil."

"Give it to a beggar!" Ad Magic snapped. "He can start a business greasing rusty bicycle chains."

"Oh ho!" Pastor Dave said. "You're a funny man, Derek. This will be a jolly trip."

"I'm going back to get Lars. They've got an X-ray machine at the Methodist clinic. Lars promised to set my thumb if there was time. It feels like a rat is chewing my whole hand off."

"I noticed the bandage at dinner, what happened?"

"I'll tell you about it on the trip," Ad Magic said. "Let me go find Lars." He started to walk back to the hotel and then turned and looked at a chicken crate that was tied above his suitcase. He walked back to the car and said, "Whose chicken is that? Is Joshua taking a chicken?"

"Oh, the chicken," Pastor Dave said. "I forgot to tell you."

"That suitcase cost me more than four hundred in Switzerland," Ad Magic said as he turned and stalked back to his room. "Fuck."

LARS sat before a cheap raw pine bureau with a small mirror, brushing her hair. She was dressed in a pair of Banana Republic shorts, Reebok Cross Trainers and a thin denim blouse. She smiled as Ad Magic came inside. "You can't go about like that," Ad Magic said, nodding at her shorts.

"Why not?" Lars said.

"Because this is Africa. How long have you been in Tanzania, anyhow?"

"What makes you think I was planning to go out like this?" Lars said. "And where do you get off getting so cheeky?"

"Because it's time to leave, only it's *not* time to leave because the water pump is out in the car. Cissy and Joshua are out at some junkyard looking for a spare."

"Affirmative."

"Well, why doesn't anyone fill me in?"

"You weren't at breakfast — "

"Breakfast! You call smoked kipper breakfast? It's all salt, bones, scales, and fuckin' fin!"

"I had tea and bread," Lars said, "with orange marmalade. We went over all of this at breakfast, Derek. Why on earth are you so grouchy? Wasn't last night relaxing?"

"I'm hung over on paregoric," Ad Magic said. "And my thumb is killing me."

Lars reached for Ad Magic's hand and examined it. "The nail is infected and it really should come off. Let's walk over to the clinic and take a picture of the break. I can probably set it for you."

"What do you mean, probably?"

"I don't know much about orthopedics," Lars said, throwing on a jacket. "But the bone is crushed. What happened to you anyhow? You're so mysterious about everything."

"I told you: quicksand," Ad Magic said. "Martha and the Vandellas. 'I'm sinkin' deeper.' "

AS Lars and Ad Magic came out of the hotel, Pastor Dave had the alternator of the Peugeot 505 laid out in the lot along with the fan belt, the water hoses and the car's radiator. "Oh my God!" Ad Magic said. "We'll be here all week."

Lars took Ad Magic's good hand and pulled him along as she took great bounding steps forward, urging him on. "That would be super."

Ad Magic laughed. "I guess you're right. I mean we're headed for Kigoma. And then — Mocherville! Let's hope he never gets it fixed."

The side road into town defined itself only by virtue of the fact that it was a darker color than the sand which surrounded it. It was packed down by road traffic and stained with oil and transmission fluid. While there were no shoulders to the road, neither was it pocked with holes. Along the roadside there were several large billboards extolling the virtues of skin bleach, dipilatories, Orange Crush, Wall's Ice Cream, and Colgate Toothpaste along with the ubiquitous Coke signs that proclaimed nothing, they were just what they were — international icons.

The billboards were interspaced by the flamboyant trees, palms, or various shade trees — acacias and balanites, under which street venders sold potatoes, onions, tomatoes, mangoes, pineapples, and enormous plantains. They sold crude salt, miswaki sticks (which the Tanzanians used as toothbrushes), and various unlikely items — "Walkman" tape players, Nike jogging shoes, Harvard University sweatshirts. Ad Magic watched a man dole out palm oil from a large tin into empty pop bottles. Another vender offered cigarettes for sale — one at a time or in colorful packets. Other venders offered a variety of cooked foods — roasted corn on the cob, roasted nuts, stews, and meat kabobs of uncertain origin. A train of African women dressed in brightly colored kanga cloth were walking along the side of the road toting various bundles on their heads — firewood, yams carried in large porcelain basins, sacks of kola nuts, stalks of bananas, hogfish. Their men walked ahead of them carrying nothing at all. This was a far sight better than Rwanda where people were reduced to eating field mice.

Bicycles and motorcycles cruised up and down the road. People stood under the trees just passing the time of day smoking cigarettes, listening to *juju* music, or playing the popular board game *kigogo* in which little wooden balls were shuffled around into slots hollowed out of a log. A child had tried to teach the game to Ad Magic in the refugee camp in Tanzania, and he promised himself that he would at some time master this game as a form of self-improvement, but Ad Magic found it to be the most complicated, difficult, and utterly pleasureless game he had ever in his life tried. It was the most awful taxing of his brain he could remember since he had to take a course in botany to meet his science requirement in college.

"Look at them," he said to Lars. "Happy go lucky, sweet, friendly. But God knows how fast that can all change. I thought I had a handle on the place but not now, not anymore. I'm going to Mocherville to file a piece on the leper colony and then I'm out of here never to return. Rwanda is just starters. All these tinhorn countries are ready to blow. And to think I used to feel safer here than at home."

As Set Benjamin Road fed into Makongoro, Lars led Ad Magic into the traffic, diesel fumes, and one-hundred-and-thirty-decibel noise. The Methodist medical clinic was packed with dozens of ailing Africans, none of whom had anything so minor as a broken thumb. Lars escorted Ad Magic into the surgery with a wave at the clerk sitting at the front desk.

As the senior physician examined the X ray of Ad Magic's thumb, Lars whipped out a syringe and began poking him around the base of the thumb with Novocain. Tears began to run from Ad Magic's eyes. "You're so violent with that damn needle," he said. "Can't you give a shot so it doesn't hurt? Like slower? You didn't even give me time to get ready — to think things over, to compose myself!"

"If I go slower, it's still hurting, isn't it?" She said. "We're all through now. Fast is better." Before he knew what was happening, Lars took a pair of forceps and removed Ad Magic's thumbnail. It was a painless operation that sounded like a piece of Scotch tape being ripped off a cold glass window. The size of the nail with its bloody root horrified Ad Magic. As soon as Lars finished cleaning out the nail bed, the house doctor was ready with a wooden splint. He fixed it to the thumb and adjusted the bone by feel. After he bandaged it, he led Ad Magic back to the X-ray machine. As the picture developed, he led Ad Magic to his consulting room where he poured tea. Lars followed the senior doctor back out to the examining room to look at an unusual pediatric case. This gave Ad Magic a chance to poke into the medicine cabinet, which sat temptingly open with a key dangling from the lock. He grabbed one of several large blue jars of morphine tablets, popped three with his tea and after he replaced it, he changed his mind and began jamming pills into his deep bush pockets. When they were bulging, he shook the jar to fluff it up and make it seem fuller and then placed it behind one of the new jars. He pulled his shirt out of his shorts to cover the bulk of his pockets. He wished he had a sea bag. A shopping cart. This was a once-in-a-lifetime score. Before him was a five-year supply of morphine. There wasn't much else worth stealing until he saw a one-hundred-count bottle of Dexedrine spansules. He poured these in his near-empty box of Marlboros and was sitting on an old leather-cushioned divan when Lars and the senior doctor came back. "All is okay," said the doctor. He carefully replaced the wooden splint with a curved one made of aluminum, secured it with an elastic bandage, and said, "Dr. Lars can take it from here."

BACK at the Hotel Arusha, Pastor Dave and Joshua seemed to have even more motor parts laid out on the ground. Pastor Dave winked at the pair and they both gave him a little wave. "Good," Ad Magic said to Lars. "We'll be here all week. Good."

"Does that mean you're happy to be with me?" Lars said.

Overjoyed at his narcotics score, Ad Magic said, "Are you kidding? I'm nuts about you. I'm in love with you. Let's go out and buy a ring. I want to marry you and live with you forever."

Lars laughed. "You're silly," she said.

He expected her to be thrilled at his admission; instead

she seemed to be mocking him. Ad Magic stared at her blankly. "So hip, so cool, so tough! You gotta heart of ice, I swear. Does life ever seem like it's nothing but a big cartoon?"

She took his good hand and led him up into her room. There, buzzed on morphine, Ad Magic became a high wire man in the circus. He was the Great Wallenda. Break Dancer Wallenda. "No inhibitions today," he said. He lifted his arms up and extended them out from his shoulders pointing his forefingers out with a little flourish. He thrust out his chin and began to walk the wire. He carefully pointed each foot forward and walked an imaginary line across the floor toe/heel, toe/heel, toe/heel. He got up on his tippy toes, then he began to backpedal as if he were about to fall. "When I was a commercial writer, I sort of flipped. Nervous breakdown. I don't know. I mean I don't know if it was all the drugs I was doing or if I was just plain crazy. I heard voices. God talked to me."

"You heard a voice from God?"

"Seemed like I did," Ad Magic said. "I was nearly killed in Rwanda. I'm getting too old for Africa. I'm over here risking life and limb and back in Los Angeles they tell me, 'Don't drive your Jaguar into the headquarters, it looks bad. We're a nonprofit organization.' I say, 'Look at how much money my letters pull in.' They say, 'All you do is sit around here all day and flirt with the girls; then you pop into your office for five minutes and write a letter.' I say, 'Well, if it's so goddamn easy, you try it. Who came up with the mealies letter? Look what I've done for you! I've put food in those empty bellies. And what the hell thanks do I get? Do you realize the cost, the psychic wear and tear it takes out of me to write this stuff? Do you think it's easy? Lars, the parishioners are donor-weary as you say. Each letter becomes harder than the last. Tell me something.

Have you ever heard the fairy tale "Rumpelstiltskin"? Have they got that one in Denmark?"

"Of course."

"Well, I suppose you think the little dwarf was a nasty man because he wanted to take the princess's first baby. Here's a man who comes along, saves her life, weaves straw into gold. Gets her married to the prince of the land. Creates for her a life of milk and honey and when it's time for her to turn over the kid as per agreement, she welshes. I got out of the commercial field where at least you know you're going to get knifed in the back — nobody pretends that it's otherwise. I thought that by doing something for humanity — I thought that by doing the right thing, I could come to terms with life but it's nothing but lies, duplicity, and them all hating me no matter how much I deliver. Yet I have been honorable and held up my end of the deal. I have brought in millions and they say, 'Don't park the Jaguar at work. It looks bad. Buy an Escort.'"

Lars stroked his cheek with the back of her hand. "Poor misunderstood genius."

"Christ, Lars, you got a heart made out of ice. Wait until you get a load of Mocherville. They've got some sorry ass missions in Zaire," Ad Magic said, holding up his hands, "but with these magic fingers I have single-handedly turned Mocherville into the fucking Hilton Inn of Zaire: air conditioners, Land Cruisers, a river launch, a pharmacy, slit lamp ophthalmology, clean water, three squares a day, HIV prevention and treatment, an immunization program, Hansen's disease eradication — the whole deal. Clothing. There's even a dental service. They have got a library. They have got classrooms. Modern textbooks. It's an oasis in Hell thanks to yours truly. To top it all off, they sent me over to this motherfucker in a coach-class seat, a violation of my contract. I have a lawyer on retainer to keep those cheap ass bastards under control. I have to pay a lawyer to protect myself from them. That's the *last* time I stand for that tourist-class bullshit, let me tell you. They can kiss my ass and let somebody else float the son-of-a-bitch. I've had it. It's been one thing after another ever since I got here. Malaria from the word go. I mean I don't even know why we are here. Every time I come back it's twenty times worse. Africa is just going down the shithole as fast as possible. People eating mice — "

"All I'm hearing is self-pity." Lars pulled off her sunglasses. "Have you ever taken lithium? Saliva is flying out of your mouth."

Ad Magic relaxed his shoulders. "Lithium? Yeah, sure. Stelazine, lithium . . . all that crap." He looked down at his shoes. "My investment portfolio is all over the joint. I've got to get on that when I get home. Maybe I can semi-retire." He thrust his lower teeth forward of his lip. Amphetamine. He grabbed her elbow. "C'mon. We've got a mission of vital importance."

Ad Magic took Lars in his arms and kissed her. "My God, you're beautiful. I love you. You're the love of my life, I swear."

In moments Lars and Ad Magic were on the road back to town. With every step Ad Magic cringed in pain.

"What?" Lars said.

"The heel bone being connected to the leg bone being connected to the hip bone and so on to the thumb bone! The thumb is killing me. I took morphine and it's throbbing any*fucking*how!" Ad Magic looked up at the sky imploringly. "Why in the hell don't you just strike me dead and get it over with?"

"Derek," Lars said. "This is insane. Stop it!"

Ad Magic was several strides ahead of her. Soon he began to jog until he came to the first fast food brazier where he bought two iced bottles of Fanta orange. He popped three more morphine tablets and swallowed them with a bottle of soda. By the time Lars caught up with him he was sipping the second bottle and smoking a cigarette.

"Do you want anything, baby? Are you thirsty? Hungry?"

Lars shook her head. "No, *baby!*"

"Look, I know what you're thinking, but don't worry; I'm all right. I was just having a little nicotine fit back there. I'm better now. Seriously, do you know where we can find a good traditional doctor? I saw a whole lane of them the other day." Ad Magic handed the stall keeper the empty soda bottles and when the man offered Ad Magic his change he told him to keep it. "Let's go!" He thrust his lower teeth forward. "The winged dragon flies through the night sky." He lifted his palm and presented the sky to her as if it was his to give. "Beautiful, huh?"

"It's not night. It's daytime."

"You can really be a pain in the ass, Lars. What a nit-picker."

A small boy ran up to Ad Magic with a shoeshine kit. Ad Magic put a loafer on the little box and while the boy started slapping on polish and working the shoe over with a stained rag, Ad Magic snapped the fingers on his good hand and worked his arms and elbows in rhythm to the popping of the shoeshine rag. "Shoeshine boy. I'm a . . . *shoeshine boy.*" After the first shoe was complete he seemed bored with the action and handed the boy the equivalent of fifty dollars while Lars shook her head in dismay. "It's all just fucking Monopoly money, Miss Nitpick. I don't have to work for it."

Ad Magic led Lars to a row of herbalist stalls in a side alley off the main road beyond the Methodist clinic. After making a pass of all the stalls, Ad Magic dragged Lars back to the one that had the most alert looking traditional doctor, an old fellow with several crusted eczema patches that he continuously worked over with the tips of his thin fingers. "The motherfucker can't cure himself, but that's not always a factor," Ad Magic said. A hand-painted sign in English advertised cures for lower back pain, impotence, toothache, malaria, and worms. He turned to Lars. "My Swahili is for shit. Ask him if he can work some *juju*. Tell him I have many enemies in America who wish to harm me and that I generally don't feel good. Tell him I need my mojo back so I can write again. My well is dry. If he's got a quit-smoking cure, have him throw that in, too."

As Lars conversed with the old man, Ad Magic shifted from foot to foot, alternately squeezing the first four fingers of each hand. "What? What?" he said anxiously.

"He thinks he can help you. Five dollars American to sacrifice a rooster. Fifteen for a goat."

"Tell him I want a big bull elephant and I'll pay five hundred dollars."

Lars translated the message. The witch doctor rose from his seat and spat on the ground. "You've insulted him," Lars said. "Now he wants twenty dollars. The size of the animal has nothing to do with it. He wants twenty."

"Seven!"

Lars turned back to the witch doctor and entered into a protracted negotiation. Ad Magic reverted to his jaw-thrusting behavior. Instead of wringing his hands, he kept checking his wristwatch. "We're late," he said. "We're late. C'mon." Lars slapped his good hand. "Relax," she said, as she continued to talk with the witch doctor. Soon both parties were laughing.

"He has a nephew that has the perfect goat."

"How much?"

"Nine dollars. I don't think I can get him down any

lower. If you can pay fifty to have one shoe shined, what's the big deal? It's just 'Monopoly money,' Derek."

"How much for the rooster? What's the bottom line on the rooster?"

Lars turned back to the witch doctor. Ad Magic glanced at his watch. "Oh hell, you're right, give him the nine. Let's get this show on the road."

Ad Magic smoked a half-dozen cigarettes in the half hour it took for the witch doctor's nephew to return not with the goat but a rooster. Lars spoke with the doctor who said a rooster was just as good. Rather than watch the ceremony, Ad Magic paid the man and handed him three Marlboro cigarettes. "Kwaheri, man. Muchos gracious. Next time h'you h'are een Bolivia, peek up zee phone h'an' geeve me hey call, dude. I weel show you zee night life h'an' get you laid." Ad Magic blew him a kiss and he and Lars fought their way through the narrow alley, turned left on the main road, and headed back toward the hotel. "You're exquisitely beautiful," he said. "You're the love of my life. I feel better already."

"You're stoned," Lars said.

"I'm not impaired, in the real sense, believe me. There's a difference."

"Why were you given Stelazine?" Lars said.

"They gave me that in the nuthouse. It's not bad. Stelazine . . . life's a dream."

"I see. 'Rumpelstiltskin' is a fairy tale, you know. An abstraction. I'm hearing concrete thinking from you."

"Let's go back to my room and do it."

"I'm having my period," she said coldly.

"We can just make out. That's even better. I like that better. You're so beautiful. Lighten up, baby."

"Okay, *baby,* but first tell me about the mealies letter."

"Fuckin' Murphy Brown! What a mouth you've got.

Shit! Well . . . the mealies letter. I hate to dwell on past glories. I've got new ones to write, but I'll tell you if I get to kiss those *mmm! mmm! goodie!* luscious lips. You know the story — everyone is playing hell trying to ship corn around the Horn what with the drought and all. Co'n 'round da ho'n. A thousand a truckload. Three years of drought. People eaten dey seed co'n, babycakes. The Somalia fiasco and so on. You wanna co'n baked muffin, it's gonna cost ya nine thousand deutsche marks. It ain't just me. None of the agencies have come up with anything that will fly. Anyhow, I got this sack of mealies in my office and I'm eating it — I mean it's better for you than the general American diet, right? But it's a joke. Like, this is what I have to eat on the pay I get and I make it into a big joke and pretty soon everybody is eating mealies, including all of the uptight assholes that I just hate and would like to knife, strangle, or shoot through the brain. This is what I really want to do, but of course I don't want to end up in jail, so what I do is mash up some Milk Bone dog biscuits. I'm telling everyone they've got protein fortified — you know, new and improved mealies and everybody is eating these Milk Bone dog biscuits and going — 'Wow! This stuff is great! This is just super!' I was getting real satisfaction to think they were eating dog food but then I read the ingredients on the dog food box — good stuff — canola oil and stuff. I tried it myself and it's like two hundred times more delicious than the real mealies. Anyhow, how do you make the problem of starvation real to most Americans who have probably never missed a meal in their lives? Pictures of babies with swollen stomachs? That only cuts it to a point. It creates donor-weariness. Overload. People *are* donor-weary. So I started sending the crushed Milk Bones out in little homemade packets that I stapled to the bottom of the letters and after the initial response, I knew I was onto a real goodie. The returns were fantastic and I began to refine the method. I went over the marketing lists. Jaguar owners, unlike myself, are typically austere types. I added coarse sea salt to the product and Bingo! We've got forty-three hundred registered Jaguar owners on our list and we get replies from twenty-one hundred and seven. The Cadillac and Lincoln crowd are comfort seekers: these got crunchy granola and brown sugar mixed with their Milk Bone. I had a little factory down in the basement and hired some street bums to crush the Milk Bones and bag them."

"What was in the Saab batch?"

"Rat shit."

Lars made a fist and socked Ad Magic on the very site where she had given him a tetanus shot a half hour before. "You bastard."

"Lars, you Danish yuppie, you. I'm just kidding. Milk Bones are bad enough. It's got to be some kind of food and drug violation — I think we sent out like forty thousand and broke all records — me and my street crew. I had this super blend that I sent to the corporate clients and that's where we started drawing down some long green. Then my boss got into the act and they started mailing real mealies and, I mean, what could I say? 'We need to use Milk Bone instead'? The curve started to drop but we were still hauling in well over triple. John Q. Citizen tastes the little sample, imagines himself in darkest Africa eating mealies far from the stresses and strains of twentieth-century America. Or something. I don't really know what the appeal was. Only that this damn letter has become an instant classic in the industry, I'm up for an award and in the meantime we are delivering metric tons of corn to the starving Masai, which is the bottom line. I mean, I could get banned if the truth ever comes out."

"Did you ever imagine yourself to be Christlike?"

"Oh ho *ho,* Lars! Don't play psychiatrist with me. Jesus was a paranoid schizophrenic. There's literature on it. I've got both my feet planted in reality."

"Hmmm!"

" 'Hmmm!' she sez. You're such a beautiful woman. You have such a free spirit — "

"Would you be willing to try the Stelazine again? The lithium?"

"Lars, don't be my doctor, be my main sah-queeze. I don't want to *hear* doctor. I can't work on lithium. Who can work on lithium? If I have to be a little crazy to do this, so be it. I'm not really in it for myself anymore. This is all part of a larger scheme."

Ad Magic hailed a gypsy cab and within five minutes they were back at the Hotel Arusha. There Ad Magic found Pastor Dave, his wife, Cissy, Joshua, and an elderly African couple sitting on the veranda sipping iced tea. The Peugeot 505 was all put together. The heat of the day was weighing down heavily but as soon as Lars and Ad Magic settled their bills they found themselves crunched in the backseat of the car with Joshua. Pastor Dave ran the motor for a moment, released the emergency brake, engaged into first, and then wheeled the old car onto the main Tarmac road leading out of Arusha.

Lars said her eyes burned and her head was pounding but Ad Magic had just caught a second wind. He reached over and massaged the back of her neck. "Are you okay, *baby*? I don't mean to ignore you but I've got a new ad coming through. There's a great deal at stake — the diabetes and the leprosy programs are real and vital concerns; we can't just let them go under. People criticize Boots but without him Zaire would be nine different countries all at war with one another. I'm still hopeful that things can turn around there. You have to be optimistic in this business.

The truth is, none of this foreign aid shit does any real good. It's all just a big waste of time. They won't do things the right way and teach the people to help themselves. We're making it worse by the day. But that's not my problem. I can't even think about that. The natural resources in Zaire are incredible. You can grow thirty-pound sweet potatoes, for God's sake. It could become the breadbasket of Africa if only we could get the roads in shape. Build a kind of jungle Autobahn."

"Derek, you're making sense but you aren't making sense. You're just talking so fast and so loud I can't think anymore. I just have to shut my eyes for a minute. I'm just absolutely drained. Please stop talking for just one minute — "

Ad Magic let his jaw jut out, exposing his lower teeth. He was totally alert on the Dexedrine, yet because of the morphine, he felt inwardly calm. He realized however that he must be doing something wrong since Lars looked absolutely frazzled. He put his hand on her shoulder. "Don't fade on me now, Lars. Keep on track. Come on, you're young, you're tough — a real trooper, remember? Twenty-two-hour days in the refugee camp — six weeks of that. You can do it. Together we can do this — *baby?*"

Lars put her hands over her ears but Ad Magic continued. "You know, Lars — shit, I should call you Erika — it's just that Lars sounds like a first name. Which do you prefer? I can't control myself, I want to call you Lars. At this moment you look like the person in that painting, *The Scream*. I mean, I don't want to split hairs but you are giving me all this grief about Stelazine and now you're the one who's caving in. Snap out of it! Don't fall to pieces on me. I'm going to have to work the refugee angle to keep money flowing into Mocherville. So much of it goes to greasing wheels. It's a pity but all of the other agencies are going to

come on like gangbusters with the Rwanda refugee thing
. . . hell, the same shit happened in Burundi three years ago
and nobody even reported it. I always hold up *my* end of
things. It's the others that fuck up. Why? Because they are
lazy. Success just doesn't come out of thin air, you know,
you have to work! I'll top the damn mealies letter. They
think they can duplicate my style, originality, and rapport
with the parishioners — in a pig's ass!"

"Derek, stop."

"Lars! Listen: Rumpelstiltskin, he goes to court with a
valid legal contract and what's Princess Heather going to
do? On the other hand, he can weave straw into gold so he
could buy anything — babies, hell you can pick them up for
a song in any country in Africa. Shit! Rumpelstiltskin's tragic
flaw was anger. You know, like he stamped his foot into
the ground and turned into a gnarled bush or something.
There's only one guy in all the land that can turn straw into
gold — "

"Derek, please! If you don't shut up, I'll die! I just . . .
can't . . . take . . . any more. *Please. Please. Please!*"

"Okay, *baby!* But don't forget: fish oil for the starvation. Sardines and mackerel. Just a tablespoon three times
a day. Works like a charm. You have to be persuasive with
the mackerel. It tastes like shit. Sardines are different.
Your King Oscar, for instance, is your premium sardine,
whether you choose the famous original style, packed in
olive oil, or the more economical brand in sild oil. Sild oil
is the oil of the herring itself. It's rather mild in flavor. What
I can't eat is a sardine packed in soybean oil. Ugghh!
Soybean oil tastes like hog runoff. You want to know if
you've got a premium batch of sardines, your first consideration is the oil. Number two, just count the fish. The
little ones are the best. I like to lay them out on a napkin
and count them. Silver, glistening beauties. Sardines are

nutrient-dense food. There's stuff in them that helps repair damaged DNA. What's bad, Lars, is a medium sardine. Six and seven to the can. Yuck, those are tough. Better get out the hot sauce, you're going to need a ton of it too. And the aftertaste will kill you. It goes on forever. You say to yourself, 'Will it *never* end? I can't *believe* this. God! It's been *six years* and I can *still* taste them.' Once I was in Russia and got a tin, opened the son-of-a-bitch up and there was like ... one huge fish inside. One fuckin' fish — "

"Please! I'm begging you. Stop!"

"One jumbo sar — "

"Shut up! Damn you, damn you!" Lars twisted away from him, sagged against the door and closed her eyes. Ad Magic reached between his legs and pulled his looseleaf notebook out of his daypack. He continued to work his chin, exposing his lower front teeth, and began to write:

Dear Mr. John Q. Public,

In the land of the noble Masai warrior on the horn of Africa, there is no such thing as social security, welfare, food stamps, or nursing homes.

Ad Magic tore the sheet loose and crumpled it up. He let his jaw jut out. "I can't do this," he said to himself. "But first, ladies and gentle, allow me to present a little Ad Magic." He leaned forward and began to speak to Cissy and Pastor Dave. "Before your very eyes I shall convert straw into gold. Yasss, folks, the hand is quicker than the eye. Watch very carefully. I am going to lean back and apply the pen to paper any moment now. Mr. Derek has to write another ad and then another and another and another, on and on forever and ever. No one will ever thank Mr. Derek for doing good things in the world. They will give him a few junky toys and badmouth him behind his back and try to fire him, but Mr. Derek is smart. He is one step ahead of them. He feels much better now. He can weave enough gold to fill Fort Knox. So do not worry about Mr. Derek. His little deadlines are mere triflings. *Heaven in motion; the strength of the dragon. The righteous man nerves himself for ceaseless activity. Creative Fire!* How's it goin' up here, Dave?"

"Splendid, Derek. How's yourself?"

"Just peachy. Sardines anyone? Miss Cissy, can I interest you in the mackerel? How about some cod liver oil?"

"We're just fine, Derek."

Ad Magic set the notebook on his knees and began to scribble:

Alabama State Penitentiary
Luncheon Menu, 5/22/95
Death Row:

Ham and Beans, creamed country peas
Corn bread & margarine
Jell-O, coffee, milk or tea

Dear Ms. Goodfuck:

The American public spends over $85,000 a year to keep a convicted criminal on Death Row. The thousands of Africans in the Global Aid refugee camp in eastern Sudan have committed no crime except to have been born poor. For this, most of these good people have been condemned to death by starvation.

With a contribution of $25 a month to Global Aid, **Ms. Goodfuck,** you can give a fellow human being reprieve from certain death. Your dollars will provide food, shelter, medical care, and hope for the destitute.

Starvation is not a pretty sight, **Ms. Goodfuck.** The

choice is yours. You can reach for your handkerchief or you can reach for your checkbook.

Be a life-saver. Write to Global Aid now. All donations are tax deductible.

Ad Magic quickly struck the last line and then looked over at Lars. She was snuggled against the window with a small pillow, snoring. She was beautiful in profile even as her mouth dropped open and a little string of spittle hung suspended from her lip. With a smile of satisfaction on his face, Ad Magic regripped the pen to accommodate his thumb splint and continued the assault on his latest direct-mail appeal. As Ad Magic's pen floated over the pad, he looked over at Joshua and said, "Dude, can I interest you in a sardine? You lookin' a bit peaked. That mingy ass chicken on the roof could use one, too, I bet. Up there shitting on my Swiss suitcase."

Joshua turned away from Ad Magic and fixed his gaze on the window. In the front seat, Pastor Dave and Cissy stiffened. Lars, who seemed to have melted into a puddle, began to snore. Ad Magic realized he had gone too far. Yet again. He repositioned his notebook and continued to sketch out his next direct-mail appeal.

Pickpocket

THESE KIDS THAT slashed the top on the Saab (ain't it a shame, twelve hundred miles on it, a black ragtop, turbocharger, five-disc sound system!), these kids call me Chop-a-Leg, which is what I had done to me. They chop a leg when the foot turns gang green. I had diabetes twelve years and wouldn't quit smokin'. My podiatrist warned me the day was drawing near, but I didn't listen. I was still out there trying to get my kicks. Now I traded the five-speed in for an automatic since when you been chop-a-legged, your prosthetic foot don't rightly feel the clutch and that can mean smash your ass!

I got a hardtop with a V-6 and these kids calling me Chop-a-Leg raked up the paint job with a blade, so now I don't have to take care parking it or lay in bed and worry about no ragtop. See, I'm new to the neighborhood and they don't know who I am. All that shit — "I got a new car, what if it gets nicked?" — is over. I got the problem defused. Those kids did me a favor. I mean I got friends, okay, who could see to it that I could park that car anywhere in the city and nobody but nobody would get near 'cause I'm a stand-up con with connections, but in my old age I find I really do abhor violence, squalor, and ugliness. And I was a kid once. I did stuff like that. So I let it slide and had a talk with those boys. It was a highly effective conversation. There won't be no more *fuck fuck* with that car.

The doctors gave me the first diabetes lecture more than a decade ago. They fine-tuned the spiel over the years. There were updates. In one ear, out the other. I figured, You're gonna die, no matter. But they were right. I got hit with the shortness of breath, blurred vision, borderline kidney function, a limp dick, and armpits so raw I got to use Tussy Cream Deodorant or go aroun' with B.O. Is that *Tussy* like *fussy* or *Tussy* like *pussy?* Heh heh.

One night after I got proficient with my new foot, I hobbled down to the basement: Peg-leg Pete. I like to go down there at night and listen to *Captain Berg's Stamp Hour* on the shortwave. Comes on at 2:00 A.M. I always know the time, right on the money, bro. Serious. I bought a German clock with a radio transmitter in it that computes with the real atomic clock in Boulder, Colorado, and from that I set my watches. I got a solid gold Rolex President — your Captain of Industry watch. I got a two-tone Sea Dweller with a Neptune green bezel, a platinum Daytona, a Patek Philippe, and so on. They all right on time. Believe it. You might think, "Why is he worried about time? 'Cause he got so little left? What is the man's problem? Like God going to cheat him out of a second or something?" When you are fascinated with clocks, it's because you're an existential person. Some guy wears a plain watch with just a slash at the noon, three, six, and nine o'clock positions, you can put your money on that man. If the watch is plain with Roman numerals, he's also a straight guy. Non-neurotic. Trust that individual. That watch is your "tell"; it's a Rorschach. If you see someone with a railroad face — same deal. Arabic numerals on a railroad face, trust him a little less. A watch with extraneous dials and buttons, don't trust 'em at all, especially if they wearing a jogging watch and they ain't in shape. This is just a general rule of thumb — your man may be wearing a watch that goes against type since his father give it to him. Wealthy people buy forty-thousand-dollar timepieces that look worse than a Timex 'cause they don't want to get taken off. The people they want to know how much their watch cost will know, but no pipehead or take-off artist will know. As they say, if it doesn't tick, it ain't shit. You wanna know if your woman cheats? There's a certain watch style and nine times out of ten, if she's wearing it, she's guilty. I swear.

A good pickpocket is very careful. I did very little time in the joint, relatively speaking, and I made incredible income. Never hurt a soul. Didn't like jail. You know, joint chow is conducive to arterial occlusions. It's all starch and fat. It's garbage and then you lay around eating all that commissary candy. Smoking. I hate dead time in the joint. Idleness truly is the devil's workshop. I was goin' nuts watching fucking *Jeopardy* up in my living room, no ciga-rettes, no action — just waiting for my stump to heal. Reading medical books. When doctors Banting and Best was up in Toronto processing insulin in 1922 they give what little they had to a vice president of Eastman Kodak's kid, James Havens, and it brought James around and saved his life. Meanwhile everybody is going to Toronto where they are trying to make bathtub insulin as fast as possible. They can only produce just a couple of units a day and they give it to this one and that one while a thousand diabetics are dying each day. One thousand a day. The treatment then in vogue was a semistarvation diet which might give you a year, a couple of months, a few days. When you are a diabetic out of control and you get hungry, it ain't like ordinary hunger. Its a sick hunger — *polyphagia*. Put such a person in the hospital and they'll eat toothpaste. Birdseed. I mean, I said I got connections and I could have gotten some of that 1922 insulin. After that there would come a phone call one day and somebody would want a favor and I would have to say yes to that favor, no matter what. That's part of the life.

Even now insulin isn't cheap. It ain't no giveaway. Shoot up four times a day. Syringes, test strips. They cost as much as three packs a day! Heh heh. But each day I get is a gift, okay? I should be dead. Before 1922, I am dead. The shortwave is an old fart's pleasure, but then I am sixty-seven years old. Most criminals don't live that long outside or in.

Anyhow, I was down there in the basement when I blew a breaker with all my radio gear going, so I went into the little power shed and snapped on the light and seen a pack of Kool Filter Kings layin' in there that I had forgotten all about. I didn't want to smoke a cigarette. Didn't need to. But you know, human nature is strange, so I fired up. I didn't inhale. Face it, it's scary the first time after you've been off. When you're standing there on an artificial leg thinking about the ambiguity of life. Tomes have been written, I know. I'm just standing there when I spotted a skinny-ass spider hanging in its web. There was dust on the cobwebs. I blew smoke on it and the spider didn't move. Looked like a shell. Dead, I figure. It's the middle of winter. I mashed out the cigarette, snapped the breaker, and went back to the radio. Three nights later, I really get this *craving* for a cigarette. I had forgotten the spider, and I went back into the power shed and smoked a Kool all the way down to the filter. It was the greatest goddamn cigarette I ever smoked in my whole fuckin' life! The one I had two nights later was almost as good. I torched up, took a big drag, and blew it all out, and the spider in the web moved like greased lightning. Jesus fuck! I seen a little red hourglass on its belly and Christ — Jesus fuck! Yow! Whew, man. But what the hell, it's just a fucking spider, black widow or no. Still it gave me a thrill and I could identify with this little mother-fucker. Your black widow is your outlaw.

After I run through that pack of Kools I find that I'm still going into the room to check on the spider. It was always in the same spot. What is it eating? I wonder. It's the middle of winter. There isn't another bug in sight. That night in bed I am so worried the spider is going to starve that I get up, strap on my leg, take a little ball of hamburger out of the refrigerator, hobble down to the basement like old man Moses, and squeeze the hamburger around a web tentacle and give the string a little twing, like it was a guitar. The spider don't move. Starved to death. I was too late. One day too late, like with my atomic clock transmissions and everything, I'm late. Chop-a-leg and all that shit. Always a day late and a fucking dollar short.

Actually, the spider was planning her attack. I believe she had the sick hunger. When she smelled that meat, she made her move and then I seen the red hourglass flash on her belly again. Seeing that hourglass was like walking into a bank with a nine-millimeter. What a rush! The spider pounced on that hamburger and gave it a poison injection. I wiggled the web a little, so the spider would think she had a live one, you know. Then I realized that the light was on and conditions weren't right for dinner. She was used to permanent dark. I shut off the light and closed the door. After *Captain Berg's Stamp Hour,* I returned and the ball of hamburger was gone. Not only that, the spider seemed to intuit a message to me. The spider was used to having me come in there and blow smoke on her and I think, Aha! I get it, you got a cigarette jones. Fuckin' A! Maybe you would like a cup of coffee, too, you nasty little cocksucker.

Piece of chocolate cake with ice cream and some hot fudge. I would like some too. Heh heh.

I peg-legged it over to a deli and bought a package of cigarettes and when I get back, I'm standing there enjoying the smoke and watching the spider — you know, chop-a-leg can't be that bad when you got eight legs — that's when I get the cold, dead feeling in my good leg, the right one. My chest gets tight. My jaw hurts. My left arm hurts. I stagger upstairs and take an aspirin and two of my pepto-glycerine tablets or whatever. Heart pills. Nitropep whatever. Put two under your tongue and they make your asshole tickle. Make it turn inside out.

I laid in my bed consumed with fear. My heart was Cuban Pete and it was rumbling to the Congo beat. It took a long time to calm down. When I was finally calm, I said, "Okay, God, I'm ready. Take me out now. I've had it with this whole no-leg motherfucker."

The next thing you know the sun is up and fuckin' birds are cheepin'. Comin' on happy at six in the morning for Chrissakes. I pursued a life of crime because I hate daylight. It's just about that simple. When you hate daylight, when you hate anything, you will develop a certain ambiguity about life and you get reckless in your habits. You overeat. You take dope. You fall in love with a bad person. You take a job you hate. You declare war against society. You do any number of things that don't cut any ice when you try to explain your motivation in a court of law or to a doctor, to a dentist, or to the kids on your block who hate you for having a new car. God didn't take me out when I was ready. I was ready but the next thing birds are cheepin' and somehow you find that you just have to go on.

I didn't even think I was listening at the time but after chop-a-leg I was at the clinic I heard this doctor say, yeah, yeah, he knew this intern who had high cholesterol. A young guy with a 344. So what this guy does is eats oatmeal three times a day. He puts some skim milk on it to make a complete protein and in three months his cholesterol drops down to 25. Twenty-five! I didn't think I was listening but it registered later. Come back to me.

I drove to the store and bought a large box of Old Fashioned Quaker Oats. I started eating oatmeal morning, noon, and night. I like looking at the Pilgrim on the box. What a happy guy, huh? I discovered that if you like your oatmeal to taste "beefy," you only need to pour some hot water over it. You don't boil it for five minutes. I mean you can, but nobody is going to come in and arrest you if you don't. For a while I liked it beefy. I also liked it regular. Once I forgot and bought Quick Quaker Oats and discovered I liked them even better. Skim milk and oatmeal. Three times a day. My leg started feeling better. I lost that shortness-of-breath thing. How simple. How easy. On the night before Christmas I sat alone in my apartment and ate my oatmeal with a mashed banana in it. What more could a person want out of life, huh? I felt so good I put on a dark Brooks Brothers suit, a cashmere topcoat, and went to the shopping mall where I lifted three thousand in green. Just wanted to see if I still had the touch. Hah! Back in the saddle again. I even boosted a home cholesterol kit. You stick your finger and put a drop of blood on a strip. Fifteen minutes later I get a reading of 42. Can you believe? I can. I sincerely believe that the regression of arterial plaque is possible even in a brittle diabetic such as myself. When they autopsied Pritikin, his coronary vessels were cleaner than a whistle. Already I have lost thirty pounds over and above the amputated leg. I take righteous dumps twice a day. I sleep like a baby. I'm a happy guy. I'm lifted from my deathbed and restored to acute good health. Sex might even be a possibility. I already tol' you, I'm sixty-seven years old but now I'm feeling horny again for the first time in years.

Every night after *Captain Berg's Stamp Hour* I continued to go into the power shed and feed the spider. She's my pal, see. I stacked all my empty oatmeal cartons in her direction with the Pilgrim smiling at her. It adds a little color to an otherwise drab decor. Heh heh.

I come out of retirement. I go out and boost on a regular basis now. I don't need the bread but I like being active. Ain't you glad to hear of my comeback? I bet you are rightly delighted. I plan on living to be a hundred. For insulin discovery, they gave Dr. Fred Banting the Nobel Prize. To keep guys like me going. Heh heh.

The spider, what it wants more than hamburger is that I should light a cigarette and blow smoke at her so she can suck it in through her spiracles and get some nicotine on her brain. Gets this look like, *"Come on, baby, drive me crazy!"* It's just a tiny spider brain. Say, "Jes' a little puff would do it, mah man."

But I look at the spider and say, *"Suffer, darlin'!* It's for ya own good. Take it from a man who knows."

Ooh Baby Baby

DOWNSHIFTING, and with his eye on the light at La Cienega and Santa Monica boulevards, Dr. Moses Galen rammed his Jaguar down from rocket speed, way down to a measly ten over the limit. There was a Chevy van ahead of him and if the driver had had the sense to *get it on,* he could have made the signal, but suddenly the van's taillights had come up red. Galen's left foot, loosely encased in a featherweight Bally loafer, pressed hard on the brake pedal, bringing the car to an abrupt, nose-dipping stop. Oh hell! Shit, man, this light was notoriously long! You could get *stranded* at this light. It just lasted forever. The Chevy could have made it with any kind of half-ass try. Christ Almighty! What a way to begin the weekend! Galen gunned the engine in frustration. The Jag's deep, full-bodied *thrag* added a certain distinctive, upscale flair to the overall roar. But the whole of it, all of the mind-numbing din of street noise, intruded into the tightly sealed cabin of the car. Too much noise. Too much traffic. Too many people on this sorry-ass goddamn planet.

Still the Jaguar was a pleasure. Its air conditioner deliciously tossed the smell of leather upholstery and Linda's expensive French cologne. He looked over at her. She had one hand on the dash with the other clenching an armrest after Galen's quick stop. He had been so intent on the traffic and his hunger that he had almost forgotten her. The way she remained in this emergency posture struck Moses as a bit theatrical but she looked and smelled pretty darn good. Pretty fine. Yeah, she was lookin' good. The sights and smells Galen most ardently longed for, however, were those of a hot meal — bacon, eggs, coffee, and a steaming platter of buttermilk pancakes topped with butter and maple syrup. He was starving but before he could eat there was this traffic jam.

Galen turned up the radio to catch the news. There was a report about food shortages in Somalia. Hell, they were starving their asses over there — *again!* "Christ, babe, we went over there out of the goodness of our hearts, tried to straighten things out, and they just end up hating us for it. What are you supposed to do? Now they're starving *again!* And that maniac from Iraq is pulling his shit, too. Haiti, Rwanda — Jesus H.!"

Linda said, "A bloodbath in Rwanda and now Somalia again. Starvation. Terrible."

But could it be worse than this? Moses wondered. It was all subjective, but could a diabetic on a low sugar jag feel any worse than those poor bastards? Galen knew he was running a sugar approximately in the forty mgs/DL range. Oh man, Somalia.

Moses had done a cleft palate restoration clinic in Mogadishu in the early 70s and before heading back to Kenya for some camera safari action, he had moved inland to practice a little general medicine. He had seen the villagers. They weren't starving then, but they were definitely lean.

Lots of undernourishment and, God, the flies! Those hefty, armor-plated, clinging mothers — you had to practically chisel them off. Well, when your house is made out of cowshit, flies will come along. Moses treated a kid that had fallen into a fire some days earlier. He gave the kid a shot of morphine and then debrided the burned skin, which was teeming with flies and maggots. Africans were good about pain, handled it a lot better than Americans, but burn pain transcended all cultures and species. Burns hurt. Fortunately the maggots, which were disgusting to look at, had kept the wounds fairly clean.

The boy, S'lad, was seriously dehydrated. Strange that he was still alive. Will to live. Some had it and some didn't. Moses loaded him up with antibiotics and when he realized that the child's mother would never be able to get the kid to a local clinic, Moses remembered the "Oath" and forsook the one day that he had reserved for his wildlife safari, and arranged to get the boy to the Italian hospital back in Mogadishu. There Moses consulted with an Italian-trained physician and mapped out a program for skin transplants so the kid would have a life. Moses also arranged to foot the bill and send him to a mission school thereafter. That had been the first day in his life that he had missed a meal and he remembered how unfair it had seemed; how completely awful. And those were back in the prediabetic days when he woke up every morning feeling like a million. He was big, strong, and good-looking in his youth and early middle age. He loved being a doctor in those days. He felt like a god and if people read that as arrogance — well, they could get off their lazy asses. You had to make your breaks in this life. Nobody handed it to you on a platter. Moses believed in himself, believed he could make a difference, and consequently he did. Last he heard, S'lad with the burns was some kind of bookkeeper in Mogadishu thanks to the bread

Moses sent him over the years. How long had it been since he had gotten a letter — "Jambo, Dr. Mo — what happening? My health is good. I enjoy smoking one box of cigarettes a day and drink too much sometimes. I have many lady friends, vast numbers. We have much sex, many times and I am liking this. *Ha! Right on, bro!* I also like watching television and movie. You're last letter is on my tv set as a Bible. Thank you for the signed American baseball. Who is Frank Thomas? Why are you not writing me? You are busy? Can you get me a job in America?" As soon as the young man began pressuring Moses for a job and emigration materials, Moses got a suffocating feeling and dropped S'lad. That had all been long before the fiasco of Operation Hope. He wondered if S'lad had managed to live through that. Or with a long list of lady friends, if S'lad had lived through *that*. AIDS was raging throughout the continent now but a war could kill faster than that virus. Well, maybe not. Now, there were fast viruses that turned you into goo and had you bleeding from every orifice three days after incubation. Made AIDS look like a cakewalk. Three days was more than enough time for someone to hop on a jet plane in apparent good health and disembark in L.A., cough for a couple of days, and then dissolve. But could that be as bad as this? This hell that was going on inside his own skin! Fuck Somalia!

Yeah. The Somalis were known for a fiercer warrior tradition than the Masai. Somalis were kicking the asses of the Peace Corps in the days when Moses had been there. You would have thought the State Department and the military would have known that the whole rescue mission had been doomed from its inception. Well, they knew better now.

Galen had been hungry in Somalia but hungry with a functioning pancreas. It wasn't as critical as this. Shit, he was shaking. In fact, how could you suffer much worse? When he got this low, just walking from the clinic to the car was like a three-month trek through the Himalayas. The simplest activity became a wrenching torment, a kind of never-ending agony.

What did it feel like to be a writhing human skeleton? After all, in the course of starvation, the body was consuming its own "furniture." But what were the readings? he wondered. Did starvation necessarily imply hypoglycemia? When Moses had been in Somalia they were eating sorghum. And some of the big bucks acted like they owned the world. At that time they seemed happier than most people he knew in L.A. That was one reason Moses resisted sponsoring S'lad, but his most basic reason was the fact that he hated close personal commitments and responsibilities. He hated cloying, dependent people. Yet Galen thought of the young man often. A life saved, to what end? He should have taken a chance and been a true friend, helped the kid out — sent for him. That way there would have been one saved for sure. Moses had been able to leave, S'lad had not. He should have taken it all the way and saved the kid. Moses had no family. The enormity of the fact of the starving millions who could not leave was just too much to ponder, as was Rwanda. Moses was something of an Africa buff. The same crap happened a few years before in Burundi only it hadn't made the news. Hundreds of thousands butchered. He had heard BBC reports over the shortwave.

Anyhow, S'lad came on too strong. Moses couldn't really blame him. If S'lad survived the war, he might easily have the virus. From S'lad to *Slim* unless he had been bullshitting about all the pussy he got. Even without those burn scars, he was no African Fabio — not by a long shot. Should have done it, sent for him. He had just fired a bookkeeper at his own clinic. Maybe he *would* send for

S'lad. Might not be a bad idea. He would have to be schooled in the ways of Los Angeles, but what the hell.

Moses switched stations until Linda Ronstadt was singing "Ooh Baby Baby." Moses remembered her doing a rendition of the "Star Spangled Banner" once before a ball game. It had been the best, and he had had a crush on the singer ever since. Goddamn, not only was she gorgeous, she had the greatest voice. What a babe! Galen worked on a lot of Hollywood people but never got a line on her. Better not to wreck things by asking around either. You needed these little fantasies to keep you going. If only he could trade that Linda for his own. God, the traffic light was lasting forever. His thoughts were making about as much sense as a Dadaist nightmare. He needed to eat.

Moments before all had been clear, now there was a bewildering congregation of pickup trucks, buses, moving vans, cement trucks, and even an ambulance at the intersection. If the Chevy van had only pushed through on the yellow. Moses wanted to get out and knife the driver for being so stupid — for being such a stupid goddamn asshole! In the low-set Jaguar, amid all the trucks, Moses felt like a bug. The heat, noise of traffic, and the fierce angle of the sun had turned the sanctuary of Galen's luxury automobile into a kind of hell. Moses almost turned on Linda and blasted *her*, but that would be no way to begin a weekend "away from it all" — anyhow, his problem was low sugar. That was why he felt so damn mean. Nevertheless Linda had been stalling at the damn hospital. Crapping around in her fool's paradise mood. Then Moses got paged at the last minute and when he straightened that deal out came the inevitable *this:* weekend bumper-to-bumper-son-of-a-bitching California traffic. Pandemonium.

He should have clicked the pager off. The "hair transplant" Moses had done in the morning called on the beeper raving that the Novocain had worn off and the pressure bandages on his head were driving him nuts. He was going to tear them off. Moses had to hand-deliver a script for Demerol to the hospital pharmacy after the patient claimed that the Percodans Galen had given him were "insufficient," and then the prick griped about having to send a driver over to pick it up, said he was going bananas and was going to tear the whole damn thing off. Those were micro transplants, Moses warned, and if he pulled off the bandage, he could kiss them goodbye along with the last of his donor tissue. It was difficult to gauge pain but Demerol was definite overkill. Still, anything to shut the bastard up and get out of Dodge. It's your hangover, pal.

Galen was going to tell Linda about the incident since the patient in question was a very popular soap opera actor who played the part of a doctor. Linda knew the guy from a night six months previous when he came into her emergency room with an Idaho potato up his ass. Question: "How did you do this?"

Linda said the potato was so large they were unable to remove it with forceps. They wheeled the guy into the elevator and were taking him up to the operating room when he finally relaxed and the potato shot out of his ass like a champagne cork. "Hot potato, everybody!" After striking up a friendship with the actor, Linda referred him to Moses for a scalp reduction and a hair transplant.

Now the guy was complaining over a pressure bandage which Moses's associate would remove in the morning once the plugs had set. It had all the makings of a funny story, especially since Linda had said he was such a nice man, so pleasant and everything, why would he want to shove vegetables up his ass? And to think of his screen persona — the way he came across as Dr. Do Right; it was the antithesis of the hysterical crybaby paging for Demerol.

Galen was fading fast. The funny story would have to wait. Hell, a potato up the ass was relatively tame anymore. They got carried away with amyl nitrate and liked to stick live gerbils up the keezer — that was the latest. Probably used white rats on party night. A potato. Hell, a potato was nothing but walking-around up-the-ass.

This goddamn traffic jam was just unbelievable. It was a goddamn, sumbitchin' motherfucker. Sugar, a mere teaspoon in his bloodstream, would turn hell into heaven, the impetuous Mr. Hyde into the reasonable, feel good, do right Jekyll. Suck! He should have grabbed some fruit at the hospital. He hated it when he let himself get caught out in the open without food. Yet he did it again and again!

To his horror Moses watched a convoy of National Guard troops passing through the intersection in large olive drab troop conveyance trucks with M.P.'s and two L.A. city motorcycle cops flagging them through. It seemed to take forever and Moses began to thump the steering wheel with the butt of his hand. This was the last straw. There were trucks as far as the eye could see. It was like that old shit when you were a kid, getting stuck at the railroad tracks while a freight train rolled by with a hundred and ninety cars. Just a half hour earlier, hunger was the last thing on Galen's mind; now he was wasted.

Galen looked over at Linda. She seemed to be enjoying the incredible traffic mess, like a child at a parade. Moses stroked her leg and said, "Tell me something, babe, how come you are always seeing these cowboys in these pickup trucks and they ain't carrying nothing in the back unless it's a Rottweiler and three pit bulls? You never see them hauling lumber or trash or doing anything practical with them. You think they get off sitting up there high up, like a judge in a courtroom?"

The Los Angeles sun was more than an even match for

the Jaguar's air-conditioning system. "Yes," Linda said. "White trash power. W'at trash, man! *Hey man!*"

Moses thumped the wheel of the Jag with a meaty palm and tried to look around the Chevrolet van in front of him. The National Guard convoy had passed and the intersection reverted to the normal rush-hour traffic pattern. Then Moses spotted a farm tractor dragging some sort of cultivator, which was so long, the tractor's turning radius forced the driver of the Chevy van to honk at Moses and indicate that he was backing up to make room. Moses had to put the car into reverse and crank his neck, which was so stiff with arthritis he could hardly move it. There was a Mac truck behind him, hard on his ass. He could only back up about two feet but he could see the driver looking at him. Moses didn't like the look. It enraged him. He felt like getting out and duking.

"It's probably some movie studio deal," Linda said, flipping the air conditioner on to "high." "You know, like a prop. Maybe they're doing an update of *Oklahoma*."

As the light changed from red to green and back to red again, the XJ6 remained nestled in the pocket of trucks surrounding the van in front. It was Galen's fourth Jaguar dating back to '61 when he went "Hollywood" and bought his first XKE.

There was a sudden squeal of tires. The very second the light had turned red, the driver of the Chevy van shot across the intersection and both Moses and Linda were able to get a full view of the farm tractor as it chugged slowly down Santa Monica Boulevard driven by an old man in a blue chambray work shirt and a straw hat. "That's no movie prop, that guy's real. God! What is real? Let's philosophize. This — *this* is my reality — this!" Moses said.

Linda Foley did not like the tone of Galen's voice. She flipped open her purse and removed a pair of spirulina Thunder Bars and tossed them in Moses's lap. Galen picked up one of the bars and read the list of ingredients. Linda's recent penchant for health foods and her New Age predilections earned her the nickname of "Moon" at Valley General. It was just a phase, this *Moon* business. Linda was a good doc and even better than that, as Moses's diabetes increasingly made sexual potency an iffy proposition, Linda was a surefire cure. Galen unwrapped one of the food bars and ate it. "Thanks," Galen said. "It tastes like crap, so it must be good for me. *W'at trash,* heh heh heh."

There was chlorophyll in the Thunder Bar. He leaned over and kissed Linda. His mouth had tasted like dragon fire and he had been diverting his breath away from her the whole time, an effort almost as exacting and complex as the worst sort of surgical procedure. She went with the kiss and placed her hand on his thigh. She reverted to her easy mood. She was a hard charger like himself but this, after all, was the weekend.

Linda and Galen had been friends for years and he was a little surprised when she came to him as a patient complaining of a deviated septum. Moses agreed to fix it, no problem, and while he was at it — what-the-hell, her nose was too damn big, she asked if he could fix that. She was so pleased with the results that she had him do a little of this and that. Her beautifully high cheekbones had formerly been a little too shallow, the firm chin had been slightly recessive, but Moses fixed that. There had been crow's-feet and wrinkles and breasts far too small, but Galen took care of that, too. Linda's body had always been fair but was even better now thanks to her obsessive workouts (she could bench press 155), and Galen's state-of-the-art liposuction technique. Linda came to Moses like the classic plastic surgery junkie — "What happened to my body? Where has all the time gone?" She was a trauma surgeon who put in frequent sixteen-hour shifts — longer when things got hairy — and she had begun to look pretty raggedy. She had been doing it for years and was suffering from a bad case of burnout. Physicians were notorious for having short life spans, and as a friend, Galen counseled her to take it easy. He had done the same thing early in his career and, like Linda, had found that whenever he was not engaged in doctoring or getting laid, his life seemed bereft of purpose. It was common enough. Now, Linda looked more like thirty than hard miles forty-two, and with her new body came a whole flood of sexual imperatives that Moses was only too happy to accommodate. A few millimeters shaved off her nose, a couple of ounces of silicone "here and there" became a passport to an entirely new world. Moses squeezed her knee. He knew Linda had fallen into a window of time where she wanted a man to see her as beautiful, lovable, intoxicating. Why, there were rumors in the medical community that she was screwing lots of guys. "The Moon Belongs to Everyone" was a commonly heard tune whistled among the nurses, amidst whom gossip ran rampant, and the way Linda threw herself into sex, with such utter abandonment, with such insatiable and varied appetites, Moses had to half believe it. He could hardly keep up with her. Behind the wheel of the Jaguar, Galen ran his hand back through his thick mane of white hair. In profile his Roman nose, his noble forehead, and his square jaw set on a muscular neck gave him the look of an aging Adonis. Simba in repose. He took a long deep breath. He was getting rummy at this traffic light. *Relax, man, breathe.* He let his head float back and tried to work out the tension in his neck. The meal would be there. Just get through this. Linda began to nudge Moses with her elbow. "Go."

"What?"

"The light is green. Go. Go!" She clapped on a pair of Italian shades against the sun's glare.

"What do you mean, 'go'? Nobody tells me to 'go.' Not like that. Not in that tone of voice!"

"Well, *I'm* telling you to go! The light is green!"

The cars and vehicles stacked up behind the Jaguar began to honk furiously. Moses reached over to the ignition and switched it off. " 'Go'?"

Linda whipped off the sunglasses and dropped her mouth in exasperation. "Stay, then. Let's stay here and die of carbon monoxide poisoning."

The honking grew worse and several cars began darting around the Jaguar, crossing Santa Monica Boulevard until the light turned red again. Cross traffic bolted forward into the intersection creating an angry snarl of honking and abrupt stops. With the power switched off, the interior of the Jaguar became like a greenhouse. Moses unpeeled the wrapper of a second Thunder Bar and munched it down in three bites. "Moon food."

"Look, buster, if you got up on the wrong side of the bed, that's your problem. You've been in a mood ever since I showed up two minutes late. How many times have I had to stand around and wait for you? And just because you're a bloody god at that damn clinic of yours doesn't give you the right to break the — "

"Doesn't give me the right to break a traffic law? If you obey every rule they got out there, you can no longer function." Moses was doing the Marlon Brando character out of that motorcycle movie, *The Wild One.* Question: *Why, whatchew rebellin' against, Mr. Motorcycle Main?* Answer: *Whaddya got?*

Linda swung open the door to the Jaguar when Moses grabbed her, yanked her back, and kissed her furiously and deeply. She fiercely resisted at first but then her lips came apart and their tongues met. When Moses came up for air he said, "I love you. Let's just do it right here in the intersection."

A traffic cop rapped on the driver's door and Moses released Linda and turned to confront the cop. Linda smoothed out her skirt and hid behind her sunglasses when she saw a smirk light up the police officer's face.

"Hey there! What's going on?"

Galen was nonplussed. "Axe-cuse me, off'cer. Ahm Doctor Moses Galen and it appears that dey is vapuh lock in th' carburetors, suh."

"Press the accelerator down and kindly turn over the engine."

Moses gave the police officer a little Marlon Brando. Moses gave him *The Wild One.*

The cop ducked down and stuck his face near Galen's. "If your name is Moses, take note: the Red Sea has parted. Move!"

The police officer stepped in front of the Jaguar and began to manually direct traffic at the intersection. When the light turned green and Moses continued to sit idle in the Jag, the officer blew his whistle and pointed at Moses, urging him forward by twirling his right arm in a circle. Behind him the Mac truck driver laid on the air horn.

"What are you waiting for?" Linda said clutching her ears. "That guy is highly pissed. Do you want to get a ticket?"

"I'm waiting for instructions from the chief pilot."

"Go," Linda said. "G-O, go."

"Thank you, my dear." As Moses pulled even with the police officer at the intersection, he said, "Why don't you go and fuck yourself, dickhead?" Galen floored the Jaguar, spinning rubber, fishtailing as he sped away.

"How juvenile, Moses — how totally lame," Linda said. "What's the matter with you?"

Instead of taking the exit for the coast, Galen made the more familiar trip home. Taking a reasonable tone he said the trip to Mendocino would be madness during the rush hour. Linda agreed, although she sounded more resigned than agreeable. "When you need to eat, it's a medical emergency. When they're starving in Bosnia, it's their own bloody fault."

That was a hot button. He had missed the meal in Somalia and missed the photo safari to save a kid's life but Galen knew he was acting like a pisser and tried to lighten his mood. "I'm sorry, babe. My blood sugar is running in the low fifties and plunging. I need . . . this may sound kind of nutty, but what I could really go for . . . what would snap me out of this foul mood . . . is — "

"Is what? Is *what?*"

"— A furburger," Moses said.

"Oh God," Linda said with a chortle. "You're so uncouth sometimes."

Galen laughed. "I'm a man of the earth, baby. I've been horny ever since you plunked your hot ass in that leather seat and started jiggling that magnificent set of implants. I gotta have it. Let's go fuck!"

When they got into the house, Moses walked over to the white grand player piano wedged tightly in the corner between the wall and the edge of his indoor pool. He rummaged through a stack of piano discs. He knew he had a copy of "The Best Things in Life Are Free" *somewhere,* but he couldn't find it. By the time he hit the bedroom Linda was half out of her clothes insisting on a shower before there was any oral sex. "Well, what's wrong with a little twang?" Moses demanded.

"Darling, what you will get goes one step beyond twang," she said.

"Hey, if I can eat two seaweed bars, 'beyond twang' doesn't scare me one bit. I'll eat tuna!"

But Linda quickly slipped off her underwear and darted

into the shower. Shit, they would be doing things her way today. Moses stood in the doorway leading into the bathroom and watched Linda shower through the frosted glass of the shower stall door. Her perfect enough body devoid of clothing did not particularly turn him on although when he looked back at the bed and saw her stockings, bra, and underwear, he felt a pleasurable twinge in his groin. He launched into the story about the TV doctor but was so weak from hunger he could not project his voice over the sound of the running water. Linda peered over the shower door and said, "What?"

"Babe, I'm sorry about that thing in the car. I felt like Jiminy Cricket in that fucking traffic jam. I feel like him now."

As Linda stepped from the shower and toweled herself off, Moses pulled off his ascot, removed his summerweight gray gabardine suit, shoes, socks, and underwear and stepped into the shower. Linda was keen on screwing in the shower and he had avoided a simultaneous shower deliberately. He was too tall for her and hated doing that number where he had to pick her up and do fuck acrobatics. As she dried herself, he turned on the water, and lowering his voice to a croak, sang "The Moon Belongs to Everyone." Moses hunched forward with his arms tucked close to his body and caused his ass to protrude comically, which it did, especially, since he had a long torso and short legs. He was crazy, running on nerves; it was so fucking bad it was funny. Halfway through the song a blacker depression than he had ever known welled up in him and he turned away, letting his voice drop off as he concentrated on soaping himself down — concentrated on pulling himself together. It was the blood sugar drop, of course. It made you crazy, made your entire life devoid of meaning — filled you with complete despair. He turned up the hot water to get his peripheral circulation going. The moment of spontaneity had passed; he should have just thrown her on the bed and fucked her. Now sex was an obstacle that stood between him and his most fervent desire — to eat a large hot meal; take a little extra insulin and he would have license to eat a Clydesdale horse.

He crawled under the cool sheets and reached for her; she had a large mouth with full lips and was one of the best kissers, one of the best at "necking" he had ever known, but ultimately he failed. Even his tongue gave out. He ended up finger banging her.

She tried to console him. "Look, Moses, it's okay. These things happen. If it doesn't pass off, you can get one of those — "

"Penile implants."

"Diabetes attacks every organ of the body, you know that. There are worse things, God knows. Anyhow, your tongue hasn't gone limp, thank you very much."

"I've got a yard of tongue and a pair of blue balls."

Moses climbed out of the bed and stood naked before the full-length mirror. Although he had once been six two, he still remained somewhere over the six foot measure and retained the mesomorphic physique of the athlete he had once been. His white hair was snowy white and he had a lot of it. He had a naturally dark complexion, no real fear of melanoma, and so he religiously maintained a bronze tan. Because of his diabetes Moses found time for a daily run or a swim, five hundred sit-ups, and at least a half hour of bag punching to keep his blood sugar under a semblance of control. He held his limp penis in his hand. "You know something, Fritz? I'm really disappointed in you. We got eight hundred and thirty-five. I thought we were going to do a thousand."

"God," Linda said. "Don't tell me you count them?

That's about the most disgusting admission I've heard in five years, do you realize that? Don't you know the score anymore? Really, Moses. What a pig."

Moses listened to this comment with curiosity. It seemed to discount "The Moon Belongs to Everyone" rumor. She struck him as a "one man at a time" kind of woman but her sexual imperatives seemed to tell another story. There were times when it seemed like she could take on an entire football team. Moses wiggled his dick. "Did you hear that, Fritz? You let Linda down tonight. Not only did you let Linda down, you let me down. Do you know why my nuts feel like, Fritz? They feel large and heavy, like a pair of metal p'tonk balls hanging in the thinnest of onionskin sacks. I've got the most gorgeous creature in the world in my bed and you have to pull a routine like this. I'm really disappointed with you. Do you have anything to say for yourself or are you just going to hang there in shame, all fourteen inches of you? It's time for the senior circuit, Fritz. Shuffleboard and dominoes."

"Four Jaguars and eight hundred and thirty-five broken hearts," Linda said, a little lighter.

Galen angled his penis in Linda's direction and spoke out of the side of his mouth in a ventriloquist's falsetto. "I'm sorry, Linda?"

"Don't worry about it, Fritz. We've had some good times in the past. You are the victim of an insidious disease. How can I fault you?"

"I've satisfied eight hundred and thirty-five beautiful women. Oh, there were a few dogs and some whores over in France and Germany during the war, but the list also contains some very well-known Hollywood starlets as well as genuine full-fledged movie stars whose names would surprise you, not out of mere gratitude might I add, for services rendered. Fate has chosen me to make women beautiful, and the first step — protocol — is to make them feel beautiful before I ever wield my magic wand. I have to fuck them! They *expect* me to fuck them. I get malpractice suits when I don't fuck them."

"Moses, I'm getting very uncomfortable with this numbers talk. Have you ever heard about AIDS? Do you ever read *JAMA* or the journals anymore, or watch the news?"

"Are you crazy, I run HIV tests on all my clients; I even did one on you. There's a virus that turns you into goo in three days' time. They're making the movie as we speak. Incidentally, what did you think of my song?"

"What song, darling?"

"The song I was singing a moment ago, in the shower. 'The Best Things in Life Are Free.' "

She looked at him blankly. "I dunno. It's a corny old song, isn't it? You're a wonderful singer, of course, and that's a wonderful sentiment. The best things in life *are* free or something — what?"

"Nothing. It's nothing."

"Then send Big Daddy over here, maybe I can do something about those blue balls. They do look a bit heavy."

As Moses approached the bed the sight of Linda's firm breasts, which jiggled slightly as she rose up to meet him — her firm shoulders; the way her chic new haircut glistened wet and shiny; the face that Moses created as "interesting," rather than beautiful per se — the sum of it all caused his cock to straighten up like a rocket. Linda grabbed the shaft with both hands, like Louis "Satchmo" Armstrong picking up a trumpet at the beginning of a set. Soon her tongue was working it over. The thought of Linda screwing a football team caused Moses to come in less than twenty seconds.

"My God," he said, "you sucked me dry. And I thought it was going to be a lost cause."

"You were really loaded," she said.

"And you like that?" Moses said.

"Yeah. It's like a little bonus. Like the maraschino cherry on top of a hot fudge sundae."

The Dr. Linda Foley of old was hardly the type to say or do such a thing — Moses simply didn't figure her for this. Maybe she *was* fucking every guy in sight. She sure seemed to like it. She kissed him deeply, causing him to taste himself, which was, oddly enough, a first for Moses and a crazy kind of turn-on. Linda wanted the kiss and soon he was on her missionary style, slow strokes giving way to faster ones. He went faster, harder, and deeper while Linda's low moans gave way to shrill cries of pleasure. Her nails dug deep into his back and Moses became lost in the experience, pain mixing with pleasure. He found himself vanishing into an abyss of ecstasy until he came for the second time and then after, found that he had to keep bucking harder and harder until she came. It became a job, a tremendous effort. When it was over, he could hardly get any air and had to sit up on the edge of the bed, panting.

"Moses, are you all right?" she said with a certain amount of professional concern.

". . . Will be. Just give me a minute."

"Are you sure you're okay?"

"It was those candy bars," he said. "What did you say was in them?"

"Spirulina. But I didn't know it could make a limp dick stiff."

Moses got out of bed and went into the bathroom. He plopped two Alka-Seltzer tablets into a paper cup he took from the dispenser near his sink. He rummaged through his medicine cabinet. It was full of old man medications — Preparation-H, Polydent, Pepto Bismol, antifungals, foot powder, Ben-Gay. In the undercabinet there were dozens of pharmaceutical samples and he knew there was some nitroglycerin in that lot. When nitro relieved chest pain you knew you were dealing with angina. It was a fair assumption, but when he finally found it, he saw the expiration date had passed more than three years before. It would be useless. The stuff was notorious for deteriorating quickly.

When he returned to his bed he said, "For a minute there I thought I was having a heart attack. But when I move around," he said, breathing heavily, "when I move around — exertion doesn't exacerbate the pain — it had to be the candy bars. Heartburn. Anyhow, I took aspirin and I've only got three years on this bypass. It should be good for ten. My cholesterol is one-five-eight and my HDLs are sixty-four. I can't have a heart attack. What time is it?"

"It's late. And you need to eat. Let me go fix something."

Moses climbed back into bed. He clicked on the television set and began counting his pulse. He was utterly exhausted. When Linda came back from the kitchen carrying a tray of roast beef sandwiches and three-bean salad, Moses was sleeping. At her approach he snapped alert. He said, "I fell asleep and had a very funny dream — "

"Tell me your dream." She was wearing his white shirt and cuddled up on the end of the bed cross-legged. She tossed her soft brown hair over each shoulder with a flip of each hand. It was already dry. Moses watched her fork away at the salad.

"I was in the army," he said, "wintertime, dark out. It was just after chow. Very cold. You could see your breath. All the GIs, I can remember them from when I was really in the army. They were still young but I was like I am now, sixty-nine years old, standing there in an Eisenhower jacket with the platoon sergeant standing on the back of this convoy truck, passing out mail — mail call. It was always a big event. Anyhow, here's the crazy part: the sergeant called out each man's name, these are real guys — my old buddies. 'Stickney,' and here comes Stickney, just like I remember him — just like it was yesterday. He moved up to the back of the truck where the sergeant was standing, reached up for his letter and opened it and then read aloud, 'Lung cancer.' It was Stickney's diagnosis, you see. Then the sergeant calls out, 'Perez, Joe. I got a letter for Perez, Joseph.' And here comes Joe Perez. He opens his letter, snaps smartly to attention, and says, 'Perez, car wreck.' Each man was reading his ultimate diagnosis. 'Hollingsworth, pneumonia,' and so on, until the sergeant called out, 'Galen.' By now I was fascinated . . . instead of taking the letter, I let the sergeant open it for me. I was filled both with dread and a kind of joyful expectation. The sergeant cried, 'Galen, HIV-positive.' And as soon as he said that, babe — I'm not kidding — I felt a tremendous sense of relief flood through me and I thought, 'Thank God, I don't have to do this anymore. I can ride off into the sunset, mission accomplished.' "

Moses flicked the TV remote and flipped through the channels watching the silent talking heads. "So what do you think of my dream?"

"If I turn up HIV-positive," Linda said, "I'll stab you in the fucking heart. I'll cut your motherfucking dick off and don't think I don't know how to do it either, buster!"

Moses was convinced by the tone of Linda's voice that the Moon *did not* belong to everyone. She belonged to him alone. He reached for her, took her face in his hands, and told her she was the most wonderful woman he had ever known. He swore his love to her for all eternity and then kissed her ever so gently. This time they slowed it down and made love with patience and tenderness, like there was all the time in the world.

Moses awoke at five A.M. and quietly padded out to the kitchen so as not to wake Linda. He experienced timidity, a kind of hand-wringing anxiety and a bad taste in his mouth that generally meant his sugar was high. Coffee would help clear his head but in the meantime there was a certain chasm of fear. As Moses waited for the coffee maker he stood at the counter, gave himself a finger stick, and deposited a drop of blood on the test strip in his glucometer. His fasting sugar was 595. This was so unbelievable that he took an alcohol swab and cleaned the tester. The second reading was 599. He went into the toilet and pissed on a dipstick to test for keotones then drew thirty units of regular insulin into a syringe and injected it in his leg. Moses swallowed a cup of coffee, ate a half piece of toast, and put on his shorts and running shoes. He walked three times around the horse trail, felt even at the midpoint, but when he got back to the house, he could tell by "feel" that his blood sugar was now perilously low. His legs were cold and shaky. Too much insulin. But that 595 scared the shit out of him. He quartered an orange and devoured five slices of bread like an inmate of Dachau. He chugged down a huge glass of orange juice and sat reading the morning paper, waiting for the sugar to kick in.

In a half hour Moses went out into the garage for his session with the heavybag. After he wrapped his hands and put on his bag gloves, Moses began pecking at the bag with his left jab. The gnawing pain in his stomach, which had started with the awful candybars, returned. Strong coffee on top of a particularly sour orange juice and then all of that orange juice. Acid stomach. Had to be. Moses was loose from the walk and was soon perspiring freely as he dug left and rights into the heavybag.

Moses had boxed for the Ninth Army light heavyweight title over in Germany just after the war. In fact, in the old days he used to tell his medical colleagues that he had won that title although in fact he lost a very close decision.

As he worked the bag he thought of Brigitte, his German lover (number 34), of the pregnancy, of his son, Werner, now a plumber. Moses met the young man once on a trip to Germany. Werner resembled his mother more than Moses. It had been an awkward and embarrassing visit for the young man and his family but not for Moses who was curious about his son, and who had sent him money when the kid went through his hippie period back in the late sixties — chump change, really — shoeshine money, nothing to brag about. Galen remembered the time he and Brigitte were walking out of the Black Forest just as the war was ending and a group of German soldiers walked past them and failed to realize that he was an American. Brigitte cursed the soldiers for their sardonic remarks, saved his life, really, by creating a diversion in their train of thought.

Moses moved into the bag and hooked at it low. He remembered how his punches bounced off Bernie Magill who had entered the tournament on a whim, without even training. The fight was scheduled for six rounds, but somehow at the last moment, it had been cut back to four. Moses could have easily whipped Magill in six, but four wasn't enough time. Magill was a farm boy, shanty Irish, and had come up hard. He was just born tough and didn't bother to train at all. Moses knew the man would tire. In fact, Moses almost took him out after three and then proceeded to win the fourth round, but he couldn't overcome the points Magill had accumulated in the first and second rounds and the first two minutes of the third. If only he had been given six rounds, like they said. If only they hadn't cheated him. If only they hadn't made it a four-round fight.

Moses planted his feet and set down on his punches. Where was Magill now? See what would happen, now. Knock on the man's door. "Hi, Bernie, *remember me?*" Moses had never really quit training. Life was hard, a fight.

Moses lined himself up against the seam of the bag and started tossing off combinations, pushing himself to see if that damn pain in his chest was angina or a stomachache. The increased exertion did not make the pain worse.

Yeah. Go out and find Magill. Run him down and kick some ass. Hostility, Moses. Well, dish it out on the bag; don't let it eat you. Let it out, ventilate it. Galen had been a lifelong bag puncher, you never knew — what if you had to put up the dukes with some street punk? Moses was older but he was still physically powerful — the strength was the last thing to go. He knew he could probably stand and trade blows with anybody for fifteen or twenty seconds, which would be as long as necessary. That is if they didn't whip out a nine-millimeter. You couldn't expect a fair fight anymore. Little pencil-neck geeks could kill you. Driving that pussy wagon all over L.A., he was overdue for a carjack. Shot dead wouldn't be a bad way to go. It would be fast. He had seen them bleed out in the E.R. It seemed painless. The shock of a bullet — you wouldn't know what happened. Better if they got you between the eyes. You wouldn't even hear the gun. Or would the gray matter, pink with oxygen, experience a half billion crazy . . . thoughts? Some kind of Salvador Dalí last-second jumble. Who could say, really? Moses was sweating freely now and began throwing hard punches.

Eight hundred and thirty-five completely different, unique, and separate pieces of poon. Most of them — the biggest proportion — angry fucks. Power fucks. How many tender fucks, Moses? How many acts of love? Well, the best one of all happened last night. It had been the best one, but Linda was just going through her phase. This affair was temporary. He remembered, "Go!"

"Go!" she had said. It made his blood boil. He danced in and out on the bag, firing hard. "Go!"

My God, it felt like a crowbar had been shot through his chest; his knees buckled but he kept his feet. In fact, the pain stood him up. What was *that*? He continued to fire with both hands. Moses had big hands, strong, solid hands that created some of the most beautiful faces, tits, and ass on the silver screen. The hands of a boxer. The hands of the artiste. How ironic. You're mine, Magill, you goddamn stupid Irish prick.

As Moses recalled, Magill was in truth not such a bad guy. He was a bully, stupid, but a clean fighter who had offered to buy Galen drinks after the fight. Magill had paid him the highest compliments. How could Moses hate him? Well, for one thing, Magill had won the fight. Magill had taught him what it felt like to be number two; it would never happen again, but it was like they said — lonely at the top. Moses had power, they feared him, but they didn't call him Mr. Nice Guy.

To screw a thousand of them he would need a penile implant. Put that on the list. He needed lots of stuff — a new heavybag, a new pair of bag gloves, a new Jag — get him a ragtop this time, a white V-12 with a black top and he could stick a .357 in the glove box in case some of the homeboys tried to take him off. Another Jaguar. Yeah. He had been the Merecedes route and felt like a bank officer. Now that he couldn't eat real food anymore he deserved his toys more than ever. And like Linda said, there were worse things than diabetes. Bone cancer, cancer of the pancreas, of the esophagus, the bladder, etc. — emphysema and cardio-myopathy. Drown for a year or two.

There was no easy death. Human organisms were tough and it was hard for them to die. That's why Moses went into cosmetic surgery — so he didn't have to look at death, even though he had seen his share just the same. In and out of hospitals every day, you just couldn't escape the problem of your own mortality. Dead wasn't so bad; it was the damn dying. There wasn't any Heaven, but there sure enough was Hell. When the shit hit the fan, nothing worked. Fucking nothing. On a good day it was: ostrich, head-in-sand. Let your prick do your thinking for you. Use a little muscle. Take of life. Too bad he and Linda couldn't drive to Mendocino, eat steak and baked potatoes with sour cream, and have some really decent wine, five hundred dollars a bottle and so good it almost tasted rotten. Top it off with a first-rate cigar.

Suddenly it felt like a flock of wing-beating chickens had been rousted from his chest, making him light-headed. Jesus! Ventricular fibrillation.

The floor seemed to come up and slam him in the face, and the sound of his head hitting the concrete floor of the garage was more that of a bowling ball than a human skull. Compared to the vise grip on his chest, the blow to his forehead was painless. He could not move. His hot sweat turned instantly cold. He had seen it all, done it all twice over — this was it; this was the death he had prayed for since he did his first rotation in a cancer ward as an intern. Because it was quick, a heart attack was *relatively* a cakewalk; still, the pain was unbelievable and he was scared shitless. He wanted to go out like a tough guy. But the Wild One was suddenly terrified. Fear overwhelmed. He began to noiselessly mouth a prayer from his youth. *May the Sacred Heart of Jesus be glorified, adored, loved and preserved throughout the world, now and forever. Sacred Heart of Jesus, pray for us. Saint Jude, worker of miracles, pray for us. Saint Jude, help of the hopeless, pray for us. Amen.*

He lay on the floor a moment. The pain was terrible but the fear began to abate. Somehow he had passed through a portal where pain still reigned over him but fear did not. He wished he could call back the prayer. It seemed like the most cowardly act of his life. It had been an act of conciliation; it had been contrary to his true nature. Moses struggled to get up, slipping in his own blood. He wanted to go down with both guns blazing. Jesse James and Cole Younger. John Wesley Harding. He could have stayed in marvelous Africa and been a Hemingway man instead of the sort who hand-delivered scripts for pain pills to TV actors. Fuckall! He fired away at the heavybag.

The pain radiated down his left arm, paralyzing it, but Moses pressed forward with his head and tossed a few right hands at the bag before the molten red lobster claw crushed harder. The pain was absolute. Moses slumped down in the fetal position and let off a small involuntary shriek, like a woman. He tried to recall it and contain it. He was afraid Linda would hear him. She was a good doc and he was afraid she might save his life.

Rocketfire Red

EIGHTEEN, DINGY ORANGE HAIR, one-fourth Aborigine, I was. A face full of freckles and a bronze melanoma tan penetratin' the depths of me epidermis. Nights I worked the tables at French Emma's Cafe out in Paddingon. Days I surfed Bondi Beach with the local blokes. Shared a flat with me cuz, Doris Platte. The digs was nothing fancy, mind you, but they was quite an improvement over Alice Springs. After graduation Dorey and I caught the first Blue Train running east from Perth and didn't stop until we saw the bleeding opera house in Sydney Harbour. Sydney: the Big Smoke. It's a bit of all right, mate — bright lights, all-night deli-marts. Discos and nightlife. Gas stops and supermarkets open Sundays. Flamin' freedom from me mum and dad, the Catholic Church, and the bloody bingo parlors of Alice. Proud to be Aw-stralian. The bloody poms call us convict bastards. Jail-birds.

As I said, Doris was me cuz. Quite lovely she was. Wanted to find fame and fortune as a high fashion model.

Listened to the BBC, she did, to cultivate her accent. I tells her, "Spit out the plum, girl, be yerself." But she was havin' none of it. Spent her wages on glad rags, makeup, ballet and modeling lessons. Never had a flamin' zac to her name. I wore me swag from home, bought a jar of Vegemite, a box of Weetabix, a pint of cream, a used surfboard, a ball of boardwax and a Speedo swimsuit done up like a Union Jack. Ridin' a bonzer wave gave me this feeling me Aboriginal gram liked to wag her chin about. Aboriginal Dream time.

In Aboriginal Dream time everythin' is happenin' all at once. Yer past, present, and future are all happenin' at the same time. Yer birth, yer life, and death are going on all at once. Dorey sez it's ridiculous to speak of spiritual bull*sh*, that the finer people will take me for a flamin' troppo, a ravin' ratbag. The bleedin' Antichrist, she sez. "They'll throw yers in an institution. You've got quite enough to do to overcome racial discrimination," she sez, "without yabbering esoteric philosophy. Men has just one thing on their minds, luv, and that's a bit of the skirt. Don't confuse them with bleedin' ideas. Anyways, just name one woman prominent in the field of philosophy? And don't give us Alice Baily or Madame Blavatsky, luv."

"Ayn Rand," I tells her.

"Cripes!" she says. "A bloody atheist, that one. Tell you what I think, luv. That little bobby-dazzler is roastin' in the fires of hell for all of eternity. And so will you, my dear, if you continue to play the jam tart for those surfing blokes."

"Don't come the raw prawn with me, Dorey," I says. "Don't do me block; I'm no drongo's potato peeler. Wilbur, Col, and Bluey are me mates and there's no more to it. It's you that's been dipping around. Commitin' the intimacy. Don't cometh the uncooked crustacean."

Doris cries stinkin' fish. Takes on her *Masterpiece The-*

atre tone. "I bloody don't give it away. There are certain career incentives, various objectives that can only be acquired in a bloke's bedroom; it's all a part of me grand plan. Accordingly, cheap morals do not apply. You only get one go in this life. Serving steak and prawn dinners to a bloody lot of stonkered drongos at French Emma's pays the rent. From humble beginnings to Hollywood does I go. It's me plan."

God save the flamin' queen! *The plan*. Dorey's road to fame and fortune. It was all she talked about walking about the flat with a bleeding encyclopedia on 'er head, "The rain in Spain falls mainly on the plain." *Gentlemen Prefer Blondes* and that lot. Eliza Doolittle, I calls her.

DOREY was Miss Alice Springs 1992. Her top bollocks were quite decent, like a pair of Queensland peaches they was; her face and hair lovely enough but Doris had long, thick legs and a high arse. Looked like an bleeding ostrich, she did, walkin' about with encyclopedias on her skull. On top of everything else, the skin on Dorey's neck looked like the flesh of a plucked chicken; she had large pores but mainly it was her bones; they were altogether too thick for fashion modeling. Built for rugby they was. Had to maintain a starvation diet, she did.

Dorey performed aerobics by the hour, then at midnight she would pop out to a milk bar for cakes and chocolate. Thirty minutes later I could hear her in the loo enjoying herself in reverse. Parking the tiger. The liquid laugh. Chundering. Parking the pea soup. Burned the flaming enamel off her teeth with stomach acids. Took out a bank loan for porcelain caps, she did, and kept chucking away.

"Clean out the bowl, love," I says. "The toilet seat is

positively technicolor. I see you've been eating corn and tomato skins again." A flamin' vegetarian she was.

When Doris wasn't playin' the whale, she drank mineral oil and did the big job: choked a darkie — a large black bowel movement that wound four times around the bowl and pointed at both ends. She was proud of 'em, too. First time she called me in for a look, she did, "Look at that then willya, luv. A proper alligator." And then soon after, she was up every half hour with a case of the toms. "Clean out the utensil, darls, it smells like an outback shithouse," I tells her. "Go to Overeaters Anonymous or you'll end up like that American singer, Karen Ann Carpenter. Think of yer 'ealth, girl."

Dorey's next go was thyroid medicine. Made her as nervous as a cat and caused her flamin' eyes to 'alf pop out of her 'ead. You could 'ear 'er 'eart thumpin' 'alfway across the room. Sounded like a woodpecker 'ammerin' on the tin roof of a backyard dunnee. After thyroid pills, it was diuretics. With diuretics she could never wander more than ten minutes from the loo, the flamin' slash house. For all her highfalutin new ways, going round with the big nobs and such, our Eliza Doolittle could indulge in the toilet talk when it suited her fancy. On diuretics it was always, "I've got to drain the dragon," or "I've got to point Pixie at the porcelain; train Tootsie at the terra cotta — micturate! Take a bleedin' piss!"

Next off she copped a bottle of Dexedrine from one of 'er mates. Jabbered away into the wee hours on that lot. "Well, how *are* you? You never believe this one, luv: Blinky, our *Bohemian gypsy,* shows up at the agency in plain gray cardigan, a white linen blouse with a neck clasp all subdued like, pearl earrings, 'er 'air done up in a bun, not a dollop of paint on 'er, pleated gray skirt, 'Gray is so elegant,' Blinky sez 'er voice all breathy like, 'Understatement is the comin' thing.' '*Victoria's Secret,* page forty-four,' I sez. 'Well, feature that!' she sez. Blinky in pearl earrings? *Imagine.* It was totally one-eighty. She must be bleedin' *de*sperate. Desleigh told her she needs a new look."

I sez to Dorey, "Who in flamin' hell is Blinky, luv?"

"Brunette from Perth with a huge pair of norks and a fat ass. Knows how to swing it about, too. Youse could knock down a house with an arse like that. But Desleigh put the fear of God in 'er. Now she tiptoes about like a schoolmarm. Can't understand it meself since Desleigh likes thems with a fat arse."

On the Dexedrine, Dorey became obsessed with doin' 'er nails, scrubbin' out the bathroom grout with a toothbrush, cleaning the fridge, doing up the windows meticulous and bouncing 'er own big arse against the walls at three in the flamin' morning.

"You needs to make a psychiatry appointment at the National Health," I tells her.

"Wot? Talk to a bleedin' freckle puncher?" Suddenly she gets to weeping. "You were as fat as a cow when we left Alice," she sez. "How do you stay thin when you quaff down so much of the amber fluid? Vats of it," she sez breakin' into tears.

It's true that the surfers like to sink a few swift ones. I says, "You could do with a few ice colds yourself, darls, to bleedin' calm down. Yer whirlin' around with the cleaning gear like a white tornado. The floor in the loo isn't yer operation room in bloody 'ospital."

"Oh, but there are germs everywhere! If I had a microscope and could give you a proper look, you might wash the plates now and then. They's dying like flies in America from the *E. coli* bacteria. Two 'undred a day or more of 'em stonkered out stiff. Perished. It's a big coverup affair."

"Them pills yer takin', Bluey says they makes a sheila

paranoid. Makes bugs an obsession. If you wants to know how I stay so thin, why not ask direct like? It ain't a mystery, luv. The water temperature at Bondi is nineteen degrees centigrade. I dunnae wear a wet suit. After a day in the surf I'm ready for a few frosties with the fellers, and I could eat a flamin' steer for dinner. Just knock off its horns, wipe its arse, and bung it on the plate, sport."

"Gad!" she says mopping off the mascara. "How disgusting!" You'll have the *E. coli* in a fortnight. And it's positively immoral to be eatin' meat. Cows an' such 'as souls same as us."

Talk about Madame Blavatsky and the fires of 'ell. Doris was a walkin' contradiction. I sez, "At least I'm not a flamin' drug addict. Give surfin' a burl and the superfluous flesh will melt away, I guarantee it. All those buggers working at the Admundsen-Scott station on the South Pole; they lays into their tucker, darls. Twelve thousand calories a day and still they lose weight. Crikey! The eats seals, walrus, and whale blubber and still lose the love handles. I seen about it on the telly. Rotates 'em back to Wellington every four months so they can put on a few stone."

The flamin' words were barely out of me gob before Doris filled a zinc laundry tub with cold water and a tray of ice cubes. It became her daily ritual. Cold as a nun's nasty she was, but the pounds melted off like snowballs in 'ell, as they say in the classics. Turned blue, Dorey did, but she smiled at me through chattering teeth. 'Er mind was focused again. She was back on the road to riches. "You really must do something about your hair, luv; it's been bloody torched by seawater and sun," she said, "and we must see about your clothes. I'll get you fixed up proper like and we'll drop 'em dead in gay Paree."

"That would be jolly," I said. "I could fancy looking like a bit bonzer. Too right."

Dorey's hair stylist, Leonard, was a flamin' pooftah from Melbourne. Leonard says me hair was tighter than a coiled spring. He put some relaxer in it and messed about with the back of 'is comb, movin' it this way and that. Washed it out and all me kink was history. "Now then, what to do for color?" Leonard sez. I tol' 'im I wanted to be blond just like Madonna. Leonard sez, "On a scale of ten, poppet, you have a base color of three. It would be impossible to make you a blond, ducky, without using bleach, petrol, and hydrochloric acid, but I have this absolutely *divine* new color from Redken called Rocketfire Red."

Shows me a picture. "Fab," I says. "Starve the lizards! Stone the crows! Bung it on!"

"Beastly!" Doris says. "You might as well lay on an inch of green eyeliner and have a crocodile tattooed on yer bum, luv. Stick a ring in yer nose while yer at it."

"Norma Jeane Baker, with her brown hair was a bit on the plainish side until she spent two bob on her first bottle of bleach. With platinum blond hair she became Marilyn Monroe, an international icon.

After my first bottle of Redken's Rocketfire Red, the proper conditioners and a little makeup, me tips at French Emma's doubled straightaway. The old gallahs pinched me arse black and blue, but fair dinkum. We was told to push the ardent spirits before dinner. Each night I went home with a bundle of the folding stuff.

I gave modelin' a fair burl but the truth is, I couldn't make a real go of it. Didn't wish to pretend I was anything other than meself. The way I sees it, the "rhine in Spine falls minely on th' flamin' pline." I mean, as they say in the classics, "When in Rome." Meanwhile Dorey was flyin' Qantas to London for shoots there and after each trip she came home ravin' about England and such, all high and mighty, like she's suddenly a member of the Royal Family.

Got sick of 'earin' it, I did. Finally I tells her to piss off. Calls me an 'ocker, she does. A convict.

I'm not a bleedin' patriot but dear ol' Oz is a far sight better than Pomland. Like comparin' 'eaven to 'ell. You can walk tall in Aw-stralia, sport. Fair dinkum. It's a bit of all right, is Oz. Yairs! I cashed in me savings and went one-fourth partnership with me surfin' mates to construct a Double A Fuel dragster. Blood Oath.

Wilbur White and Col was iron workers and built the dragster's rails with various materials purloined from their work sites. We picked up a 1957 Chrysler 392 Hemi block, mounted it on the front end and bunged on a fuel-injected blower. Just messing about we built a racer out of pieces. Bluey's old man owned a car repair shop and we spent all our spare time there listening to rock music and monkey wrenching. Bluey was one of Aw-stralia's most fearless surfers. A blond Adonis. 'E was a good driver on a motorbike or in a big sedan. Had speed of hand, foot and eye but when he got into a fire suit, helmet, mask and gloves and sat in the tight roll cage of *Pieces,* 'e went pale with claustrophobia. He red-lighted in his first two qualifiers and racing the next fortnight 'e threw *Pieces*'s clutch and flywheel. Bluey took a two hundred twenty mph trip up the stream of effluent in a barbed-wire canoe sans paddle, 'e did. Rolled her three times. Cut up 'is legs, 'e did; broke 'is knee. Punctured his bladder and near sliced off 'is sausage — 'is Willy, 'is John Thomas. The virile member. 'Is snorker. 'Is beef bugle. Just like the bloke in America, John Wayne Bobbitt. Sixty-two stitches in 'is trouser snake.

We was all short on the old lolly after the demise of *Pieces* and we was without a driver after Col and Will copped a look at Bluey's mutton. The medicos sewed up 'is sausage but said it might be a while before 'e would crack a fat, let alone jerk the gherkin, or run the risk of goin' blind exercising the ferret. Tol' Bluey it could be a year before 'e'd take 'is next hop in the horsecollar, if ever. Bluey liked 'is bit of skirt. Dipped around like a belt-fed mortar. Col sez Blue could bang away like a shithouse door in a gale. I took a fancy to 'im and prior to the smash, almost let him get into me knickers. Kissed me proper like, 'e did. Me cheeks got hot and me 'ead swirled. But after hearin' Dorey goin' on about germs and the flamin AIDS virus night and day, knowing 'ow Blue chased the gals, and because of me strict Catholic upbringing, I gained me senses an' sent 'im packin'. Then with a bandage on 'is mulligan, 'e was dead off shagging, and surfing as well. Looked as lonely as a bastard on Father's Day. Claimed 'is life was a bag full of arseholes. "She'll be all right, sport," I says. "Wotcher?" But it was a rotten cop for Bluey all around. Felt terrible about it, 'im being me mate, and fancyin' 'im as I did in the old time romantic way of sentimental movies.

YOUSE might think that would have been the end of drag racing, us being stoney and Blue fair crooked, but me old Aboriginal gram snuffed it. Shot through she did. Passed away in 'er sleep. Died peaceful like at ninety-two. Mum found 'er with a smile on her gob at sparrow's fart. Gram didn't have enough swag to hang on a nail but she left me a harlequin opal she found in the strip mines near Cooper Pedey when I was just a nipper. Worth more than anyone thought. I quickly converted it to the green stuff and bought various racing parts — a new bell housing, magneto, clutch assembly, flywheel, and a proper set of tires. Wilbur and Col welded together a new set of chrome-moly rails whilst Bluey's dad bored out the Chrysler's block and threw in a new set of rings. In spite of what happened to Blue we mounted the engine on the front of the dragster;

rare is the driver that will anymore, since the engine and front end parts can become deadly shrapnel in a smash-up, but the front-mounted engines are quicker an' without sponsors we needed every advantage we could get. We rechristened *Pieces* with a bottle of Ned Kelly whiskey. Named 'er after me hair dye, *Rocketfire Red*. She was fair beaut, a regular humdinger, and while the lads weren't keen to drive 'er, I was. We spent our last rarzoo on a barrel of 90 percent nitro-methane racing fuel mixed with 10 percent alcohol — $65 a gallon that lot, and when youse figure seven imperial gallons for a quarter-mile run, our entry fees for the Blue Mountains points meet, spare parts and what all — we was fair skinned.

THE lads and I spent so much time monkey wrenchin' the engine, the brakes was our last consideration. Me parachute was me brakes and I packed it meself. Let me tell youse, shooting the tube at Bondi or catching a great wave up past Cairns, along the Barrier Reef, is fair dinkum, but runnin' a quarter mile at 299 mph is like 'avin' all your birthdays at once. Flamin' colossal. Took the prize, we did. After which we loads *Red* on the trailer and stopped at the first pub for a few foaming frosties. I was as dry as a dead dingo's donger from the heat of the strip and me nose was still bleeding from all the "g's" I pulled at the top end of the track. Col says four "g's" will cause most people to bugger out, but a driver will never know if he's up to it until 'e races. I hardly got dizzy but after the race I was dry enough to drink out of a Jap's jockstrap. Chug-a-lug. Chug-a-lug. Had a skinful, I did, and made love to the lav that night. Cried Ruth, I did. Hit the crash cot as soon as the lads dropped me home. Had to place me foot on the floor to stop the swirlies. I called in sick at French Emma's and laid low the whole next day.

Swore off the neck oil for a solid week. Absolutely flaked, I was. Buggered.

With our winnings we tossed another new set of rings in the Chrysler to boost the compression, bought three sets of spark plugs, a case of oil, and had just enough left over for the ferry crossing and entry fees for the races in Hobart, Tasmania. For the trip Wilbur made Marmite sandwiches on Wonder Bread and wrapped them in wax paper. We 'ad to sleep in Blue's flamin' Holman. The mosquitoes was somethin' ferocious. Won first prize, we did.

A week later we won the trophy at Canberra, and the following week we took first in Adelaide. Halfway down the track in the final race, a flamin' wallaby shot across the Tarmac. I accidentally hit the parachute release but won the race anyway. In the papers, the feller placed second said it was bad enough losing to a sheila, a bonzer one at that; but it was dead humiliatin' to get beat by a homemade dragster with its parachute wide open.

Col was a bit schicker at the Victoria Regionals, misplaced the front end weights and I did a quarter-mile wheelie. Me clutch was a bit loose. We lost that race but there was a picture of *Rocketfire Red* screeching down the track with the front end in the air and me rear tires smokin' in the morning edition of the *Melbourne Sun*. We went on to win the Queensland Finals in Brisbane, and in less than two months, we had risen from virtual obscurity to national prominence. We beat professional racers sponsored in full by the lager and soft drink firms. These blokes showed up at the track not only with a trailer full of spare parts, but fresh engines they could drop into their dragsters if they blew one qualifying. No sponsors would give us so much as the sniff of a fart, we done it on our own. We was monkey wrenching in between races. Pulling plugs, adjusting the air/fuel mixture on the fuel injectors, messin' with the jets, checking the tires for air pressure. The bloody tension level on the track was incredible.

THE '58 Chrysler 392 block has a hemispherical head with a round combustion chamber. It is still the bloody best racing engine you can buy. The pros buy identical duplicates for $40,000 American and have them shipped over complete in every detail. To the drivers with major sponsors, blowin' an engine qualifying scarcely matters so long as they win. They've got forty minutes between races to drop in a fresh engine and a first-rate pit crew to do it. There was just the four of us monkey wrenching on *Red* and without decent spare parts, forty minutes weren't long enough to do the job up proper.

I drove *Red* with a light foot lest I throw a rod through those rebored cylinders. We placed third in the summer nationals at Broken Hills when the favorite driver got a case of the nerves, red-lighted and disqualified. *Full Tilt Boogie* seen their chance after this and fills their tank with hydrozine and nitro. Only a flamin' fool would do such a thing since the two chemicals combine to make up nitroglycerine. If you don't keep it dead cold, the fuel tank can explode like an atom bomb. Col and Wilbur seen their pit crew icing *Boogie*'s engine on the sly, a sure sign they was up to somethin' devious. Col tells me to blow out the cobwebs in the last qualifier whilst Bluey says if I let it all go and dust the engine we wouldn't finish in the money. We was flamin' stoney and had a list of creditors as long as yer arm. Blue was dead right, of course, but this was the flamin' Australian Nationals and I 'ad to let the flags out. I threw the smoke and *Red* ran bonzer. The Chrysler engine held. We beat *FTB* with a 4:99. All yer birthdays at once? Starve the lizards! *All* me birthdays at once, mate! Fair beaut. We lost the finals by a tenth of a second. Finally tossed a rod in the Chrysler an' cracked three pistons. Toasted 'em. But good on. A bunch of monkey wrenchers and we almost beat the corporation. Whacko-the-diddle-o!

WHEN Bluey's mutton remained numb past Australian rules football season and well into cricket, 'e got stonkered an' jumped off the bridge in Sydney Harbour. I was good to 'im, all this while, featured 'im as me feller even when Wilbur says to forget it. Blue don't want to settle down. In truth it was me blood 'e couldn't get past. Fact of me heritage. Fact that I was partly a dusky. Experienced me share of 'eartbreak when I sees he doesn't fancy me and multiplied it when he died. Gone off me food.

Before 'e snuffed it, Blue tells Col, "It's bad enough walkin' about with a tube up yer doover, or wearin' a diaper all the time, but what's life if you can't dip the dagger now and then?" This is what he said on the night precedin'. Blue must've changed 'is mind after 'e hit the water since 'e swam 'alfway to Manly before he was struck by the last ferry returning to Sydney. Got chopped apart by propellers. Made the headlines. "Three-Time Surfing Champ Drowns!" After the funeral Col buggered out of town. Took a construction job in Fremantle. Wilbur stayed in Sydney to work in the garage with Blue's old man. *Rocketfire Red* is under a tarp in the back of the lot. I didn't care for drag racing anymore, surfing neither. Not after losing me feller, Bluey, nor me ol' gram. Life got stale, it did.

Then one day Desleigh Davidson gives me a jingle. Met the lady once or twice at the modeling agency with Doris. Desleigh says she wants to arrange to have me picture done for the magazines. An Aboriginal female drag racer was the angle of the dangle. I tol' her I was done with that lot, but she offered me a bundle of green, so I sez, "Yairs, why not?" They makes me out to be a full-blooded Aborigine. A regular Machiavelli, was Desleigh. Soon I was a cover girl for the best Australian fashion magazines. "More beautiful than Evonne Goolagong. The next new great face!" and all that bull*sh*. From Sydney I began to fly Qantas to shoots in London, Paris, Rome, Berlin, and Los Angeles. Twenty years old. An overnight sensation. Made the *Sports Illustrated* swimsuit issue, I did. Shootin' the tube at Bondi with makeup on me face and me hair done up in mousse. That was the angle of that dangle. Yairs! Desleigh, a bloody Machiavelli, she was. Took 'er straight fifteen percent, too.

Never was ambitious. Didn't care a wit about fame and celebrity. Didn't really care all that much about the folding stuff neither — why bother? The taxes are something atrocious. Desleigh says that to become successful one can neither explain nor complain. She's got a point. Who wants to bleedin' hear it? Still, it's up at five A.M. and gettin' beautiful. In this bloody business you 'ave to get up a bleedin' hour and a 'alf before you hit the flamin' cot. I sez, "Desleigh, I'm half shagged. I'll be old before me time."

Tell us about it, luv. Strewth! "Success doesn't come out of thin air," she sez.

Few will believe it, but I was never a jam tart — a potato peeler. Blood oath. To be beautiful for all men, I can give myself to no man. Don't know what an orgasm is and don't care to. Must be me Catholic upbringing. Or maybe I might like orgasms too much and end up jumping off the harbor bridge when I can't have 'em no more. I think of Blue a lot. Could feature myself having sex with 'im that night 'e tried to get into me knickers. Wished I had.

I think of me Aborigine gram and me life back in Alice when I was a wee nipper on me gram's knee. I think of the fairy tales she told me an' 'ow life was in the old days —

pioneer times. Gram liked to chin wag about dream time. Said I was the only member of the family would catch on. Too right, she was.

In Australian Dream time everything makes perfect sense. There is no judgment. Thems that massacred me ancestors will receive no eternal judgment. Neither will your Mother Teresa win a Brownie medal; she's just playing her part in the cosmic play. Doing her bleedin' job. Good and evil all happen for a reason. Of this I'm certain. I'm givin' it to youse straight. Me vision is true. Quite genuine. *Dinki-di*, as me gram said. But Doris was dead right; such talk is upsetting. People think you're a raving ratbag. A danger to the social order.

Waiting tables at French Emma's, I was, at the minimum wage, and now I'm painting meself up like a peacock and having me pictures for all the lovely magazines with their articles about sexual orgasms, the G-spot, and clitoral stimulation. It's not only a common bloke like Blue wants in me knickers. I've had proposals of marriage from dukes and lords and such. Billionaires from Texas and Saudi Arabia. Movie stars and jet setters. Doesn't bother them a bit that I'm partly Abbo, an Australian dusky — half caste. All of them comes on with a line of bull*sh*. Tells 'em to piss off, I does. I may come from Alice Springs, Aw-stralia, but I weren't born yesterday, as they say in the classics.

Without me makeup expert, me hair stylist, and fashion-designed clothes; without me bottle of Rocketfire Red, I don't look a whole lot different than your average bonzer sheila. So the next time you see me mug in a high-fashion magazine, gals, don't go running off for plastic surgery. The whole business is done with mirrors, shadows, and air brushin'. Don't sit about moony-eyed wishing you were someone different or somewheres else; there's a glorious life right where yer sittin' now. When yer take a deep reflection an' look into yer 'eart, you'll see that everything is *dinki-di*. You'll find at last that the true home you've been searching for everywhere is in yer own backyard. Blood oath! There's no need to go on bloody Walkabout to discover the truth.

Me last ride in the dragster I copped a Captain Cook. Saw it all coming: fame, fortune, celebrity; the death of Bluey; Doris packing up in a huff when I became more famous than her. She may never forgive me for it, she mightn't, but she's basically apples. Married a barrister back in Alice where she has two nippers wot's taking medication for hyperactivity, a turquoise budgie, and a swimming pool. Twenty pounds overweight. A devout member of the church; she hasn't the least shred of Christian forgiveness in 'er 'eart. Me gram was right. There was none that would understand Dream time except yours truly.

Driving *Rocketfire Red* at the Nationals I seen me birth, me whole life and me death in 4.9 seconds. I saw flamin' everything. The stocks to buy, the horses to bet on, and the date and location of the next major volcanic eruption, but me lips are sealed. It would be wrong to take advantage. Australian Dream time. I seen Blue and me gram and everything is aces. Always has been. It always has been. Never featured meself driving racing cars or me mug on the cover of shiny magazines but it was all God's doing, not me own.

Thems that's out to reform the world has their priorities. wrong. Seeing things from the wrong angle. I mean they flamin' well give it the hurly burl when they should go easy. Like I says, everything has already happened anyway. So anyways, me dears, there you 'ave it. I'm just a 'umble lass from Alice Springs, Aw-stralia. I'm 'ere to tell yers that under the Redken's Rocketfire, I 'appen to 'ave a brain wot thinks deep thoughts. I'm not a flamin' troppo, a glamorous jet setter. I'm nobody's jam tart. The strict Catholic upbringing. I guess it's the reason this sex queen is a flamin' virgin! As chaste as a nun. How's that for irony, 'ey? It takes a bit of fortitude when every other bloke on the street wants in me pants and every gal is wonderin', "What's she like? What's she about?" As I said, there's a brain contains deep thoughts under this head full of processed hair. So I sat down to write out me story an' spell things out for yers. There's nothing mysterious about me. I'm just like youse. I knows fame, youth, and beauty is fleeting things. I haven't let celebrity go to me 'ead. If I did that, me life would turn into a hatful of arseholes; so I'm the same as always — pure apples. Just another bonzer sheila from kangaroo valley. When I pack this modeling lot in, I hope to find a proper bloke, the ol' fashioned way, traditional like, go to the flickers and eat ice cream sundaes, get to know 'im proper and then settle down someplace quiet an' decent like an' raise a family.

When youse comes to the Land of Sunshine, stop in Sydney and order the steak at French Emma's Cafe out in Paddington. Enjoy a few chilled tubes of Foster's and then 'ave the twenty-four-ounce filet. Melts in yer mouth, it does. Just tell the cook to knock off its horns, wipe its arse, and bung it on the plate. It's beaut, sport. The entire menu is crash hot. Fan-bloody-tastic. Good on yer, then. I've 'ad me say. Waltzin' Matilda and all that lot. Whacko-the-diddle-oh! Hey!

I Need a Man to Love Me

HER PHONE WAS ONE of those black, old-time heavy jobs with a Bakelite dial, the base made out of ceramic or something — granite maybe . . . lead. It was like, heavy-and-a-half, an anvil. Seemed like a moron's phone if you don't know her, since in her condition she could barely lift it and it was getting all but impossible to dial. The left hand was super bad. No fast-draw Billy the Kid hand; it had no strength whatever. When it worked, when all was optimal, it was a cold blue claw and she could hook things with it. Captain Hook. People saw her mickey mouse around with the old phone and there was no sympathy.

The right hand was a little stronger. Not a lot, but it was her bread-and-butter hand. As the years passed it also got weaker. She wasn't Stephen Hawking yet, or like that guy with the left foot, Christy Brown, but close. That's why she liked to keep everything about her the same — the environment the same. This house, this home, her all-her-life home, forty-seven years in a shotgun shack. Okay, don't get morbid — the once cheerful, and still not such a bad . . . bungalow, was home. Period. The doors and windows were now secured with metal bars, a little crack action down on the corner but, hey! — that's New Orleans for y'all. Two bedrooms, a full basement, the add-on front porch done when her father was still alive. Busy beaver with a paintbrush and flower gardens was he. Her dad, Corliss, had a mania for tidiness, and her mother, too, which made the latter hell on wheels when the diagnosis came through; when they learned that she would be crippled for life. Turned her mother into a pisser.

First memories. Let's see . . . she could remember walking when she was maybe four. Just a little, you know. Ugly prosthetic shoes. Then the wheelchair. Oh Lord, your bony ass could get sore in one of those, day after day, even under a pile of lambskin. So how could a mother not love her only kid? Well, it wasn't that Lou Ann didn't love her, it was just that with Lou Ann being a perfectionist and all — there was a certain ambiguity, and when you have to wait on somebody hand and foot — a certain amount of resentment and you start feeling like a slave. You start feelin' that way because it was true. Corliss rose to the occasion and Lou Ann, too, after he passed on. Finally! Lou Ann *finally* accepted the situation and tried to make the best of it. On top of everything else there was all the stress and strain of an adult daughter living with a mother, but what are you going to do? Then Lou Ann ups and dies. Her faced looked like a fried prune in the coffin. A face like dried goatshit. A final accusation . . . like, "see what you *did* to me!"

Her dad had been a concentrated good guy, had a different temperament, but Lou Ann really never could take it. Corliss was dead now fourteen years — Lou Ann, three, leaving her to get by with daykeepers. Quite unlike her temporal home — her scrawny, dilapidated body — the house was still in good condition. You take a normal human body, you could abuse it with drugs, alcohol, tobacco, and junk food and still it would last longer than practically anything. It would last longer than a Westinghouse can opener, pair of Levi's, or a Panama parrot. The average human body lasted longer than just about everything you laid eyes on except a house. A house could last . . . this house. But not the puny body that was hers. The house was still going strong. Sell it and she'd have two years in a nursing home and then indigent — a ward of the state. What happened then? You probably went down pretty fast. Some night, hooked up on a heart monitor, you know, one of those Jamaican nurse aides — *Fuck dis shit, I'm going out for a cig'rette. A Parliament cig'rette. Yeah, I want to have me a Parliament cig'rette. You could let dis here bitch die in the meantime. So what. World gonna miss her? I doesn't think so, daddy. Seriously doubts it.*

Mabel? Have you been out smoking again?

No, sir, I sure hasn't been smokin', I been right here, honey, like I s'posed to be. Turn my back an' she stroked out, thass all I know.

She would be under clover and the house would still be going strong. It was a waste of money keeping the yard so perfect. Putting on the vinyl siding — whew, she got jobbed on that one, but the salesman was so nice — man, that motherfucker *poured* out the charm. Oh well. It did look good. The roof needed work. Maybe next year. If there is a next year, huh? There wouldn't be any tomorrow if she could implement the plan, but she was an ol' scaredycat in regards to the plan.

Anyhow, there was the illusion of safety in keeping everything approximately the same. Better the old phone than something new. A brand-new, glossy, plastic featherweight phone would be a kind of formal acknowledgment, open up a two-lane highway from the pineal gland and pump out the death hormones. Dead wasn't so bad but dying like this was a bitch. A real live sumbitch and then pfffttt! So much for this incarnation. "Dear God, what was I supposed to figure out forty-eight years in this wheelchair?" Forty years plus of staring at the ceiling in silence, looking out the window, staring at the wallpaper, listening to classical FM radio, and looking at her face in the bureau mirror — a pretty face once, now not so hot, not with all of the makeup in the world. Bust the damn mirror. Stare at the ceiling, stare at the floor. Drink gin and watch TV. She never got out much but she knew life all too well, this life this . . . shadow cave and from her life she could extrapolate. Nobody but nobody was happy. They might think so, but they were wrong. When you got right down to it, they would rue the day they were born. Ho, ho, ho. Don't believe it? Wait and see. Ain't nobody escaped dying. Yeah, everybody wants to go to heaven, but ain't nobody wants to die.

Bobby was back in town. A blast from the past. Just out of prison and he lays a diamond necklace on her, a little trifling he picked up. He barely hits the streets and he's stealing again. Came over that afternoon, hardly says hi, and suddenly he's on the phone trying to buy her a new refrigerator 'cause the one she's got is "too loud." Whoever heard of such a thing? Too loud. That was pure Bobby. "But I spent a lot of money on that refrigerator. It's not even a year old."

"Yeah," he says, "and it just goes to show ya, they've been making refrigerators for years and listen to it. How can you even think? It's loud in jail, let me tell you, but that refrigerator is a killer. Good heavens, child, that machine is putting out Richter waves. What we gonna have to do here is go with the foreign made. Japanese."

"What, a Panasonic refrigerator?"

"Along those lines, darlin'. All I know is they don't take over the damn house. Believe it. I'm a thief. I'm in a lot of kitchens in the dead of night and I hear refrigerators of every make and description, and at these times I'm glad they are loud, but I didn't come over heah to steal and that thing is overbearin'. It's aud*acious* and it's jes' a kitchen appliance. An object. So where does it get off? What right do it have?"

Bobby hopped on the phone and started making calls. Placed "on hold," he craned his neck around the corner and said, "America cannot make a refrigerator anymore. What are they but a damn box, a compressor an' some shelves and trays? People graduating from Harvard with degrees in engineering — you would think they could make a better refrigerator! Somebody ought to look into it and develop a whisper-quiet line of kitchen appliances. That fridge you got is loud, darlin'. The German ones are much better an' the Italian ones does look peachy but for a combination of quiet and style, my personal preference is Japanese. You know, the president of Japafreez*or* over they in Tokyo will bring every new model home and live with it. He will ask questions of the family. Say to the old lady, 'How you liking this fridge, baby?' Say to the kids, 'How you liking this fridge, honorable son, honorable daughta?' And these are not crude people, we dealin' with. They won't march directly forward with a bald statement lest they give offense. It's like a damn tea ceremony gettin' a straight answer since they are very civilized people. That's the way of doin' when you got seven million to the square mile. Maybe the son will get bold and say, "Why, it's not a bad refrigerator, suh, but the ice does tastes like dishwa*tah,* they is mold on the *ched*dar, the Popsicles is gooey, an' the damn thing *hums* too much.' 'Just as I thought,' Mr. Japafreez*or* will say before he hops into his Lexus su-preme dream and drives back to the factory at eleven o'clock at night, rolls up his sleeves and gets down to business. He is wishin' someone would invent a pill so he never has to sleep; so he can work twenty-three hours a day. Make it better. Make it better! No ice in the Jell-O, no mold on the cheddar cheese. Make it quiet. Get the *texture* of the Popsicles right. Make it pretty. None of those avocado paint jobs that looked all right in 1968 but became the worst color in the world a year later. The only American that clever, industrious, and hardworking is yoah dope fiend with a two-thousand-dollar-a-day heroin habit."

Bobby gave her a look like, "I've been in jail for almost four years, but even I know that one," and then suddenly he's talking turkey with a sales representative. Oh yeah — the automatic defrosters cause all the racket. They've got side-by-side doors or over-and-under. Gallon jug capacity in the door. Egg storage, also in the door. Colors. Cubic footage. Automatic ice maker.

In less than an hour, a delivery truck showed up and Bobby and the delivery men, smiling Asians in neat blue uniforms, tore the packing box apart and transferred all her food from the old refrigerator to the new one. There wasn't much — lettuce, baloney, milk — the usual. Bobby watched them with intense interest. "We Americans underpower our motors, don't you think? On a hot day, that ol' thing is huffing constantly. It's sufferin' from emphysema as we speak. The poor Little Engine that couldn't. Soundin' like a D-6 Cat with a Kotex in a Coke can for a muff-a-ler. Ever since I walked in the door it has been causin' me great psychic duress. I believe that my nerves are more than slightly frayed. That I am a bit edgy. Forgive me for rattlin' on so. I'm somewhat overcome. Perhaps I should make the switch ovah from regular coffee to a decaffeinated brand."

A worker plugged in the new refrigerator and flipped on

the power settings for the freezer, the meat drawer, and the main compartment. It was virtually impossible to hear the motor but Bobby placed his hands in the freezer and proclaimed that it was working. "Black is a' ace of a color, don'cha think? Pretty *cool*, huh?"

He paid the delivery men with a roll of crisp one-hundred-dollar bills. "Thanks evah so much, fellas," he said, handing them each an extra hundred. "Here is a little kiss goodbye for such fast and courteous service. The world needs more people who take special pains to get things right." He gave them a hand in gathering up the packing materials and then as they rolled the old refrigerator out to their truck, he waved goodbye.

Geez! The size of Bobby's roll made her paranoid. He had to be printing money again. Thirty-four months in prison and he comes out and starts committing serious federal crimes. He would never learn. The diamond necklace — bought with phony money or stolen outright? Don't ask. It was merchandise. It gave her a small thrill to wear it but she really didn't want the damn thing or the new refrigerator either. Ultimately it would be nothing but guilt and depression.

It was sad to see Bobby do this but there was no need to drive him off with a lecture. And she had to get in the rest of her Carl and Maizie story. Those two were under her skin like bugs but it was hard to talk about it with all of the refrigerator stuff going on. Her story was rambling and incoherent but Bobby was quick; he got the gist of it. She felt better to get it out, and he listened with empathy. He kissed her tears away and carried her to bed, pulled back the sheets, white satin sheets, and Bobby remembered. Said, "White satin sheets and an ultra-firm Posturpedic. One hundred percent goose down pillows. I often thought of you in these delicious circumstances while I was racked out in jail. You here, me there. Muslin sheets, a foam pad, and a steel slab are hard to take in your middle age; one develops delicate sensibilities as the years go by. Don't you find this to be true?"

It had been so long since a man touched her she practically came when he picked her up. He brought her to orgasms that were like epileptic seizures and dropped her into a deep and peaceful slumber from which she hoped never to return. Daykeeper #2, Lucille, came by to cook supper and help her with her toilet. After an hour of TV, Lucille put her to bed where she discovered a note from Bobby.

He promised to call back around nine and he did call, exactly at nine. "Hello." Somebody actually, finally did something they promised they would do.

"Hi."

"What are you playing? What's that music?"

"Mozart."

"Mozart? How *long* since Mozart? Time gallops anymore, even in jail. A year is a day." She heard him flip his Zippo, click the little carbon wheel and heard the small dull *bap* of ignition, a small explosion. She could picture the orange and blue flame. Then she heard him click the lighter shut and take a deep drag off a cigarette, exhale, and then fuss with his mouth, picking small strings of dark brown tobacco off his tongue. Bobby smoked straight Gauloises. He said, "Has what's-huh-name gone? The helper."

"Yes."

"Yes?" Puff. He really sucked on a cigarette. Really liked to smoke. He said, "Ain't it frightenin'? All alone for the night?"

"No, this is the best time. Why did you rush off? Why did you leave?"

"I hate to admit it, but whenever I am at liberty, it

seems I am ever on the prowl for hard narcotics. When I am thusly focused, Hercules, Gilgamesh, Sir Galahad — none of them boys has got nothin' on me." Bobby sucked on his cigarette. He said, "This guy, your gentleman friend, Carl, sounds a bit *snakey* if ya ask me. I'm truly appalled by the way things have gone funny since I've been away. You just can't trust anyone anymore. Even your square johns are becoming dangerously unpredictable."

"Oh God! I'm so messed up I can't think straight," she said.

"Your best friend runs off with your boyfriend. I would guess you would be messed up. I don't blame you, darlin'. I thought you said he was married — Carl was married. Tell me about his precious wife?"

"She hasn't got a clue. She's just *out of it*. Doesn't know a thing."

"They always know. What do you mean, doesn't know? They always know. I mean you can't imagine it because you're in love with this rattler snake. You are not bein' objective. You're blind to the whole deal."

"I can hear you smoking. Aren't you supposed to quit smoking when you've got diabetes?"

"Yes; it's one hundred times worse. I cannot drink. I cannot eat so I'm going to smoke, take the narcotic and defile myself in all other ways possible. I *am* a rebel, you know."

"The Leader of the Pack," she said.

He laughed at this and went off on a rap. "Kind sir, your leathers, Levi's, an' your motorcycle boots are quite nasty; your tattoos look like Haitian voodoo, your hair is all greasy and that beard is a fright. The very smell of you is revoltin' and if looks could kill, I do believe I would be dead. Everything is quite in order, we are all of us conformists of one sort or another, but tell me, whyever did you get a foreign-made chopper? How are you going to be a bad ass-kicker on that high-windin' Japanese piece of shit?"

"You inflicted that refrigerator on me and now you're Jap bashing!"

"Truly, darlin', a two-cycle engine is an offense to the human ear. Your Harley-Davidson rumbles in the lower ranges. Whenever I steal a bike for a job, I search out a Harley. They have become utterly dependable in recent years, an' if you are spotted in the commission of a crime, the heat will fall out on the biker groups, not yours truly."

She said, "What kind of drugs did you get? I've got downers. You could have asked me. I miss you."

"I called to discuss your heartthrob, Carl. Being a dangerous criminal sociopath has given me insights and advantages in the field of human dynamics. With a complete lack of moral values I have an edge over just any ol' Tom, Dick, or Harry. I can read deep into the human heart, darlin'. I have a few helpful pointers for ya to consider. I am about to *elucidate*. But let us first recap the situation: Carl just tells you that he doesn't like havin' such a 'limited' relationship. Although he will always love you and carry a special place in his heart for you, he can't bear to lay eyes on you again — "

"And Maizie is in love and I have to listen to her because I'm still dependent on her. I have to listen to her 'goo goo' crap. God! I just want to strangle them both. Somebody ought to take that cocksucking bitch out in the bayou and set her on fire."

"She's 'goo goo' 'cause he took her to heaven."

"Burn them! I'm serious."

"I believe you are. Your whole life, you have to be genial and pleasant. From day one you have to be nice, but you aren't a dependent person really . . . actually, if you could move around, if you were mobile and could ambulate at high speeds, you would be more like a barracuda. A muncher operatin' outside the boundaries of conventional morality, wreakin' havoc and mayhem."

"You got it. I have to play nice. I'm sick of it."

"When I came by I was a trifle drug sick and somewhat inattentive to your concerns. Set 'em on fire? Out in the desert? Why, I don't shock easily, darlin', but I'm still blushin' over the phone at those profane words you have spewed out in such a poisonous and vitriolic fashion. Mercy! You had mah ears flamin'. But you don't let people walk on you. You get it back. I hear what you're saying."

"God, Bobby, I'm sorry! I've never been like this. I'm so full of hate. I am almost afraid of all the hate and meanness I have inside."

"Remember that time out in the backyard when I had — I think, I had drunk around the clock and showed up drunk and we drank that whiskey, and then we went and got more? We went down to the Shannon's Tavern together and you kept pissing about how I was going to dump the wheelchair, but I had presence of mind. I wasn't that drunk. You were pissed. I saw 'set 'em on fire' that night."

She sighed. "That was a great night. A starry summer night. Van Gogh's *Starry Night*. Alcohol and I'm-in-love LSD. I think about that night all the time. I don't remember anything about getting pissed."

"That was 'Light My Fire' night. I remember details. That was the night that *defined* my life. Actions proceeding from that night set me on a course from which there was no turning back. When I was in the joint I used to play Robby Krieger's guitar riff from the middle of 'Light My Fire.' The cut from the Doors' *Double Live Album*. When I was in the joint I played it several hundred thousand times on my Walkman and in it discovered the true meanin' of life. I know all about *the thing in itself* which exists in all things — this evil thing, this will to live on a planet where all is so blamin' nasty. Pain is the positive thing, the essential thing. Dear me, I *do* get carried away — so much for philosophy. You ever see Carlos, or Way-out Willie anymore? Hey, c'mon, baby. Say somethin'. Hello dere? Hello? Hiya . . . my name José Jimenez. He he heh. My name is . . . Walter, the performing Walrus. Ork! Ork! *I'm gonna love ya, baby . . . all night long.* I hope my mustache isn't too stiff and that you don't find my breath offensive at close quarters. Hello dere? Excuse me, missy, do you have a breath mint? A bottle of Scope perhaps? I may be a greasy ass walrus but even I find a steady diet of mackerel and codfish repulsive to the palate. Ork! Hello dere, ladies 'n' gentlemen. I'm Wally the performin' Walrus and, gee, hey, isn't this a great night? Are dey *many here among us who feel that life is but a joke?* Oh yeah, y'all a bunch a existentialists, ain'tcha?"

"Oh, Robert, cut it out."

"You didn't even know 'Carl' and we had our laughs. We had good times. He wasn't even in the picture. This big hurt is going to pass off, believe me."

"Carlos is in prison," she said. "Willie . . . I don't know." She heard the Zippo click again and could picture him with the cigarette perched in the center of his mouth. "Yeah, Carlos is in the slammer and Way-out Willie took a powder."

Bobby said, "Is that so? I figured them to be dead by now. They have exceeded my most extravagant expectations."

She took a sip from her bedside wineglass, popped down a couple Dramamine along with four Stelazine tablets. Robin's egg blue pills chased with more wine. She thought of Carl. Carl was a square, there was no denying.

Bobby said, "You're at that point where you don't think you can get over it again. You can do it once, twice, three times and then you lose the stomach for it. Does that make any sense?"

"I don't know — " she said. "I don't know if I can make it anymore."

"To give someone trust or credibility, you listen to them and then buy into what they tell you. When you know what they say is true, insightful, and that it feels right, over a period of time — as you come to know them, when they become your friend, you take on faith whatever else they may be pushing. As a criminal psychopath I learned that this is a vital, an essential truth. In the beginning what you had with Carl was really all on the level. Then they start lying and you believe them because you need to believe. That's why suckers buy snake oil, baby. That's why life is so damn tricky. It's the reason people get paranoid. They've got good reason. If that was his picture in your room, the man is involved in real estate. Razor bumps and halitosis. White on white tie. Diamond rings on his pinky finger. Why, I can scarcely bear to picture such a gross and horrible presentation of vulgarity. How could ya fall for a straight john like that? A pigeon like that? Well, that is water over the bridge. He's your boy. Then suddenly — whoa! This other passion is cooking for Maizie. Come to think of it he's having fantasies about her for a time and vice versa — subliminal, can you dig? until there is some event where the two of them are alone together, one thing leads to another and they are both fuckin'. Let's not call it 'making love,' let's call it what it was, all right? Fuckin'. Probably did it in the missionary style the first time. That's how it usually goes, no improvisations or anything too darin'. All that exotic fuckin' — all of that comes later. Anyhow, he means no harm up to a point and then he has a choice to make. They're probably surprised to know you got hurt feelings! I mean they are so much into themselves."

She finished off her glass of wine and felt it warm her, it was a subject she was sick of, yet obsessed with, and this was another perspective. Nice of Bobby to try and cheer her up, but she was just so sick of it . . . all.

Bobby continued. "I mean, he's probably got an old condom in his wallet. Just in case. They commit the intimacy. Maybe precede it with some fellatio and cunnilingus. They are really feeling 'up' because they are doing something clandestine — naughty, sneaky. What a thrill! I mean now he's cheating at least two ways and this is really exciting. Are you feeling angry?"

"That," she said, "but more objective than usual. Disgusted."

"Fucking like a couple of dogs in heat. Get out a hose. You know, everybody does it, but they don't want the world to see it. And the reason they don't want the world to see it is because love manifested on this vibration is of a low order. It really isn't love, it's just lust, one of the cardinal vices in the Buddhist scheme. Don't you just envy them?"

"God, no! What are the other . . . cardinal vices?"

"Anger, avarice, and indolence. The cardinal virtues bein' chastity, generosity, gentleness, and humility. Plato's celebrated virtues would be justice — "

"Valor, temperance, and wisdom."

"Very good. I thought propriety was in there but you may be right. The prison library is rather inadequate. That's neither here nor there. Carl and Maizie. Together they feel as one. This is rapture in the backseat of a car. You feel like you're missing out on something? Smellin' kinda funky in that backseat."

"What are the Christian virtues?"

"What is this? You tell me."

"Faith, love, hope — "

"I'm not a Christian, but it seems to me that if you can have sympathy for another human being, the walls break down."

She took a deep breath and swallowed hot salty tears. "He *took her to heaven*. And you're right, she acts like she *is* in heaven, remember? Don't try to give me aversion therapy — 'it stinks in the backseat.' "

"You say you wanna set them on fire out in the desert — that's the downside of all this shit. Part and parcel. That's all I'm saying. Think of them like dogs in heat, it's easier that way. And never, but never, get involved with a married man."

"My options are very limited," she said. "I always imagined being carried away by the passion. Swept up in kisses. You're wrecking the whole deal for me."

"This is not *Gone With the Wind*. This is a couple of dogs in heat. These two are bad. Give me the match. Has Carl got kids?"

"Three."

"That's splashing bad karma all over the place. Poor Carl, he needs *this* and he needs *that*. Fucks his kids, fucks his wife, fucks you — he's a *sorry motherfucker*. And you feel guilty crapping around with a married guy, right? *Why* would you mess around with a married man? You are not without blame, here. I get caught boosting and I do my time. I know the rules."

"You're right," she said absently. "He always needs this and that."

"And he didn't have the balls to come right out with it. He's doing it incrementally. I could go over there now and shoot him right between the eyes if you have an aversion to flame. He won't know what hit him. Where does he live?"

"I'd like that. In a way I'd like that, but — "

"You're a barracuda. I'm not lying. Little Anthony and the Imperials. 'Tears on my pillow, pain in my heart; that ain't you. The female Steven Seagal, I'm not lyin'. Where does he live, I'll get him tonight? I got my ball-

point and paper ready and I'm in possession of untrace-
able firearms."

"No, Bobby," she said wearily. "It wasn't nothin' no
more than an everyday two-timin'. I jes' been down, I guess.
Robert, it's so good to hear your voice. It doesn't seem like
four years, it seems like yesterday."

"They were troubles yesterday. We always got troubles.
Walk around on this planet and you're gonna have troubles.
Only the mind does amazing things. It forgets the pain.
You see pictures of people in the death camp — some guy
points a camera at them and they smile, or somebody shows
you a picture of Johnny and he's smiling and somebody
says, 'Yeah, we took that photograph four days before he
blew his head off with the twelve-gauge.' Life is tricky that
way. Fools you. I could do it, you know. I could blow my
head off. Once you make your mind up to end it, they say
you feel incredibly peaceful and infinitely wise."

"When Johnny gets on the other side. What happens?"

"Nothing."

"You say 'nothing.' Like before you were born?"

"Just like that."

"What if Johnny gets over to the other side and finds
himself in a pile of shit. A pile of shit he can't get out of?"

"No, baby, this is it. What you see is what you get. You
get this. So anyhow, Johnny with his twelve-gauge. Maybe
somebody says a certain thing and he don't take out the
shotgun but three years later gets cancer of the pancreas.
Don't have the nerve to die *now*. Don't got the balls for it
anymore. Suffers excruciating pain. Termites eatin' outcher
insides. Ya know? Johnny should have shot himself *then*.
The part of him that can see in the future told him *then*. I'm
not saying you should always follow your heart, but these
unconscious drives are probably more correct than we will
ever know."

She took the heavy receiver and shifted it to her other ear, cradling it against her shoulder. Poised on the edge of her bed, she reached over with her right hand and poured herself another glass of wine. She opened the drawer of her night table and pulled out the rest of her stash. She couldn't believe what she was doing. The plan. Her grand inspiration was fast becoming a reality. She never thought she could pull it off but she was doing it, taking charge.

"I could never shoot myself," she said.

"It's the fastest way out," he said.

The Dramamine had hit her fast behind all that wine. She picked up four more Stelazine tablets and swallowed those with more wine. Like Dramamine, Stelazine had an antinausea effect; it would keep her from puking. Plus, it could really make you blotto. She looked at her pills: her cache of Librium, glossy black and green capsules — five hundred or more; Valiums in blue; Xanax all pearly white; red and gray Darvons; Ludiomils in good-morning-sunshine orange; tricolored Tuinal in red, redder, and baby blue; drab brown Triavil in the 4-10 proportion; there were pastel orange methadone diskets (just two); some chalk white meprobamate in the generic — wipe-you-out-for-sure; multicolored Dexedrine spansules, passionate purple Parnate; there were her Nembutals, and the sea green, let's-do-the-job-up-right Placidyl gel caps (Baby Dills) — the pills and capsules suddenly became an object of immense beauty, a treasure. It was better than unearthing a pirate captain's sea chest filled with glittering gold doubloons, shimmering jewels: emeralds, rubies, diamonds and chips of anthracite coal — better because pills did things. Drugs altered sensations. They could alter the worst sensation — permanently. They would do so . . . presently. All you had to do was swallow. What a relief to commit. To finally end it. She felt the richness and depth of color of the pills down to the roots of her hair. Pills so beautiful they made her hurt down to the roots of her hair.

Maybe it was the wine. No, really, it was the pills hitting home. Taken with wine on an empty stomach, they probably dissolved in seconds. She would have to make fast work of the cache and after she asked him what his plans were, she began swallowing the various pills and capsules with wine, ten at a time. It was like working on an assembly line and her hand began to tire. She got down thirty and had to rest a moment. She poured another glass of wine and was quickly back at it. This was her job. Her last job.

She heard the Zippo go off again. He was smoking. Thinking. There was too much of a dead space. He didn't know what to say. He was trying to psych her up and was out of gas himself. He didn't realize that he had made the final act possible. She was proud of herself. Your friends do sometimes come through. "Isn't that some bad shit at the refugee camp in Zaire?" she said merrily. She grabbed at the pills as the colors suited her mood.

"Yeah, bad. But if I'm laying in the gutter shitting and puking my guts out — and I have laid in gutters and done that, baby. Nobody comes along — no foreigner comes along with an IV tube to save my black ass. I ain't even expecting it."

"Geez, you sent me a postcard from Kinshasa, Zaire. What a great stamp. I got that card and I couldn't believe it — the Congo. He's in the Congo having an adventure and I'm stuck here. I used to wait for your letters, and the mailman, he was always so nice — when he came down the street — I'd be in the sun porch, he could see me — he'd give me the high sign when he had one of your letters. One week you were in Africa and the next week it was Finland. I thought, What is that boy doin'?"

"*That boy* got fucked up on some bad dope in Africa

actually. Pretty postage stamps is all they got in Kinshasha, believe me. Man, twenty lifetimes ago; but that's how life tricks you. You're thinking he's in Africa having an adventure and it's horrible in Africa — back home watching the Atlanta Braves by the air conditioner is where it's at. Everybody always thinks they're missing out. It's an illusion."

She felt a surge of resolution and finished off the fourth handful. She could see that it was impossible to take all of them but at least the barbiturates were in, the methadone was in, most of the Valium. Her stomach felt like a bowling ball. But she didn't feel *that* fucked up, only just a shade past mellow. When is it going to hit? Why hasn't it hit? What happened? *When is this fucking show going to end?* She pulled a half pint of Gordon's gin out of her nightstand drawer and grabbed another handful of poison. It was time to get serious. You could never be too sure. Then a big wave hit her and suddenly she felt like she was blowing out to sea. It was a good feeling. It involved a long expanse of time.

She heard a voice. From far away. It was Bobby. Sounded like he was a million miles away. His voice rang with a subtle twang of desperation. "I said, 'You really sound fucked up.' What kind of downers did you say you had?"

She said, "I didn't say."

"I'm asking."

"Fifteen years' worth," she said.

Shut up! Don't let the cat out of the bag now. Medic I. Stomach pumped. Is that what she wanted? Was this just a hysterical gesture?

"Fifteen years' worth. Are you serious?"

"Why?"

"Just let me in alone in the pharmacy with a grocery bag and five minutes. That's all I ever asked of God."

It was hard to judge, but Bobby sounded scared. Her head swirled.

Bobby said, "I just called to say goodbye, darlin'. I'm about to shuffle off the mortal coil. I'm headed fo' Booga-lousa where all is ultimately bound and from whence none return."

"That's why you scored?"

"Yes. To get the nerve up. Ever since I committed to the idea, a curious sense of calm *has* descended on me and I have felt somethin' like happiness for over a week or more, but now, however, the stark reality of the act has me alive with fear. If I take your meanin', you on the same path over some damn man. That's foolishness, abominable folly. I would not have announced my intentions. I was going to tell you I was headed for Chile but you let the cat out of the bag. I will not dissuade ya."

"It's too bad about the refrigerator. No one's going to use . . . it's not Carl. It's — "

"It's just a whole string of *Carl*, ain't it, darlin'?" He lit yet another cigarette. She could hear ice cubes rattling in a glass. Bobby said, "I can't hear you, darlin'."

Another wave swept over her, leaving her calm, un-afraid. It seemed like a long time had passed. An epic. She weighed ten thousand pounds. "Are you on the nod?" she said.

"Shot some scag. Mozart . . ." he said. "You paralyze the high cerebral processes and mortality ain't such a biggie. No! Let me rephrase that: You paralyze the *alligator* brain and the higher cerebral processes engage in an ultimate clarity and *then* you can overcome the will to live which is seated right they-ah at the base of ya skull; you see the thing in itself in its true colors. Nay! Indeed, you feel it in the very core of your bein'. Forgive me, my thinkin' is gettin' sloppy. It's all very simple. You anesthetize and the decision to live or die ain't a whole lot harder than choosin' between chocolate ice cream and butter pecan. I have been practicin', but I must confess, I'm a trifle shaky whenevah I try shovin' the barrel of this nine-millimeter in my mouth. Th' taste of gun solvent an' cold blue steel is rather vile. I wonder how those fellas in the classical literature and the history books could fall on they-ah swords without the benefit of narcotic. Was they valiant? Why, I hardly does think so."

There was another long pause. She punched the stereo remote a dozen times. It was becoming too much of an effort to speak. The CD changer clicked and suddenly the Moody Blues were doing "Nights in White Satin." A very long time before it had been *their* song. Now he was back into the Doors and what did she have beyond *The Best of the Doors*? And how could she possibly find it in this kind of fucked-up condition? Or get to it? Even now she was still doing her whole ineradicable thing, running her game: trying to please someone other than herself. She let the phone drop next to a stereo speaker. Bobby was Wally the Walrus again.

It took considerable effort but she was able to gulp down a last few swallows of gin and edge over away from the side of the bed. Some of the liquor rolled off her chin down her neck, over her satin pillowcase. Her special crystal nightcap goblet fell to the hardwood floor and smashed.

Shit. Bobby spent half his life behind bars and what did he know really? She knew what it was like to fall back into the inner darkness of the self. To implode nights and come to every morning like reconstituted misery. Come crawling back in the day cell of the puny withering body. She knew all about the black holes of the self. She knew all about prison, about clocks and calendars. She knew single soul-crushing seconds that lasted months of Sundays. She knew sixty-second hand sweeps that *were* life plus ninety-nine; hours of agony like twenty lifetimes of Methuselah; weeks that tormented like furnace years on the surface of Mercury, months of frozen black solitude like lost ages on the icy black moons of Pluto. All the while thinking about "why me?" and "poor me." She had heard the sound of the sun and the silence of the crystal moon reflected in still mountain lakes and that did not change a thing. Nothing was altered. It was a very bad deal and then on top of everything else, you had to die. *Why has God done this thing to me?*

She was no Helen Keller. She had never been up for any of this. Thanks to all of the pills and booze there was, at last, that wonderful sense of detachment. She could take the scissors and cut the thread any time now. Should have done it years ago but *finally* . . . the sentence was almost completed. Some people work in that damn gold pit in Brazil, some people sharecrop, some go to jail and . . . some contract muscular dystrophy. That's how it was. From the telephone receiver, Wally the Walrus was singing "Hookah tookah my soda cracker? Does your mama chaw tobacco?" Then his voice snapped sober and he said, "Oh, fuckall! *Let us stop talkin' falsely now, the hour's getting late.* Are you there, sugar? Or are you not there? Are you they-ah?"

She was too fucked up to speak. It was getting difficult to breathe. That's what happened when you o.d.'d. Your lungs filled up with water and you drowned. She thought you fell unconscious first. You were supposed to. Oh, well, at least it didn't hurt.

Bobby recited Bob Dylan, "*Outside in the cold distance, a wildcat did growl; two riders were approaching and the wind began to howl! . . . Yeeowwww!*"

She heard the report of a gunshot. God! Bobby! She tried to call his name but was so stoned she was crosseyed. Floating on the ceiling she was, looking down on the scene, looking at herself. She could hear her father, Corliss. Oh, Daddy, she thought. Daddy! My daddy!

It was just a neurological illusion. A psychic defense

against the ultimate fear. A Freudian defense mechanism — denial. Apparent reality.

"Nights in White Satin" was still playing on the CD. She had hit the replay button at least a dozen times, so she couldn't gauge time by counting the cuts on a disc. Her vision was too blurry to see the clock, but she could see the colors of the music stream out of the stereo speakers like streaks of red, white, yellow, and blue neon. Each note shot out into the air like a colored needle that compressed itself as its flight was spent, and then crystalized into a bright filigreed atom before it popped with a sharp electric snap and disappeared. *Electricity cost less today, you know, than it did twenty-five years ago! A little birdie told me so.* What *was* electricity?

The plan called for Mozart but . . . Bobby. Shit, Bobby. In the long run, take a friend, a really good friend over a lover any day. And if not a friend, then a dog. Maybe when she hit the other side, it would be like spirits and stuff and she and Bobby would meet and be together again with fresh, young healthy bodies. After all, they were checking out together. Practically within the same hour. She hoped he had the soul strength to hold it together and wait for her. Some of them just evaporated and disappeared and some others turned into angels. How did she know that? Suddenly she knew that. "Hiya, fancy meetin' you here." She and Bobby could walk hand in hand into the promised land. Not that physical bodies could reconstitute.

God! What if she ended up in a horrible pile of shit on the other side? An eternal pile of shit. Another truth hit home. The only hell she would ever know was about to end. In fact, it was over. She felt warmth and love. She wondered if there was a heaven. Seemed very likely now, contrary to what common sense had previously deemed. Hey, you see all this shit through the glass darkly until checkout time.

She felt light; soul on a string — a mere seven and one-half ounces. Truffles. Fluffy perfumed lace hankies. She felt warm. It was good. Bliss. Finally.

All she had to do now was wait for the next wave, wait for it to heave her up and carry her away. Just let go and ride out that breaking white crest into eternity. She was waiting for the next wave. Emerald wave, surfer girl.

Hang ten!

Pot Shack

"SHAKE AND BAKE" was much more than what you might call a gung-ho Marine. Second Lieutenant Baker took it one step further. To another realm altogether. This man could drop down a "junk-on-the-bunk" faster than the legendary Sergeant Chesty Puller ever snapped a four-fingered salute off the brim of his Eisenhower piss-cutter. Lieutenant Baker could put out a "junk-on-the-bunk" faster than Doc Holliday slapped leather in the O.K. Corral and pumped hot lead at a half dozen or so of the Clanton Gang from the nickel-plated barrels of his single-action Colt .44's. Dropped them Clanton boys like sacks of cement. This was how fast and emphatically Baker could lay out his gear. He could strip down his M-14 and reassemble it blindfolded faster than any other man in the company could complete the said feat with benefit of 20/20 vision.

Baker's boots and shoes were spit-shined like glass. The lieutenant could go through a tin of Kiwi dark brown shoe polish and a can of Brasso in a month whereas for most

Marines said quantities of the above were quite enough for a four-year tour. Give Baker a compass and a topographical map and one could bear witness to — indeed, become a part of — the elusive, semimystical Tao of military science. Such were Baker's leadership skills that his every thought, word, and action could propel a lesser personality into self-less, right actions in the service of the Big Green Machine. Under Baker's influence a Marine no longer thought about himself and his personal woe or travail, that Marine gladly followed orders for God and country. Even misfit individualists such as myself were mesmerized by Baker.

In garrison Baker always wore a fresh set of starched utilities with a blocked cap. Starched and ironed them himself. His creases were sharper than the standard issue Gillette Super Blue double-edged razor blades. Blake was not impressed with the laundry services available in Oceanside, California. But then when you wanted to be the most squared-away Marine that ever lived, how could you find satisfaction from a commercial laundry service? On a hot day after noon chow, Baker would take his second of three shaves, brush his teeth, shower, douse his armpits with Right Guard and change into a fresh uniform. Moreover, he passed the true test of a lifer in that Lieutenant Baker actually *liked* Marine Corps chow. He ate seconds of the grilled liver on Tuesdays, the fried rabbit that was served on Thursdays, and was the only man in the regiment known to eat the sliced carrot and raisin salad on a regular basis. I came to believe that if Lieutenant Baker had lived in ancient Greece and served the Spartan army in the most minor capacity, the Spartans would have won the Peloponnesian War and changed the subsequent course of Western civilization. A man austere enough to endorse grilled liver, fried rabbit, sliced carrot salad, or the ham and lima bean C-rats is capable of anything.

The lieutenant often took his meals with the enlisted men. He got to know them and care about them. He committed none of the unforgivable sins of the typical second lieutenant. Baker was smart enough to know that when he *didn't know,* he didn't have to pretend otherwise. At these times he would defer to the advice of anyone with a brighter idea, even a common private such as myself. Baker had a broad, wholesome, and charitable worldview, and of course, all of the Marines loved this guy. He was almost everything an officer should be. So it was only natural that when he came up for promotion to first lieutenant, he was passed over. We were slowly gearing up for Vietnam and the Marine Corps, in their infinite wisdom, determined that an officer working in S-1 that couldn't qualify at the rifle range would be better off selling refrigerators at the Sears store in Topeka, Kansas, than, say, maybe doing a shitload of paperwork in Saigon. On the other hand we had a captain who should have been selling refrigerators on the South Pole. Captain McQueen.

McQueen nailed me with thirty days mess duty after he strolled through the barracks one fine morning and spotted my open wall locker. It was a mess and I got mess duty. Thirty days of mess duty per year was allowable for anyone under E-4, but the pot shack was a special hell reserved for the worst of the shitbirds. Captain McQueen believed I was of this species because I hadn't been using enough Kiwi dark brown and Brasso. I wasn't spending enough of my clothing allowance on starched utilities. Furthermore my rifle was in "disgraceful condition," a special court-martial offence! Captain McQueen was of the opinion that the drill instructor that passed me through boot camp — Parris Island boot camp, mind you — was a moron. Captain McQueen said he must have been one "sorry-ass, piss-poor motherfucker" to let a "fucking shitbird" like me squeak through. What was the Corps coming to? And so forth. Furthermore, I was "the most piss-poor, sorry-ass excuse of a Marine" he had ever seen, and furthermore, if he wasn't in such a good mood, he would court martial my ass, have my single stripe removed and see if thirty days in the brig would motivate me along the lines of housekeeping matters. I had never heard quite so many *motherfuckers* come out of a gentleman's mouth, delivered with such vituperation and in such a short period of time since boot camp.

McQueen wasn't through, however. Who *was* my D.I.? And what the fuck was I doing laying on my rack reading *Ring* magazine and *Batman* comic books at nine hundred hours?

I stood at attention and barked off a lot of "yessirs" and "no sirs" and hoped that Captain McQueen would get a sore throat from screaming and just go away. I prayed he would not open my footlocker, which sat tantalizingly before him with my Master padlock hanging open on the footlocker's hinge and clasp. McQueen was in an energetic mood and kept on screaming as he upended my footlocker and spilled its contents onto the concrete floor of the barracks. But instead of spotting my lid of grass which spilled into plain view, McQueen reached for my Gillette double-edged safety razor and ordered me to dry-shave. I do believe such an act of torture is against the Geneva Convention Rules, especially when your Super Blues have gone three steps beyond "dull" — I mean, it brought tears to my eyes to have to shave in such a fashion but I complied anyhow, artfully kicking a pair of dirty skivvies over the lid of grass as I finished the job. Then I commenced to explain to Captain McQueen that I was a boxer in special services and that the reason I hadn't shaved was the fact that I had a fight coming up in three days. "A close shave will lead to a cut on my nineteen-year-old baby-pink face! Sir!" I said that the reasons I was reading *Batman* were both literary and psychological — I was about to go into battle, one-on-one with a Navy boxer name of Goliath. I said that Sergeant Wright, my D.I. back at Parris Island, had won the Navy Cross in Korea and never tolerated slackers. I was quite relieved to have the lid of grass concealed and confident that the boxing coach, Sergeant Myers, would take care of this mickey mouse hassle since Myers was tight with the colonel who himself happened to be a boxing buff. I was penciled in as the light heavyweight even though I had lost two of my last five fights. I smoked, drank, and had quite a gut going in addition to my grass habit. The team's only possible winners figured to be the Menares brothers, Sammy and Flash — twins from the Philippines, a featherweight and lightweight respectively, and our best bet, the middleweight, Hector Greene, who was fifteen pounds lighter than me and my chief sparring partner. Hector could punch harder than me and he was all but impossible to hit. I hated working with him. I figured my own chances against the Navy fighter as pretty much nil, but as a member of the squad I was free to train and sleep as I pleased and to be relieved of all duties extraneous to boxing. I tried to explain this to McQueen.

The captain understood my explanations to be altogether so much smart-mouthing and after a twenty-second phone call, I was over at the chow hall in white cotton mess clothes with a little fluffy white hat designed to prevent the quarter-inch hairs of my jarhead from falling into the massive pots and pans the cook's assistants kept hauling over to the pot shack by the tens and twenties.

The pot shack was a steam room barely big enough for two bantamweights, a box of Brillo pads, and the steady flow of pots and pans. It smelled of hot rancid grease and on the perimeter of the pot shack, where the heat fell from the

110 degree Fahrenheit core range, to the 80s and lower, and where the whitish-yellow grease congealed and was smeared all about the floor, it got into your boots, into the cuffs of your pants, on your white apron, on your hands, hair, and face. Where I worked with the pressure washers, the grease atomized and I breathed so much of it through the course of a day I was seldom hungry. The other Marine in the pot shack with me was a grunt from Oxford, Mississippi, larger than myself, and for the first couple of hours all he said to me was "Watch out, goddamn it, and hurry the fuck up! We runnin' nine mahls behind. Gait the cob oucher ass, boah." Mississippi had three teeth in his head, the most prominent being the lower left canine, tooth #22 as it is known in the trade. Due to severe gum recession and lack of collateral support, Mississippi's #22 tooth drifted to the center of his mouth like a tusk. It was about the size and shape of a Bolivian plantain.

My partner had a constant can of Coke going, which he referred to as "sar'dah"; I believe something in that popular beverage's secret ingredients had stripped the enamel off #22, making it amenable to stains. Mississippi smoked enough straight Camels to color it a kind of Boston Baked Bean brown. To watch Mississippi finger #22 or caress it with this thick tongue was just about enough to put me off the fried rabbit or grilled liver let alone a cold can of ham and limas. He said there was a cavity in it and he liked to keep it wet, like a beached whale, otherwise it hurt like shit. Since he was shy about twenty-five teeth, he wasn't the world's best enunciator, and because of his thick southern accent, I was able to ascertain little else of what he said. Nonetheless it took only about forty-five minutes before I was hating him as much as or more than I hated Captain McQueen.

Just before lunch the breakfast pots and pans were finished and one of the cooks signaled for us to grab some chow — bolt it down in the upright position, actually, since in the few moments we were away a new mountain of stainless-steel, brass, and aluminum cookware filled the pot shack. By midafternoon I was moving back and forth on the pot shack's slippery duckboard at all times very much aware of where my partner was standing and as I began to match his output, he began to hate me just a little less whereas my loathing for this lowlife hillbilly had no bounds.

We took the early supper and then worked until midnight finishing up the dinner pots and pans and the green marmite hot food containers that the mess crew brought in from the field where they had been serving the grunts on night maneuvers.

I staggered back to the barracks and put in a piss call with the night watch, fell asleep in my clothes, and when a Marine with a flashlight tapped me on the shoulder at two A.M., I jumped out of bed and made my way through the dark back to Mess Hall Number Three. A new guy, fresh from San Diego, was standing guard and called out, "Halt, who goes there!"

I was no seasoned Marine but neither was I in the mood for this kind of mickey mouse, so I said, "Bugs Bunny, motherfucker!" I heard the private chamber a round and thought a bullet in the back of the head wouldn't be so bad the way things had been going ever since I joined the fucking Crotch. The question *"Why* did you join? Why *did* you join? Etc. *Why did you fucking join?"* came up a lot in my interior monologues. It was my impenetrable Zen koan. I had not been coerced to join by the court; I was not a psychopath and I did not join because I became temporarily insane after a girl two-timed me. The pay was something like eleven cents an hour, so it wasn't for the money. I was not drafted but actually *joined* — of my own free will, sober and in full possession of all my mental faculties — the United States Marine Corps. I was convinced that such a fool as myself had never lived.

Mississippi was already dripping with sweat as I stepped inside the pot shack on my second day and pulled on my rubber gloves, which I later realized were useless and gave up altogether. "Whar th' fuck ya been? We nine mahls b'hind!" Liked to have smashed him in the face for about the ninety-fifth time in the last seventeen hours I had known him, but I reminded myself that the Marine Corps has some very bad places for people who don't get with the program. There was the brig McQueen threatened me with, which was pretty much like hell without the fires. There were the chain-link dog cages behind the brig where they threw you in naked except for your drawers, cotton, and where they cooled you off with a fire hose if you complained about the accommodations. Rations in the dog kennels consisted of three slices of stale bread and two canteens of water supposedly followed by a full meal every third day and then back to bread and water. My recruiting sergeant didn't exactly promise me a rose garden, but I certainly wish he would have told me about those dog kennels and the brig chasers with big biceps and billy clubs most of whom looked like close relatives of Charles "Sonny" Liston the then current heavyweight champion of the world. I wondered if my recruiter had any colored glossy brochures entitled "The Brig and Its Environs"; I would have liked to have seen them before I joined. I might have changed my mind and done something more sensible like joining the Foreign Legion.

Mississippi was sweating so bad he had his shirt and apron off. He was a redhead with plenty of freckles. There was no gut on him. He was rangy and muscular from humping the boonies. He had the standard USMC tattoo on his left deltoid and above that, emblazoned on his arm, was the name "Nudey." I took note, grabbed a fresh Brillo pad, and got busy. Just at the very moment the last of the jerricans were done, the cook's assistants bore down on us with sadistic grins and huge pots and kettles from morning chow. Some of these kettles, had they not been scrubbed so fastidiously, day after day, year after year — had they been blackened with soot, they would have put you in mind of kettles out in the dark jungles of Africa or the Amazon in which cannibals could cook two or three missionaries, a dog, and a mess of root vegetables all at once. And there were so many of them. And they kept coming! I tried to emulate Lieutenant Baker and get into the Tao of the pot shack. I tried to become a part of its essence, lose my identity, become a molecule or an atom — detach and just flow with it all, but that second day, all twenty-two hours of it, was just a complete motherfucker, pure and simple. Seventy-nine thousand, two hundred seconds of motherfucker.

I was back to the rack at midnight. After a suitable dose of self-pity, about 4.0 seconds, I fell asleep to the lullaby, earth-shaking sound of 220 artillery fired by grunts running night maneuvers. Dreamed I slid from Southern California all the way down to Patagonia and fell off the bottom of the globe into an abyss of dragons, toothy lizards, Gabon vipers, and black Norway rats crawling with typhus fleas. There were scorpions, Tasmanian jumping spiders with sharp ivory teeth, and various other eight-legged, predaceous arachnids with bad attitudes. Horrible as it was, this dream was preferable to the flashlight in the face at two A.M. I got up, took a quick piss, and then ran through the chill night air to Mess Hall Number Three watching red tracers arc across the skyline. An illumination round lit up the night like a full moon and I spotted the private fresh from San Diego standing guard again. I caught him smoking and told him to fuck off before he even challenged me. He just gave me a sly grin. We were both just a couple of shitbirds and we knew it, so why jack around? There was enough hassle for everybody as it was.

Inside I expected green marmite cans up-the-ass and I was more than right. The ensuing shift in the pot shack was very much the same as the preceding, except that I was even more tired and the color was leached out of my hands as they were filled with dozens of stainless-steel slivers. I began to long for the dull, sluggish, futile, languorous and aimless days of life on the boxing team. The pot shack was nothing but hustle.

That afternoon, Sergeant Myers, the boxing coach, showed up while I'm struggling with a grungy-ass pot caked with mashed potatoes. "Where in the hell have you been?" he says.

I started to explain about my underuse of Kiwi shoe polish, Brasso, and rifle cleaning gear when Mississippi shot me a look of hatred for my falling output. Myers said he would talk to Captain McQueen and after he left, like a prisoner on Death Row, I began to entertain the slight hope that the governor might be a commie liberal opposed to the ultimate punishment. Or that Joan Baez would sing a sweet song to Lyndon Johnson, have him crying his eyes out and soon dispatching *Air Force One* to pick up such an intelligent, sensitive and promising young man as myself, and send me to Harvard College on free government scholarship after a two-week vacation at Camp David.

That night as per usual, I went to bed at midnight. Piss call at two. The green marmite cans, followed by aluminum bowls used to whisk scrambled eggs, mix pancake batter, and concoct hamburger and white gravy on toast, e.g., "shit on a shingle." There were frying pans from the officers' mess filled with crusted egg, bacon and sausage grease, empty pans of biscuits 'n' gravy, and an endless supply of hot greasy bakery trays the size of solar satellite panels. There were large ladles, spoons, carving knives, and peculiar little dagger utensils that looked like Pygmy spears. Then came the marmite cans again and the beginning of the lunch mess. If you were lucky and you really hustled you could squeeze in a piss and a cigarette about three in the afternoon. The heavy shit came down after that — the supper mess was worse than both the breakfast and lunch jobs together. Mess Hall Number Three was feeding a couple of thousand men a day. We were doing double duty since the Fifth Regiment was ready to ship out to Vietnam and their chow hall was already secured. Mess Hall Number Three was feeding those troopers as well as our own. Still, the Marines working the scullery could clean up the mess hall exactly two hours after the last Marine was served chow and they could go back to their barracks, smoke cigarettes, and grab an hour of sleep before reporting back. They could take a shower or have a game of volleyball. The action in the pot shack, however, was unending. I began to fantasize on the various ways I would like to murder Captain McQueen.

To the Marines pulling mess duty in the scullery, Mississippi and I became objects of mystery, fascination, and much speculation. We looked like a couple of Haitian zombies only we moved faster. Even the worst of the shitbirds were never condemned to more than three days in the pot shack. Geneva Convention. Soon I was pushing my second straight week and Mississippi, I don't know how long. There was no salvation from Sergeant Myers and of course, no intervention from that wonderful, talented, and elegant entertainer, Ms. Baez.

I really began to think it would have made more sense to join the French Foreign Legion. They had better uniforms and the thought of a posting in Sidi bel Abbes, Algeria, had a certain romance to it. I mean North Africa, check it out: the Atlas Mountains, desert sands, the pyramids, the Sphinx, Berber nomads, camels, date palms, and a policy of "no questions asked." There was the tradition of General Patton, Field Marshal Rommel, and T. E. Lawrence. Of course all I know of Patton came after the fact, when I saw George C. Scott in the role, slapping some poor soldier across the face for cowardice in an otherwise boring movie. Peter O'Toole's movie *Lawrence of Arabia*, which I saw prior to my enlistment, was a lot better. Lawrence, like Baker, seemed to have discovered the elusive Tao of the military arts. The harder things were, the better he liked them.

I decided the best way to murder Captain McQueen was by sleep deprivation. I heard it took about three months to kill a man in such a fashion. I would force McQueen to stand at attention in a brightly lit cell. Whenever he blinked his eyes more than twice in a week, I would order one of my legionnaires to hoist him up by his heels and whip the soles of his bare feet with a sackful of centimes. "How long are you going to make me stay awake, mon Commandant?"

"I'm going to make you stay awake until you die."

In 1964, Camp Pendleton was nothing but a hundred square miles of Quonset huts and lots of scorched foothills with names like "Little Agony" and "Big Agony" and "Sheepshit Hill." These were hills the Marines humped and were named accordingly. Big Agony was very bad, Little Agony could half kill you, and a run up Sheepshit Hill required rock climber's gear. It was nothing but foothills and Quonset huts and one shade of green. There were no camels or palm-infested oases choked with humid vegetation. There were no magnificent sweeps of desert with buzzards flying high in the arid blue sky. There were no nights when you could see magnificent soul-inspiring constellations of stars. There was just the fucking pot shack where every day was a repeat of the day before.

Mississippi kept awake on Coca-Cola. I did so by drinking thirty plus cups of coffee. I had my head in so many pots and pans for so many days, I was beginning to hallucinate. Once when I accidentally knocked over a full can of Mississippi's sar'dah, he grabbed me by the throat with his left hand while he dug his thumb in my eye and squeezed my face with his right. "You ever do that again, I'll kill your fuckin' Yankee ass, you Yankee cocksucker."

"Yeah! Yeah! Yeah!" I said.

Mississippi was a scary guy. On a prior occasion I tried to get neighborly and he took a swing at me for calling him "Nudey." It was a good punch and I was tired but because of trained reflexes I was just able to give him a head slip. He tried to follow up with a left hook but I had my hands up by then and stepped away from the punch as Mississippi slipped on the soapy duckboard and knocked himself cold when he banged his head against the sharp edge of the steam compressor's floor brace. I let him lie there as I resumed my activities. When he got up about ten minutes later, he had a goose egg on his forehead and there was no more fight in him. I told him to get his fucking hillbilly ass in gear. "Sleeping on the job, why mercy me," I said. "Get up. We're nine mahls behind. Get the cob outcher ass!"

Mississippi liked to talk to himself. He liked to refer to our beloved Corps as a "goddamn, green, sumbitch, cocksuckin' motherfucker."

On this matter he got no argument from me. But his negativity was infectious. By the third week I had passed through the anger stage and became a neutral Haitian zombie. While I was used to the marvelous nuance, versatility, and precision of the word "fuck" and lived in a universe where "fuck" was every other word, more or less, all of

Mississippi's "cocksucks" and "motherfucks" delivered in a toothless drawl were making me a very depressed zombie. I could see no light at the end of the tunnel.

One afternoon just into the fourth week Second Lieutenant Baker poked his head into the pot shack and said, "Who did this to you?"

I said, "It ain't no biggie, sir. Just pulling a little mess duty here."

Lieutenant Baker said, "Go back to the barracks, take a shower, and get some rest." He turned to Mississippi and said, "The same goes for you, Marine."

The way it turned out, the way Lieutenant Baker got past Captain McQueen was this: everybody from the Fifth Regiment who hadn't qualified at the rifle range in less than a year was pulled off the line and sent to the range. Lieutenant Baker went to the colonel with a list of men who had not qualified from our own platoon and although it should not have been, my name was on that list. The reason I had a chevron on my collar had to do with the fact that I shot the highest score in my boot camp platoon. That chevron separated me from being the lowest thing on the planet, a private in the Marine Corps. Being a private in the USMC is a couple of notches lower than being an untouchable in India — lower than a harijan haricot with a case of AIDS, wet leprosy, and halitosis. You could be an E-1 in the Army, Navy, Coast Guard, or Air Force but you would not be so low. In 1964 a private in the Army could just as well be some guy from Yale who just earned a doctorate in astrophysics and got drafted. A man could join the Navy and actually see the world, or a man might join the Air Force because of the food or training — but the Marines? I already listed the reasons: forced by law, insanity, and two-timed by your woman.

The next morning a troop transport left for the range at

0510 hours. Lieutenant Baker, Mississippi, and myself were on that truck and as we waited for dawn in the freezing chill, huddled in our lined field jackets and blowing on our frozen fingers, a range coach came by with a carbide lamp to blacken our rifle sights and flash suppressors. As soon as the sun cracked the horizon, the field jacket came off and sweat began to bead on my forehead. Two hours later it was running down the crack of my ass.

The one thing the Marines can do better than anyone is shoot. To qualify at the range you must be able to shoot in the prone position, the seated position, and in the standing offhand position. You must shoot in rapid fire, and within the context of a more relaxed time frame, at various distances up to five hundred yards. Using your rifle sling, it is possible to hold the rifle steady and draw a bead. The Marine Corps shooting technique involves four phases. Breathe, relax, aim, squeeze. This is known by the acronym BRASS. It works for just about everyone. I mean, it's got a far higher success rate than Alcoholics Anonymous. As we practiced our shooting I could immediately see what the problem was with Lieutenant Baker. He would take the deep breath, blow it out, and then aim. But instead of squeezing the trigger, he would jerk. The reason for this had to do with the BRASS technique. Just after you take a deep breath and blow it out, relax and aim, time stops. Your concentration becomes so intense that all of time stops from here to the farthest reaches of the Milky Way. From here to all hell and gone. The next part should be easy, you just squeeze, but in the millisecond of stop-time, Lieutenant Baker's eyes would glaze over as he went past the Tao of military science and entered the realm of cosmic consciousness. When his brain finally screamed for him to inhale, he would jerk off a round and miss the target altogether and then look at you with a stupid blank stare.

Mississippi, who turned out to be a pretty decent fellow after a good night's sleep, and who happened to feel rightfully grateful to escape the pot shack, tried to teach Lieutenant Baker a method of shooting he learned plunking squirrels, possum, and deer in the sloughs and piney woods of his homeland. He had Baker line his finger along the edge of his M-14 barrel, point it at the target and then let his eye follow his finger to the target. This worked very well for the officer until we got back to the five-hundred-yard line. There, in spite of his thick G.I. glasses, which were so ugly they were known as "birth control devices," Lieutenant Baker simply could not see. But he was shooting so well in the closer ranges, we figured he could kiss off the five hundred and still qualify. On that day, at showtime, Baker, who had failed so many times in the art almost every Marine excelled at, panicked and shot high, missing his target completely at the two-hundred-yard prone-position rapid fire. By the time we moved back to the five hundred, Baker was pale with the knowledge that he would have to shoot a perfect score to qualify in the least of categories, that of "marksman." No doubt he was also thinking of the refrigerator and appliance department at the Sears & Roebuck Company in Topeka, Kansas.

I, on the other hand, had never shot so well in my life. After we collected our brass cartridge casings, Mississippi drew up next to me and said, "He ain't gonna hit the broadside of a barn, boah; what say ah put five rounds through the bull's eye and y'all pick up on the other five?"

"That's a Rog," I said. "That's a definite."

I was shooting four positions to the right of Lieutenant Baker while Mississippi was directly next to him in the fire lane to the left. When the butt pullers yanked up the targets we all commenced firing. Mississippi grouped five rounds in the heart of Baker's bull's eye. Then it was my turn. I grouped three shots in the same spot then put a round low into the second ring. I cursed myself. Even if I made my last shot, Baker would not qualify. Mississippi tossed me a look of disgust. I shook my head in disbelief and proceeded to put the next round in my original group. The targets went down and came up with white paper ribbons showing where each shot had scored. The field observer studied Lieutenant Baker's target with his binoculars. "I'll be a son-of-a-bitch. There's eleven rounds in that target." There was a quick conference with the range officer, who said that someone must have shot wide, most likely Mississippi who was directly to the lieutenant's left, and who had hit his own target a sum total of four times. Mississippi was cursing, pretending like he was highly pissed with himself.

My range observer pulled a chocolate doughnut out of a white sack, took a sip of hot coffee, and said, "You could have had a nice score, Marine. Too bad you blew it." A group of nonshooters had congregated around me in the hope I might shoot a perfect score. "Nerves," I said. I had my chance to be a hero and then just like that I was suddenly just another fucked-up PFC in the Big Green Machine. I think the fact that I knew I could have enjoyed a little ego enhancement is what caused me to blow my next to last shot at Lieutenant Baker's target. I was a victim of ambiguity.

Then the range officer announced that Baker would *not — roger, he would not —* have to repeat the five hundred. Because of the tight grouping in the heart of the bull's eye, the range officer deemed the eleventh shot on Baker's target to be a stray and qualified the man.

When it dawned on the lieutenant that he passed, when he realized he would be promoted to first lieutenant and could re-enlist and go to Vietnam where the life expectancy of a platoon commander was about eighty-nine seconds, he became the happiest man on earth. Everybody was whooping it up and slapping him on the back, even me. You go a year without smiling or experiencing a single endorphin passing through your brain, a smile can be a very exhausting exercise. I had a sore face for three days but in my heart I was glad because I did what every Marine would do, I helped a buddy. All the guys in our platoon threw a little party for Baker when he got his silver bars. We chipped in and bought him a new rifle cleaning kit. Never saw Baker after that party. Much later, when I got to Da Nang, somebody told me he got greased the second week he went out on the line. You might think selling appliances in Topeka, doing anything in Topeka, Kansas, would have been preferable, but Baker, who was assigned to the rear echelon, volunteered for the line. I believe he died happy. I do not suffer from guilt for helping him get there without proper marksmanship skills. Topeka would have been his pot shack. Would have turned him into a Haitian zombie.

Captain McQueen continued to carry a hard-on for me. Most of your run-of-the-mill assholes have better things to do than sustain a grudge but McQueen was the king of assholes. Not only was I off the boxing team, I lost my gig as a typist in S-2. Got sent to the grunts along with Mississippi where I began to go through the Brasso and Kiwi dark brown at an accelerated rate. Mississippi got his three teeth pulled and was fitted with his first set of government-issue dentures. With teeth in his mouth he was altogether impossible to understand but one night when his gums were bleeding and he pulled his dentures out, he told me the story about his tattoo. He said he had no recollection of getting it and had no idea who or what "Nudey" was, but whatever, he didn't like it. Mississippi's real name was Homer Haines. "Homer" of course was a fighting word right up there with "Nudey." The grunts who knew Mississippi called him "Bud."

In the infantry, I soon humped my gut off and in the process I learned that there were officers that were such nitpickers they made Captain McQueen seem like a pure candyass. Mississippi said he had him a mind to join recon. It was bad there but it was fair. I was young with less than a year in the Corps and more than three to go. Time was dragging heavy on my ass. So when I ran into my old buddy Jorgeson, my mainline man from the Island, and he too said there were openings in recon, where they take awful to a whole new level, I introduced him to Mississippi. We all got good and drunk at the EN Club, talked about jumping out of airplanes and shit, and then as soon as we ran out of beer money, we went over to headquarters company and signed the transfer papers in a hot second. A *hot* second, bro.

I'm not stupid, and I'm not pleading drunk. I don't like awful. But awful/awful can sometimes be very interesting.

Dynamite Hands

JUAN FLEW Johnny Pushe coach class up to Washington State to fight Seattle's light heavyweight, a white kid got him a record of 20–0 called Irish Tommy Wilde. The word was out: This guy is so bad he eats glass for breakfast, pisses razor blades, and shits hot gravel. Truth is, his handlers had fed him some easy targets to develop his confidence and get everybody all whipped up for payday, but Tommy Wilde still had to undergo the test by fire. Sooner or later you got to show or got to go. People want to know if you got juice. Some of that *boom boom*. They want to know if you've got that essential thing.

Our guy, Johnny, looked to be that test, proof positive. Johnny was kind of a perennial number nine, a solid fighter but no puncher, a guy with a weight problem, known for carousing. Juan and Lolo chewed on toothpicks and shrugged like what-tha-fuck when Tommy Wilde's business consortium came by to check out the action. Juan knew they was coming and had Johnny go into the locker room and drink a full gallon of water. Johnny comes out to meet them smoking a cigarette and by the time Wilde's people left, they were rubbing their hands in glee. They had Johnny figured for a sure thing. Flying back to Seattle, they were probably already lining up their next fight, some headliner action: Atlantic City, Vegas, Tahoe, whatever. They were going to recoup their investment and march straight to the title. Didn't know jack shit about the fight game, and their mind just wasn't on Johnny Pushe.

This was not lost on Juan. He is a shrewd guy, and he was still hungry. Although he had come close, he'd never taken a fighter all the way. He had a burning desire, and Johnny, with Johnny, you know — hey, just maybe. You till the soil, plant the seed, fertilize, and pray for the right combination of sunshine and rain. And hope God is smilin' down.

Juan ran his ass ragged getting Johnny in almost decent condition. He worked harder than Johnny. Lolo was always kidding him about it. "Here come Juan, look at heem go, mon. Roadrunner!" Juan was a trainer by day, Johnny's babysitter by night, and on the graveyard shift he was a bakery distributor. Training Johnny for this fight, he did nothing but hustle. Kept Johnny out of clubs, away from nooky, away from every temptation. Got him up at four for a run. Back for his shower, fixed him a couple of soft-boiled eggs, toast, and a pot of green tea for breakfast. Then he set the alarm clock so Johnny could rack out until noon. All Johnny had to do was get up and drink some more tea, lounge around for a while, read the paper, and then down to the gym at three. After that it was rare steak and vegetables, a little TV, and to bed at eight, with Juan crashed on the couch mapping out strategy. Each day the pounds were coming off Johnny and he was getting stronger both physically and mentally. Training for a big fight is no day at the beach. Boxing, you do it right and it's a holy activity.

I did my part by showing Johnny how to juice up his firepower. I showed him punches I learned early in life while I was doing a little sabbatical in Mexico City Correctionals. This one old dude stood me against the wall in the prison yard and showed me all about dynamite hands. It's not a secret really, just something that went out of style. Fighters now are into weights, Nautilus and shit, and more concerned with looking nice and buffed out than winning fights. They can get downright vain.

Anyhow, what you do, you put your left hand against the wall not quite fully extended and you press with all your might. It's an isometric thing. Clamp your jaw and press so hard you think you're going to crush your teeth. You do the same with the right. Same thing. You do your hooks, uppercuts, you go through your whole arsenal. You do each punch in sets of five, three times a day. You won't get big biceps, but one day, all of a sudden what you got is a pair of dynamite hands. That *boom boom* I was talking about. Pure TNT.

I showed this to Johnny and he got real curious about it. Pretty soon he had a right hand like the hammer of Thor. Before I came along, he couldn't crush a grape, and suddenly he was ringing everybody's bell with this punch, which, on top of having thunder in it, was sneaky fast. Johnny didn't tell me thanks or anything. He just said, "I always wondered how a Mexican with skinny arms could punch. Huh huh huh!" Johnny is a smart guy in his way, but he laughs like he's got an IQ of 52.

Another good thing they did — why Juan had to babysit — Johnny went six weeks without sex. Modern guys say it doesn't make a bit of difference, but if you go six weeks without sex you will become just a little bit mean. Johnny is a cool 'n' easy guy but for this fight he had an edge. I know. I drove him and Juan to the airport in my beat-up Cadillac

and Johnny was spitting fire. Mean. You could smell hormones in that car. I ain't lyin'. The very air around Johnny
had electricity in it. Sparks were flying off the man: Frank-
enstein at charge-up time. *Zzzzt! Pow! Bap! Boom!*

A bunch of us guys from the gym watched the fight over
in Lolo's living room. It was an ESPN main event. The plan
was for Johnny to work up a lather in the dressing room,
shadowbox for six hard rounds, and then go out and nail
this guy. Catch him cold. This is what Juan came up with
when he crashed on Johnny's couch to baby-sit, when he
was suffering from sleep deprivation, when he was red-eyed.
It was sound thinking. Johnny knew he'd better catch
Tommy Wilde cold, 'cause no matter how hard he trained,
he wasn't gonna have the gas for ten rounds. The plan was
a gamble and we all knew it, but it was the only way. Wilde's
people were expecting a hope-you-get-lucky boxing match
from an over-the-hill, no-ambition, no-punch, no-gas-tank
number nine. Wilde had cash dollars on his brain and was
already thinking of the light heavyweight title as his right;
he was shopping for real estate, talking to investment bro-
kers and picking out kelly green boxing outfits and emerald
jewelry. He wasn't concentrating on the here and now. He
wasn't expecting tough-as-nails from Johnny Pushe, and he
sure as heck wasn't ready for dynamite charges bouncing off
his jaw. But then we never stopped to consider that Irish
Tommy Wilde might have a little *boom boom* himself.

It was a great fight. Johnny started clipping early. He
wobbled Wilde in the first round, then dropped him twice
in the third, and almost put him away in the first few seconds of the fifth. Johnny didn't take a backward step. He
bulled forward, strong and confident, but Tommy Wilde
wasn't exactly running away. It wasn't like he was a sucker
for a straight right, a left hook, or whatever, like he was
making some kind of stupid mistake over and over again.

His trainer was top class; it was his management who failed to scout out the situation. Wilde fought real good, but Johnny was onto the man's patterns. He was doing the high calculus of the ring. The way he was setting this guy up was inspired. But then after the seventh we started to worry. The glaze cleared from Wilde's eyes and Johnny was running on fumes by now.

The referee was on the take, that was obvious. Whenever Johnny put his man in hurt, the ref was stalling to reinsert a mouthpiece, retape the man's gloves, warning Johnny for borderline punches and actually taking a point away for an alleged low blow. Then Johnny went down on a slip and the ref gave him a standing eight — almost called a TKO. It was outrageous. After we saw this referee, we knew the fight couldn't go to the cards because the judges were in the pocket. It had to be a knockout or nothing.

Johnny started to sag after seven and Wilde, young and tough, came on in a big way. But then Johnny found something down deep and he took over again. Like he drank a six-pack of ass kick or something. Showed some heart. As soon as it looked like Johnny was going to put on the kill, Wilde would come back. We were in the wave and then out of the wave. In and out. Out and in. It was fucking crazy.

Nobody expected Johnny to extend to the full ten rounds. When they gave Wilde a split decision, oh, man! There was big-time depression in Lolo's living room. As high as we got, we got that low. We knew the price that had been paid — roadrunner! — and to end up seeing our guy getting robbed, man. There ain't no justice in the universe, any fighter knows that much but — oh, man.

WHEN Johnny got home he didn't cry about losing since with all those knockdowns on national TV, he knew he would get another shot. He'd got a reprieve from the short-order-cook vocation. We gave him a hero's welcome when he came back to the gym. He'd won the fight, of that there was no doubt, and we wanted to hear his story. You see one of the best fights in your life and you want to hear it from the man's lips.

Instead, what Johnny told everyone about was how he sparred with boxers at the Monroe Reformatory afternoons, about all these rough motherfuckers in prison and then about how Juan drove him up near Stevens Pass every morning so Johnny could run at a high altitude and store up extra red blood cells — the cells that carry oxygen. Johnny told us about waterfalls and shit. Mountain vistas and shit. The prophet comes back from the wilderness and starts talking about bluebirds and squirrels. I'm not lyin'.

He said Juan had him running twelve and fifteen miles up there on backcountry timber roads. He said, "Yeah, no shit, one morning I'm running up this road, a one-lane dirt job, and here comes this *bear*."

Scotty, a lightweight of Ugandan origin, said, "Whoot the fook you talkin' aboot, Johnny, a fookin' bear?"

"It's no lie, man, this was a big-ass bear. I measured this sucker, 'cause I figured I'd tag him on the end of the nose with a jab — maybe a double jab, and then come over on top with a right. I'm hoping the bear's nose is tender, like they say the bull's is. What the fuck do I know about live-stock, right? I'm not some fuckin' Montana-head. I'm a civilized person that grew up in a city! What the fuck would *you* do? Tell me about your fight strategy, man."

"You got to improvise," I said, "when the shit hits the fan in such a fashion, and do whatever. Fall down on your belly and pretend like you're a sack of greasy old, dirty old clothes."

"Play the possum," Chester said. "If you was Goldilocks, went into the cottage and ate the Quaker's oatmeal?"

"Hey!" Lolo says. "Chester, you're crazy, mon."

Chester's eyes flared. "That's right. I'm crazy. You got that straight. I'm crazy, man! I'm a crazy motherfucker. Goddammit, that's for sure." Chester bit at a piece of tape hanging from his left handwraps, cocked his head at a right angle and looked off into space in a vacant way. The way he stood there smacking his lips, biting at the tape, made me think he was going to have a fit.

Everyone got quiet; it was the look we sometimes saw on his face before he had a seizure. Suddenly Chester stuck his left hand in his right armpit and began flapping his elbow like he was a large bird of prey with a broken wing. He began bobbing his head and started a kind of high leg-pumping action like he was trying to follow a Jane Fonda exercise video. Chester's dance was antithetical to the salsa music coming from Cuba's boom box, but it didn't seem to matter. He screamed, "I'm *crazy*, man!" He cried, "*Ahh feel good!* I feel nice, sugar and spice, now!"

Meantime, Johnny was still staring at me waiting to know if I had some strategy for fist-fighting a bear. He held onto his own beat and waited for Chester to stop making noise. No matter what Chester did, Johnny considered Chester as little more than outer environment. Johnny was still running on stacked-up hormones, acting highly pissed. He kept on moving in on me, violating any reasonable concept of personal space. The other fighters looked away from Chester and began to focus on the two of us.

"Double jab and a right over the top," I say.

Johnny laughed and said, "Right, an' hope you get lucky. A double jab and a right over the top. I sure as fuck ain't gonna rassle it."

Chester said, "Hey, Johnny, was it one a' them *grizzly* bears?"

"I don't know, fuck! It was just a bear. I don't know classifications, I told you. A big fuckin' bear, all right? He comes flying down the road right out a' nowhere."

"Whachew do when you seen that bear, Johnny?" Chester said. His voice was husky from an old injury to the larynx.

"Roadrunner!" Lolo said with a crooked, goofy smile.

"I wiggled, man," Johnny said. "I did the electric slide trying to spook that sumbitch off. But he comes right down on me. I started backpedaling until I could turn and run. Then I set a world record for the mile run wearing combat boots."

"Roadrunner!" Lolo said.

"That's right," Johnny said. "I don't know — having a bear chase you, you survive it, it's good information. I stand before you today with no deep gut fear of any man alive."

Chester slammed a speed bag with the butt of his hand. "Rassled a bear at the carnival, man. Cuba and me was drunk. He put me up to it, man, encouraged me to play the fool. Afterward I stunk so bad my ma made me towel off with gazzoline, man. A bear on you as bad as a skunk. Funky, man!"

"Hey!" Lolo said. "Let Johnny tell the story."

Chester puffed up. He walked over to the tall yellow windows by the fire escape and looked down at the traffic outside. "Lolo always tellin' everybody, 'Hey!' Fuckin' *'Hey!'* Fuckin' Lolo, you 'hey'-in' me out. Everybody in the fuckin' gym be sayin', *'Hey!'*"

"Hey!" Lolo said. He always held a gym towel around his neck and now he took it off and made like he was going to snap Chester on the ass with it. Chester scooted back.

"There he goes with 'hey!'" Chester squared his shoulders and did his take on Lolo. "*'I goes up to this guy and I tells him, 'Hey!'* 'Cause fuckin' Lolo be a bad motherfucker. You hear what I'm sayin', make his voice go *'hey!'*"

"Let Johnny tell us about the bear. How about it?" Lolo pulled the cord from the boom box and the bag punchers and rope skippers and the fighters doing calisthenics all gathered around Johnny, who said, "I ran the four-minute mile. The next thing I knew, it was gone. Crazy son-of-a-bitch. I mean he *had me*. I checked out a Marlin Perkins tape; they can do thirty and they're highly unpredictable. Even that one in the cartoon, Yogi or whatever. He ain't normal. He's in serious need of psychiatric care. I mean, I don't want an individual like that livin' in my neighborhood. Fuck all that save-the-grizzly shit. They ought to kill all of them. What the fuck good are they, anyhow? Here I am now with another loss on my record." Johnny was saying this like he was unhappy but it was just an act, you could tell.

Lolo said, "Johnny, man, they're good for the planet. God put them here. They're good for the ecosystem."

"Good fuckin' how?"

Suddenly, Lolo had his fingers out, tabulating. "They go into hibernation, then come out of it all grouchy, eatin' the salmon and stuff. Gooseberries. And then there's also what's-his-hat — Smokey. Mon, only you can prevent forest fires."

Chester began to laugh. "That bear showed Johnny the law of the jungle."

Johnny turned to Chester. The tightness in his shoulders melted away, the jive dropped out of his voice and Johnny took on a scholarly air. He spoke slowly and deliberately, in a whisper. "I lost my color vision. Everything happened in slow motion. I was running away but it wasn't doing me any good. With one swipe of the paw, I'm gone. Pound-for-pound, a bear is one of the strongest things alive. One swipe of the paw and man, it looked like he was ready to snag me, too. I was thinking, it's strange, but I was thinking, Good, this motherfucking life is over. I don't have to go through no more, get old, rot with cancer, become a bum or whatever it is that's in the cards for Johnny Pushe. I don't know, for the first time I don't know how long, I experienced peace."

"That was before the fight. Now you ain't scared a' nobody," Chester said.

Johnny brightened. "I carried that slow-motion business into my fight. I seen his punches coming in and slipping them was the easiest thing in the world. I had all of the moves, man. I'm not braggin', but it was a great night. Win, lose, who cares? I got so fuckin' high. Chester feels good? Hey! *I* feel good, motherfucker! It was beautiful. I can live the next three years off that night."

JOHNNY picked up his headgear and mouthpiece and headed for the locker room. Like, that was it. That was the story. Meanwhile, in spite of a sore hand which had already been broken twice, I was gloved up to go in with Chester when a brash, mouthy black kid from the Kane Street neighborhood came in with a retinue of friends in gold chains, leather jackets with fifty-five zippers each, and White Sox ball caps worn backward. This guy said, "Where's Johnny Pushe? I need some work."

Juan was not running a big-time gym, we were used to walk-in trade like this. Lolo said Johnny was in the shower, and I heard Chester say, "Hey, I'll give you some work. I'm Chester Werthe."

Kane Street screwed up his face. "Chester? What kind of name is Chester?"

"Chester Werthe, you motherfucker. I fought 'em all. Get your ass up here." Chester started to drool a little and grunt, rocking back on his heels. For a minute I thought he now might be about to have a fit, but then he leveled out. Before an epileptic attack, Chester makes strange noises, like a man drowning in air. Like an animal in rut. *Mmm grrr mmm!*

Because of my hand, I hadn't planned on doing much more than move with Chester, so I said okay, and relinquished my ring time. Suddenly this new guy was in the ring throwing serious leather. Lolo was calling, *"Tiempo, tiempo!* Time!"

He hopped up on the ring apron and went over to the new guy's corner, where all of his pals were whooping it up, and if you didn't know it before, by now you knew there were some serious cocaine vibes in that corner. Lolo pulled at the gym towel he wore over his neck, dipped his head low and whispered to this guy. "Hey, what's the matter with you, blood? Lighten up. That's Chester. He takes Dilantin, mon." Chester heard this and said, "That nigger ain't hurtin' me none!"

Kane Street said, "Nigger, I had you stagglin'!"

"You don't tee off on Chester," Lolo said. "And no racial remarks. Act like sportsmen!"

"Well, he's in the ring and he's standin' there. I want some work."

"Call time," Chester said, chomping his mouthpiece and giving his headgear a little slap with his glove. His eyes locked on his opponent with grim determination.

You could see that Lolo was ambivalent. He wanted to let Chester have his self-respect, but Chester was brain-damaged. His epilepsy came from a right hand I landed on his temple during a fight over in Paris, France.

Chester still had something of a name then. He was the number five WBA middleweight and I was a fighter on the way up, but just another Mexican with a string of knockouts, which is a hard act to keep going. Anyhow, Chester's opponent sprained his ankle — actually this French fighter was scared after he got a look at Chester's fight clips and faked an injury. Juan had me flown over on two days' notice. Flew me over to fight a stablemate — a friend. Juan was better than most, like I said. He was pretty straight, but really, that was low, and I was low to go for it.

Chester fought with absolutely no regard for his own welfare. His face was so ugly he didn't care what happened to it and that's how he fought. Like angel dust, like PCP. The French guy saw Chester's fight clips and lost his nerve. He didn't know Chester was shot — you wouldn't — but I was sparring with him every day and I knew it, and I also knew that he was weak from making weight. I knew that when Juan had put me in as an alternate.

I thought by taking him out quick I would be doing him a favor, but what I didn't calculate was the effect of the crowd on Chester. For a crowd, he could rise to the occasion, and we got into a hellacious fight, Juan working his corner and Lolo working mine. It seemed so strange. I mugged the poor bastard. I got him drunk and then I nailed him with the worst kind of punch — the one you don't see coming.

Four days unconscious didn't help, neither him nor me. Chester got a $7,000 payday — it wasn't nothing but shoeshine money, popcorn change. I saw a Judas payment around $2,500. Chester was just an accident waiting to happen, but it gave me a rotten feeling.

Max Baer, Ray Robinson, and Emile Griffith killed men in the ring — Ray Mancini — it happens. When you are a boxer, putting people in trouble is your business, but I knew Chester and I had to live with him. I should have said I wouldn't fight a stablemate. But I was greedy for fame and fortune. I won't deny it. Most likely the same thing would have happened to Chester in a bar or back alley for no payday at all. It's just that it wouldn't have been on my conscience.

I was thinking of this and of how far Chester had fallen when Lolo clicked his stopwatch, called time again and this guy who just walked in off the streets started nailing Chester, formerly a world-class fighter. Kane Street was a counterpuncher and he was letting Chester walk head-on into his punches. Mugging him. Getting him drunk.

Chester couldn't adjust, couldn't slip, or duck, bob and weave, side-to side — nothing. He never could. He just pressed after the new guy in a balls-out windmill assault. This had worked a few years back when he was in shape and rang up a string of knockouts, but he had since been anni-hilated mentally and once that happens you're a shot fighter, pure and simple.

I was gloved up and ready to get in there to take care of business, clean some house, but Chester called for another round. Lolo was running back and forth frantically. Like, where's Juan? I was thinking it, too. Kane Street danced out to the middle of the ring and greeted Chester with a flurry of uppercuts, dumping him on his butt. There Chester sat like a little baby that wanted to cry but couldn't get the breath up for it. From the look on his face, you could tell he finally knew that he had gone from world-class to a fighter who couldn't even make it as a gym rat anymore. It was a terrible thing to see.

Lolo was helping him out of the ring when Johnny Pushe, freshly showered and back in his street clothes, took one look and picked up on the situation. Johnny pulled off his jacket and jumped into the ring in his Levi's, T-shirt, and Nikes, pulled on a pair of sixteen-ounce gloves — no mouthpiece, no Vaseline — and said quietly, "Let's go, man. I'm Johnny Pushe and I'd be honored to work with you."

They touched gloves and then Kane Street got uppity and hit Johnny with a right hand lead the very second Lolo called time. This was a bad mistake. I jumped down from the ring apron and stood along the wall and watched as Johnny commenced to commit homicide on the new guy. I mean, I'd been going go give it to him, but I wasn't going to kill the man.

Johnny said, "Is that all you got, bad boy? If that's all you got, your black ass is in trouble." Johnny egged the man on. He said, "Give me a shot, man. Show me some stuff, bad boy."

As soon as Kane Street attempted anything more complicated than a left jab, Johnny uncorked successions of punches. Even when the black kid held his hands up and danced away, Johnny scored with punches, snorting like a bull as he fired. When he got on the bicycle and just tried to survive, Johnny made things even worse for him.

The black boxer's entourage was silent. Just when it seemed that Johnny would put him away mercifully, he backed off so that the kid couldn't quit without losing face totally. "Are you tired? Are you a girl?" Johnny taunted. "Come on, man!"

Kane Street moved in firing. One last try. Johnny carried his hands down at his sides, and was slipping punches slicker than shit. He tagged Kane Street with hard shots, allowing him to recover sufficiently before throwing more. He beat him on the arms and shoulders. It was like overnight mail: The new guy wouldn't feel it until the morning. When Johnny got bored with this, he landed serious thunder, dropping the black fighter on the seat of his pants where he hung in the corner with one arm on the lowest rope, his left eye completely shut and his upper lip looking like he had just chewed on a nestful of hornets. Like Lolo says, it ain't nice to make denigrating racial remarks, but this guy looked like a Ubangi that just did a one-on-one with an African honey badger. "That was fun," Johnny said, tapping the downed man on the top of the head. "Come back tomorrow and I'll show you some more neat stuff."

I HAD to get out of the gym. I was wondering if I had the heart for any of this anymore. Johnny had done the right thing. There's more kindness than cruelty in a beating like that, and Kane Street was now free to pursue his other options — frying hamburgers, running for Congress, or whatever. At least he would no longer harbor illusions that he would become a fighting champion. I was not so sure what Chester was thinking, only that he couldn't feel "so good — so fine" any longer.

It was a cold night for October, and outside there was a bad moon hanging in the sky like a fat ball of silver white pigeonshit ready to fall out of the skies on me like bad karma. Normally I like the full moon, but not that night. I went out and got drunk. Didn't sober up for a couple of weeks.

THE next thing you know, through the clamor of popular demand, Johnny got a rematch with Irish Tommy Wilde. *Aye an' begorra!* A promoter in Belfast coughed up some of that long green, and Juan saw to it that I got a slot on the undercard.

I couldn't believe that Juan had agreed to take a fight on Saint Patrick's Day in Northern Ireland. But the money was good. Juan said it was the only way you could pack a house and draw that kind of payday. However, Johnny was going to need a knockout more than ever. If not, and if

Tommy Wilde didn't get him, the fight mob would. The Guinness would definitely be flowing on Saint Patty's day.

In the paranoia of coming off booze myself, I was thinking that Juan wanted me in shape only so Johnny would have somebody to spar with and he could cut costs. I was also worried about my right hand, twice busted. The orthopedic surgeon who set it the last time had told me no more fighting or I would end up with a fucking claw. Because of the hand, I was learning a whole new technique. A whole new style. I squeezed a racquetball and took calcium tablets to make my right hand stronger. Green tea. Boiled eggs. No sex. Steak and veggies. *Zen and the Art of Archery.* Johnny was over at my place every morning at four in his combat boots and his hand weights, and we went out running together.

It's funny how you lie to yourself. When I'd seen Johnny fighting Tommy Wilde in Lolo's living room, I was wanting it so bad I wished I could become a little four-inch man and jump right in the TV and take over in that seventh round. At that moment, I had my first sense of freedom over the thing I'd done against Chester. If I could have got in that fight, Tommy Wilde would be six feet under and I would be pissing on his grave. But seeing Chester on that floor had scared me so bad I guess I had to get drunk to tamp that freedom back down.

I RAN into Chester downtown one night after an AA meeting, at the most down-and-dirty meeting in town, in fact, and hence the most interesting, but in a bad part of town. Here came Chester with Kane Street and his bunch. I could see that they were all fucked up on dope and that Chester seemed to have gone down fast and hard. His clothes were especially bad, he was unshaven, his hair was hanging down in greasy dreadlocks, his nose was running. His face was puffy and the sclera of his eyes was covered with burst red blood vessels. He had gained bloat weight, and, wearing a full-length leather coat like the rest of the gang, he now looked short, like a dwarf.

I had an AA companion with me, going out for coffee. One of Kane Street's boys started in on her. I tried to look them off when Chester recognized me. "It's my man," he said. "Hey, man, whatchew say?" A distinctive odor of vomit, booze, garlic, and reefer emanated from the bunch. The other young men, who did not recognize me, stopped and sized me up in a confrontational manner. My date said, "Do you know these people?" I looked Chester in the eye and said, "No," and led her away, crossing the street to my car. Chester called after me with a voice like gravel and ground glass, "Hey, man, we really got it on over there in Paris, France, didn't we, man? We wuz rumblin'. Hey, man! Hey!"

I looked over my shoulder and cried, "You gave me six kinds of hell! You was bad that night!"

Chester cried, "Number five in the world, daddy. Never can take that away from me."

I TOLD Johnny about Chester later, as we did a predawn run through the streets of L.A. We were throwing out punches as we slogged through the wet streets in our sweats and combat boots where gasoline rainbows glistened on the black asphalt with the reflection of shoe-store neon, of orange tungsten streetlights and ghostly blue restaurant bug-zappers. The last of the diehard nighthawks were still on the prowl and some motherfucker yelled, "Hey boxer-man! Come on back here and I'll *fuck* your ass!" And Johnny laughed and said to me, "Right." And I laughed, too.

"Chester is history," Johnny said. "Forget him. Hanging out with coked-out thugs. They'll all be dead in a year. You gotta know that. Fuck 'em."

"I never felt right since I put him out over in Paris. Never thought that Juan — "

"Juan was doing you a favor, my man." Suddenly I felt like Johnny was talking down to me. Patronizing me. I was talking to him straight and suddenly he's some big hero. It is necessary for a fighter to become grandiose, expansive and entertain images of omnipotence on a certain level, but it is also important to keep a cool head and know how things are. How they really are.

So I told him, "I got ranked but I got guilty. I felt responsible. It screwed me over — "

"I picked up on the vibe, man. And now you got it out of you. You hear what I'm saying? I knew you was going to say that, and I'm glad you said it. The trouble with you is that you're nice. Nice people. Man, go be a social worker and hold the motherfucker's hand if you want. If my mother is in the fuckin' ring, I'm going to destroy. I'm going to murder. I'm going to kill. 'Cause that's it. What's the matter with you? What the fuck, man."

Johnny threw a lightning combination in the crisp, thin morning air and then broke away from me running at a six-minute-mile pace. We'd started out on this run buddies.

And then suddenly it came to me. I had my juice back. I'd been giving Johnny more trouble in sparring than Tommy Wilde gave him in his last fight. When he shut down on me like that, just like that, I saw that he knew it. He was thinking we might end up in a situation like what happened with me and Chester, that we might end up fighting each other for real. Stranger things have happened — and after all, this is just business. But what happened to that "no deep gut fear of any man alive"? It hurt me to think that he could see me doing that again, fighting a friend, but when I seen him shut down on me, he wasn't my friend anymore.

I thought about that old dude in the Mexico City jail that showed me dynamite hands. He was the coolest motherfucker on the planet, and I don't even know his name. I remembered watching him pulling his sweatshirt off one afternoon. He was going to show me some moves and when he did this, when he lifted up his T-shirt, I saw that his entire abdomen was covered with razor slashes. Like the bear had got him. I knew the slashes were from razor fighting and when he saw the astonishment on my face, he just laughed like he was saying, "Don't worry, pachuco. I can show you how to do this." I saw that he wasn't just some convict. I saw that he was a holy man.

Johnny, that motherfucker. Coming on like he was Sugar Ray Robinson, acting like he was going to blow me away, leave me in the dust. Pissed me off. You don't ever want to piss me off, get me riled. Like Johnny said, you survive the bear, it's good information.

I felt the thing in itself surge up inside, and I blasted by Johnny like he was standing still. I continued to pour it on, running up the crest of our biggest hill where the sun was there to greet me as it peeked out from the eastern horizon.

My legs, my lungs were burning like liquid fire but it didn't hurt. I was beyond the realm of pain. It's all right there, all you got to do is take it. I was plugged in again. I could feel that *boom boom* churning. The sun at the top of that hill, it said, "Angel, go out and get you some. Go out and show them something!"

I'm thinking this is going to be a really fine comeback. This time out I'm going all the way. This time I'm gonna become what you call a regular household name. Hey!

Acknowledgments

I would like to thank the Guggenheim Foundation for their support in helping make this collection possible.

I would also like to thank my book and magazine editors. Foremost among these I wish to express my love and gratitude to Deborah Garrison of the *New Yorker* who has helped me turn out much of my very best work. Her poetic vision and her faith in me have been invaluable, and words are insufficient. I would also like to express deep gratitude to Dan Menaker, Robert Gottlieb and Ms. Tina Brown of the *New Yorker*.

Thanks to Alice K. Turner at *Playboy*, whom I love, love, love! Alice continues to teach me much about the craft of writing. Her critical acumen and remarkable sense of humor, infinite in its range, make rewrites a form of play. I am indebted and grateful.

I would like to thank Colin Harrison at *Harper's*. In addition to being a great fan of his fiction, I am in awe of his abilities as an editor. As with Deborah and Alice, Colin has looked deep into my raw material, and like a geologist wandering over vast stretches of barren desert, has discovered and blueprinted underlying structure from my pages, making major overhauls possible for me.

No less thanks to editors who have been very generous with me in various and many ways. These include: Jennifer Barton at *Harper's*; Will Blythe and Rust Hills at *Esquire*; Lois Rosenthal at *Story*; Renée Vogel at *Buzz* and Mike Paterniti at *Outside* magazine.

My book editors at Little, Brown and Co., Roger Donald and Jordan Pavlin, have never failed me. They have been so gracious and easy in manner, I have come to take for granted their supernatural feats and their infinite patience. At Little,

Brown I would also like to thank Geoff Kloske, Becky Michaels, Mike Mattil, Peggy Freudenthal, Steve Snider, Amanda Murray, Charlie Hayward, Bill Phillips, and a defector to Putnam's, but a true inspiration and lasting friend, Ms. Mih-Ho Cha.

I would like to thank my wife, Sally, and my friends Jon Jackson, Don Fotheringham, and Richard Fisher for being my first readers all these years, and for encouraging me.

God bless my mother, Marilyn; my sister, Cindy; my brother, Mark; John Jones, my uncle, an inspiration and vast source of material. I thank them all for their emotional support. Thanks to The Doors and Arthur Schopenhauer for their artistic inspiration. Thanks to North Thurston High School in Lacey, Washington, for providing me with sanctuary some eleven years. Thanks to my dear grandmother, Margaret, who lives with me in spirit, as does a former teacher of English 101 from the University of Hawaii, R. J. Williams, who told me I should become a writer along about 1966. He did not tell me how long and lonely the trip into the interior would be and for this merciful omission, I would like to thank him especially. I'm sorry that he isn't here to bear witness.

Thanks to Candida Donadio, one of the world's genuine saints. Her ability to recognize quality in all things has been vital to my success. Additionally, Candida's friendship has been responsible for expanding the narrow spectrum of happiness that is available to such gloomy, hypochondriacal existentialists as myself. Along those lines — thanks respectively to Wyeth/ Ayerst Laboratories and Stuart Pharmaceuticals for further expanding that narrow channel of joy by manufacturing Effexor and Elavil; drugs so good they feel illegal. Thanks to my dog Shelby who also makes me feel pretty good.

Thanks finally to my readers, and I say this from the bottom of my heart because it is the most important thank you of all.